D0489284

RONNIE TURNER grew up in Cornwall, the youngest in a large family. At an early age, she discovered a love of literature and dreamed of being a published author. Ronnie now lives in Dorset with her family and three dogs. In her spare time, she reviews books on her blog and enjoys long walks on the coast. *Lies Between Us* is her debut novel.

Lies Between Us

RONNIE TURNER

ONE PLACE. MANY STORIES

This novel is entirely a work of fiction. The names, characters and incidents portrayed in it are the work of the author's imagination. Any resemblance to actual persons, living or dead, events or localities is entirely coincidental.

HQ
An imprint of HarperCollins*Publishers* Ltd
1 London Bridge Street
London SE1 9GF

This paperback edition 2018

First published in Great Britain by
HQ, an imprint of HarperCollins*Publishers* Ltd 2018

Copyright © Ronnie Turner 2018

Ronnie Turner asserts the moral right to be
identified as the author of this work.
A catalogue record for this book is
available from the British Library.

ISBN: 9780008322991

MIX
Paper from
responsible sources
FSC
www.fsc.org   FSC™ C007454

This book is produced from independently certified FSC™ paper
to ensure responsible forest management.

For more information visit: www.harpercollins.co.uk/green

Typeset by Palimpsest Book Production Ltd, Falkirk, Stirlingshire

Printed and bound in Great Britain by
CPI Group (UK) Ltd, Croydon, CR0 4YY

All rights reserved. No part of this publication may be reproduced,
stored in a retrieval system, or transmitted, in any form or by any means,
electronic, mechanical, photocopying, recording or otherwise,
without the prior permission of the publishers.

This book is sold subject to the condition that it shall not, by way of trade
or otherwise, be lent, re-sold, hired out or otherwise circulated without
the publisher's prior consent in any form of binding or cover other than
that in which it is published and without a similar condition including this
condition being imposed on the subsequent purchaser.

For my family – Team Turner –
who are always cheering me on.

Not all love is pure
Not all love is kind
Not all love is true
Some love is blind

Chapter 1

Miller

Let me tell you something I haven't told you before…

One, two, three, finger by finger, I squeeze down into the soft, pale skin of her neck.

Four, five, six…

She reaches out and grasps and grasps at thin air, small fingers searching for some salvation, even as her young face submerges and her lungs fill with water.

Seven, eight, nine…

It doesn't take long. I stroke her hair and smile into her frightened brown eyes.

Ten, eleven, twelve… I squeeze down until her arms grow limp and the last moments of life bleed into nothing.

Thursday 19 March, 1992

They come to you in waves, the wives clutching their hands to their chests, the husbands folding their arms in front of their stomachs, heads bowed, all wearing expressions they deem suitable for the occasion. Unbidden, they are trespassers on your grief and it's as if they've pulled their expressions from their wardrobes, along with the black clothing they donned this morning. But their otherwise perfect appearance is bereft of the most crucial component: sincerity.

You and your parents barely notice. You accept their condolences and pats on the back with good grace, but I can see behind the well-mannered veneer to the part of you wanting to be left to the solitude of her absence. I've lost count of the times I've witnessed them smile, stroke your cheek and mutter to your parents, 'Brave little soldier.' You only nod and force a smile onto your lips, awaiting the next chorus of 'Ohhs' and 'Ahhs,' closely followed by the ensuing pulse of 'Such a shame, such a terrible shame'.

As they leave, the expressions they wear already slipping, I walk up to your house and ram my nail into the puckered scratch that runs across my forearm, tears of pain slipping down my skin. Smudging them across my face, I knock on the door and wait. When you appear, you take in my appearance and I yours. Despite watching from afar all morning, I hadn't realised how your posture has slumped, nor how your eyes are rimmed red.

'I'm sorry, mate,' I say, and like those before me I pat you on the back and smile; a mechanical act but an acceptable one.

You nod and step aside: an invitation into your home, to share in your grief, but most of all an invitation to comfort you. If only I could, properly. If only I could gather you up in my arms and stroke your short brown hair, kiss each of your fingers and banish the pain. The desire to do all of this, my beautiful boy, is nearly impossible to ignore. But I must. You need your friend. You need the person I've given you. You need the illusion. The good-little-boy pretence. The neighbour. Not me. Not the oddity. I realised a long time ago who I needed to be and what I needed to do to achieve in

2

life. You don't have to look hard to see that 'good boys' go further. They get what they want when they are as sweet as me.

It doesn't matter that this is a pretence, though. Even being with you as someone else is good enough for me.

My hand lingers a second too long and you pull away, but you do not close the door. I follow you into her bedroom, where I can see you and your parents spent last night. Wads of used tissues are balled up like confetti across the bed. The pink duvet is rumpled and creased. And already, her posters are beginning to peel away. Strewn across the floor are her things: bears, dolls, storybooks, the shrapnel of four years of her life already slipping into the past. You perch on the bed and look at it all, hands tucked beneath your legs so I can't see them shake. I sit close – this way you can feel me beside you. The smell of cheese and cucumber sandwiches wafts from your mouth. I imagine you ate them to assuage your mother's concern, each bite tasting of ash on your lips.

You look at her toys and books, your lips parted in an 'O' shape as if you can't quite believe the ferocity with which life has taken a swipe at your family. Tears trickle down your cheeks. My hand itches to wipe them away but I keep myself in check and instead pat you on the back again. That is the limit, the boundary. You slump into me as if I have stolen your remaining strength and begin to weep. And even as you do this, you are silent. We sit like this for what seems like hours. But it can't be because when I leave you in her room, the sun is nudging its way into the middle of the sky. I take off down the street, words that have been bandied about by the neighbours repeating themselves over and over again in my mind:

'Sweet girl. Funny girl. Happy girl.'

I stop and look back at your house. Through the crack in the curtains, I can see you, curled up in your mother's arms, bright-red cheeks scarred by the pale tracks tears have made down your skin. Your mother rocks you to and fro. The last vestiges of strength that have kept you on your feet all morning burn up and slide away. And I turn away and smile.

Sweet girl. Funny girl. Dead girl.

Chapter 2

John

Tuesday 17 November, 2015

John Graham lovingly ties the red bow in her wavy brown hair and breathes in the sweet scent of his daughter, treasuring these swiftly vanishing moments before he has to put her down and watch her grow again. Now she is six years old. A bright, bubbling age in which every exhalation carries a sentence tumbling from her lips, and the hodgepodge of styles she favours catches the eyes of passing strangers. But soon she will be seven, soon she will be eight. And in no time at all, she will be gliding through their house cloaked in the confidence that comes in with the tide of adolescence, a red stripe of lipstick glistening on her lips, fingers adorned with bold rings and earplugs stuck in firmly like oversized earrings. But for now, he revels in the love she is not yet embarrassed to give.

'Daddy, can I have some crisps?' She peers into his eyes, and John laughs, knowing even before she asks the question that his answer will be yes.

'OK, sweetheart, but you have to ask Mummy first.'

She gives him a firm nod and crawls out of their makeshift tent, trailing behind her the hem of a dress five sizes too big. 'Don't trip!'

'I won't, Daddy.'

John pulls himself into a sitting position and lets his eyes roam across the fabric of their tent: three duvet covers pegged together and tied to a hook in the ceiling, joining Bonnie's three favourite cartoon characters in a splash of garish pink. She'd woken him and his wife, Jules, that morning with a trumpet call of excitement because she'd had a 'really, really, *really* good idea'.

Despite the way his back lets off a volley of cracks when he crawls out of the tent (he's in his thirties; he's allowed to have aches and pains now, surely?), he can't bring himself to regret even a minute of building the monstrosity with his daughter that morning. And he can't imagine a better way to celebrate his book becoming a bestseller than with his family, curled up in a *very* pink tent.

John closes his eyes and listens to his daughter rattling around in the kitchen cupboards, his mind floating back to yesterday when his friend Don called to congratulate him. He has worked hard to get where he is. The path of an author was one paved with blood, sweat and rejections. Mostly rejections. *Deception*, his latest thriller, is climbing the charts and, after a clutch of published books, he finally feels happy with what he has made for himself.

Bonnie hurtles into the lounge, stumbling over her dress, gripping a packet of crisps in her fingers. 'Mummy is making sandwiches!'

John wraps his arms around her and pulls her, giggling, onto his lap. 'Oh, is she? Are you going to share those crisps, monkey?'

She grins. 'Yes, Daddy.'

John kisses her head and pops a crisp into his mouth, smiling at Jules as she carries a platter of sandwiches into the lounge. She has managed to retain the youth people their age seek out in overpriced lotions and potions. Her skin is smooth and clear, hair bouncing with the rhythm of her gait, eyes bright and curious. She still looks like the Jules he met in his youth, the young woman he knew, with a certainty in the centre of his bones, that he loved, and would love for the rest of his life. They had moved from their home county to the rush of Oxford as soon as they were able, clutching delicate dreams like paper hearts in their hands. In the spare time they managed to hook away from work, they sat side by side, Jules painting to her heart's content and he jotting down his stories, their fingers brushing when they leant back to judge their work.

John runs a hand over his face, fingers picking out the lines and wrinkles in his skin like the brushstrokes in one of Jules's paintings. He hasn't aged as well; the sun has wiped a blanket of freckles over his cheeks, drying out his skin and making him look older. But he doesn't mind. Jules and Bonnie seem fine with the way he looks. And they, in addition to Don and his parents, are the ones who mean the most to him.

'Here we are.' Jules beams, settling the platter on the duvet they have laid across the floor. Her hands find a way to her swollen stomach, tapping a loving rhythm to their unborn child. John is looking forward to meeting their baby with an intensity that sends a tremble through his body. Who will it look like? Who will it be like? Bonnie repeatedly tells them she is going to dress it up in one of her princess dresses. Complete with as many bows and frills and sparkles as she can find.

'You have some paint on your neck, sweetheart.' He gestures to his wife's skin and smiles. He is proud of her, proud of the way she runs her successful gallery, proud of her for juggling a career with a family. It isn't always easy but they share the care and chores and it works well for them. They have found a pattern and a routine that eases them into the day and eases them back out with enough energy left over for each other.

Jules wipes the paint mark off with a rub of her finger and

says, 'I'm going to look like a Smurf if I get much more on me!' Bonnie giggles, nestling deeper into the duvet.

John shuffles to the edge as Jules lays herself down, a sigh slipping from her lips like a secret whispered to a friend. He wraps an arm around her and she wraps an arm around Bonnie. And like this they stay, until it is time to start the day again.

Chapter 3

Maisie

Thursday 14 January, 2016

'So, how was your day?'

Maisie Green runs a hand through her hair and stifles a yawn, sinking back into the sofa cushions as the ache in her shoulder shoots sharp fingers of pain down her back. 'Good. My new patient was transferred today so it was a bit hectic. How about yours?'

'I'm trying to think of a really funny anecdote or something to give you but it was terrible. Bill had to break up this brawl, then he got a glass of red thrown in his face, and somehow managed to blame it on me.' Ben, her partner of three years, chuckles and props his feet on the coffee table, leaning his head back on the sofa cushion.

Maisie smiles, dropping a kiss on his cheek, loving him for transforming any unpleasant situation into something that tempted a giggle rather than a tear. 'That sounds rough. One day we'll win the lottery and you'll be able to tell that boss of yours what you think.'

'Can we win it in time for my shift tomorrow?'

'I'm not sure I can pull it off that quick.'

'That's a shame.' Ben weaves his fingers through hers and grins. 'How is everything else at work?'

Maisie is an ICU nurse and her days are usually divided between assessing her patients' conditions, monitoring and safeguarding their care, acting as an advocate for them and their families, and supporting them through the veil of turmoil that cloaks their lives. So much of what she does is emotional. Yes, she administers medication to her patients, bathes them, and cleans and tests the equipment that keeps their bodies ticking over while they heal, but she also has to be on hand to advise, support and talk to her patients' families, stapling together their pasts with their panicked new lives.

Maisie has seen the varying shades of grief and loss. Wives, husbands, mothers, fathers, people from all walks of life... her job is to help them cross the border into this clinical world of disinfectant handwash and soggy tissues. It's a savage world, one in which they're no longer authors of their fates, but living with the influence of brain scans, bed sores, antibiotics, drips, and the sudden impulse to pray when they haven't prayed before. She has seen men and women clinging to hope with steel in their fingers, chanting comforting words, hands shaking and lips wobbling. They walk up to her, telling themselves that today – today! – she'll give them the news they're hoping for. Today, they'll sit beside their loved one and no longer have to cling to hope, but feel it, truly feel it. For the first time in a long time it will seep into their bones. For the first time in a long time, they will find the parts of themselves they thought they'd lost.

Maisie squeezes Ben's hand and smiles. Although Maisie knows she shouldn't share her patient's details, she trusts Ben implicitly. 'Emotional, exhausting. My new patient, Tim, was attacked and found in the middle of the street a couple of weeks ago. At least that was what I was told. The detective investigating didn't tell us much else. They're not sure whether it was some random attack or something premeditated. They're looking for the culprit now but I don't think they're very optimistic about finding him or her.'

'That's terrible! How are his family coping?'

'They're struggling. Heidi, his wife, is broken up. He was in a coma until two days ago; now he's progressed into a vegetative state. She can't quite wrap her head around it, I don't think. And she's heavily pregnant – only a month away from her due date – with a little kid at home.'

'God, poor lady.'

'She's dealing with it well. She's a strong one, I think. And she has the support of their friend Watson. He seems like a good guy. I really feel for them both.'

'How long have she and Tim been together?'

'Fifteen years.' Maisie nods, thinking of Heidi with her wild blonde curls and bright-green eyes, black bags hanging like small thunderclouds beneath. She'd stood over her husband's bed, hand sailing back and forth between her chest and swollen stomach, as if it couldn't quite decide where it needed to be. For the most part, she simply looked lost. Someone suspended in a state of shock. But, for a moment, all of that had given way and Maisie had thought she'd glimpsed something else. A swift shift in expression, a bowing of her shoulders, a balling of her hands, lips thinning to pale strips of ribbon, fear-laden eyes locked on the floor, then suddenly skittering across the room as if searching for the source of a noise. It was as if a film of something had settled across her face, a reality, a truth that, for a few seconds, was laid bare for those around her to see, all before her composure returned and she wiped away this look like she would wipe away dust on a shelf.

Maisie didn't ask Heidi why. She didn't want to intrude on her grief. She had never seen a reaction like that before, not from the other distraught wives who sat weeping by their husbands' sides, or the girlfriends who looked like big-eyed children as she gently explained treatment and tried to buoy their hopes. Heidi wept for her husband, fear and pain painted clearly across her face, but there was something else too. Something she was trying to keep hidden.

Her friend Watson, a tall, bearded man, fetched her tea and snacks although they were only pushed to the side and steadily grew into a small tower of food. He constantly held her hand, his eyes finding their way to Tim, his fingers removing a tear from his cheek when he thought no one else was watching. Maisie spoke words of comfort and eased them into a new world as she had done with so many others before.

Some families struggled to talk in front of the patient but, when they did, it soothed their fears and lightened the atmosphere. She always asked them questions that allowed them to open up a little more easily. 'Jam or marmalade? Rainy days or sunny days? Cats or dogs? Which does he or she prefer? Tell me the simple things.'

'I hope this chap, Tim, recovers. Does he have a fair chance?'

'He does but then it's early days. Heidi was telling me this really sweet story about how he injured himself when he was little and his mum bought him a pair of Mickey Mouse socks to cheer him up. He kept them on for weeks, literally, wouldn't take them off because he thought they were lucky. He still has them.' Ben inches down the sofa, resting his chin on his hand. 'His daughter had to read this story out to her class a few months ago – she was so nervous. Apparently Tim washed his socks with a pair of her own and told her she'd have some of his luck. It worked a treat because the little girl pulled it off.'

'That's adorable.'

'Mmm. Heidi's not sure about letting her visit Tim. It's tough. She had a mishap at school – a kid pushed her off the climbing frame and she broke her hand so she's feeling a bit vulnerable. Heidi's worried it might be a bit much for her to see Tim like that. Sometimes it helps, sometimes it just upsets everyone. Always depends on the people.'

'What do you think?'

'I think it's worth a shot if it helps the little girl.' Maisie nods, visualising Heidi's expression; how, despite fishing for a look of calm, her anguish had been brushed across her face like black paint over a white wall. Her reaction to seeing Tim was one of the strangest Maisie had experienced. She had cared for countless VS patients over the years, and each one seemed like a shell, their personality replaced with an abyss that crippled those around them. In her precious moments of quiet, Maisie sometimes wondered if it would have been easier if they had stayed in a coma for ever. At least then they'd look as if they were sleeping. In a vegetative state they were watching, moving, reacting to the environment around them. But it was only reflexes, would only ever be reflexes. Until the brain had had a chance to heal, Tim would still be lodged firmly in the landscape of his mind.

'What about the friend... Watson? How did he seem?' Ben heaves himself off the sofa and jogs into their tiny kitchen where he boils the kettle, swiping a strand of brown hair from his eye.

'He tried to cover it up but you could see he was heartbroken. He was supporting Heidi, making sure she was comfortable, fetching her snacks. I think he seems really sweet.'

'Do you want some tea, sweetheart?' Ben hooks the handle of a mug with his finger and raises an eyebrow.

'Yes, please. Fancy cracking open the good biscuits?'

Ben winks, shooting a mischievous grin her way. 'You're a bad influence on me.'

She laughs, tucking her feet under a blanket. Rivulets of steam spout from the mugs like smoke from twin chimneys. Ben passes her a mug and props a plate of custard creams between them. 'I have an early shift at the café tomorrow. I can drop you off at work if you want to go a bit earlier?'

'That would be lovely, thanks!' She nestles into his arms,

nibbling on a biscuit and delighting in his warmth after a day on the ward. As an ICU nurse, her job entailed keeping a tight lid on her emotions, building a wall, brick by brick, to enable her to remain professional, but sometimes, when she least expected, cracks rocked through her defences. And it was at times like these, when she could curl up with Ben and leave behind her life in the hospital, that she found the sense of calm she needed to relax.

Ben wraps his arms around her and deposits a gentle kiss on her head. And Maisie savours it – savours the small pause before this day ends and a new day begins.

Chapter 4

Miller

'Tell me a story. Tell it again.' That is what you used to say, sitting by my side, bright-blue eyes peering up at me, thirsty for knowledge, for an insight I could give you. I called them stories but they weren't. They were facets of life only I could see.

The neighbours clocking each other in the street, bidden, despite trying to avoid each other with the utmost stealth, to stop, smile, chatter through clenched teeth by a need to be perceived as polite that is almost tangible. As if they are in pain. But it is not pain. Only disdain.

The man who watches his girlfriend laugh and throw about gossip like tinsel at Christmas, impatience boiling under his skin, shooting glares in her direction. But she doesn't see them, and her friends don't see the bruises that mark her skin like different-coloured counties on a map. Later she will pay for every word that passed her lips.

The mother on the sidewalk, fondling her newborn baby. Yes, that is what you see, but you miss the husband standing off to the side, frustrated eyes staring not at the woman but at the baby. His baby. You miss the pursing of his lips and the balling of his

15

fists, you miss the jealousy that pours from his muscled body like steam. Jealous of the attention and love his baby receives from its mother. You miss the truth in its brutal, disgusting form. Far better to only see the sweet picture. But by missing the small things, you miss everything. *Everything*.

'Tell me a story. Tell it again.' Shall I tell you mine? Shall I tell you who I was before I met you? Before you exploded into my life in a riot of colour and noise and happiness. Before I took *her* from you in the water that day and slotted myself into the place she left behind.

I'll start with my family because you know the beginning is just as important as the end.

Sunday 1 January, 1984

The girl squeals as she is hoisted into the air by her father, eyes alight with the simple pleasure of his unconditional love and devotion. Her mother stands to the side laughing, hands – nails long and lacquered – clenched into an elated fist at her chest, as if she is trying to stop her heart from leaping out. She watches them, proud of her husband for his surprising skill at handling his own child, proud of her child for her beauty and innocence. When the father props the girl on his left hip, the mother joins them, arms round their shoulders, fingernails tenderly caressing their faces, one third of their happiness. One third of their lives. Their love. One third of their family. A family of three. Or so it seems, standing as they do, ignoring the boy who hangs on the outskirts wondering why that circle of happiness doesn't extend to him.

I spend hours watching them, noticing the finer details of their family. *Theirs,* not ours. It is always the three of them. The father is besotted with his bundle of freckles and blonde curls. The mother is besotted with them both, and neither notices the boy to the left, peering up at them, seeking affection, validation, encouragement. The boy who sneaks into their bedroom when he has a nightmare only to find their little angel already there, snuggled up to her parents, who even in sleep wear smiles.

I stand there for what seems like hours some nights, wishing I could see into their dreams. But then why would I need to? I already know who would be there.

Father plants a kiss on her cheek – his little angel, Mary. She giggles and squirms in his arms, swinging a podgy arm around Mother's neck, consumed with joy. Mother takes her from Father and the girl nuzzles into the space between her neck and collarbone – so perfect for a child's head. She pats her back and swings from side to side. To and fro. Dancing in their circle, proud of one in a brood of two.

Something I have always found fascinating is this: we share so much of one another. DNA, characteristics, mannerisms. Her eyes are my eyes, her nose is my nose, her lips are my lips. We are nearly the same person. We eat with our fingers even though Mother and Father tell us not to. We smile the same, laugh the same. We are one. And yet, if we both cry she is the one who is kissed and hugged and loved until the pain has passed. She is the one in the circle, I am the one outside. Sweet, angelic, innocent Mary.

I wonder if it is because I am not special. Not someone who catches the adoring looks of neighbours and friends. Someone who, if they do something wrong, is given a forgiving, sympathetic look. Nobody ever likes the odd boy, the strange boy… the naughty boy.

Once, when we were playing in the garden, our plastic toys strewn across the grass, slightly more on her side than mine, Mrs Taylor sauntered over, cheaply produced clothes and badly applied make-up not boding well against the backdrop of her newly permed hair. She looked at us, smiling even though it looked like a wince, and said loudly, 'The little dears!'

Father grimaced and forced himself to look at her slightly

17

uneven features, desperately trying to tame the eyes that flitted to the wart sitting sentinel under her left brow. 'Good morning, Mrs Taylor? How is Mr Taylor? Good, I hope. Sunny today, isn't it? Enjoying the fine weather?' The words tumbled out of his mouth, one after the other, as if he was trying to fill the space where an apology should have been. His eyes found her wart again.

'Oh, good, *good*.' She brushed away the questions like flies from her T-shirt. 'And how are these *lovely* children?' She knelt down and made popping noises into thin air. As we were hidden by her mass, if anyone had walked past it would have looked as if she had lost her mind. 'Oooh. Aren't *we* a pair of cutie pies?!' She was talking to us both and yet her eyes peered at Mary, who looked back at her with a slightly bewildered expression. Mother and Father came over, sharing a look behind her back. 'And how *is* little Mary Moo this morning?' She poked her in the ribs, like an animal in a cage. Poke. Jab. Poke. Mary, confused, grabbed a pebble from the ground and popped it into her mouth, grinning.

'Mary!' Mother screeched, eyes widening, rushing forward, picking her up as Father prised her mouth open. The pebble dropped at Mrs Taylor's feet, covered in saliva. She stared at it in shock, stumbling back, affronted.

Mary grinned, a string of spittle hanging from her mouth. Father wiped it away and awaited Mrs Taylor's reaction. She came forward and tickled Mary's cheek with hairy fingers, her features growing horrifyingly animated as she whispered, 'What a *special* girl!'

Mother returned her to the ground and they looked at a cat across the road. I reached out and pinched her arm. She whimpered, tears forming in her eyes. I pulled away as they turned back round, and smiled when I saw I had left a mark.

I stand by the staircase in our small detached house, watching them, wondering why, if we are so similar, if we are nearly the same person, why I'm not wanted and loved and tickled and poked? Why am I not as special as Angel Mary? I watch them, their happiness drowning me, wondering what makes me different. What makes me the oddity?

Monday 2 January, 1984

I run my fingers down her blonde braid as she plays with a doll, permanent grin etched on her face, enjoying the pull and tug of my fingers. I watch her, studying her mannerisms, her expressions, the way she laughs, the way she sticks her thumb in her mouth and sucks – as if on a lolly – when she is thinking, the way a frown creases her forehead when confused. Mother is cooking in the kitchen, stirring soup, tapping her nails on the worktop. Do you know, I lay awake last night imagining ripping them off, prising her nail away from her skin and taking it between my teeth, feeling the soft shell of the varnish crumble in my mouth. When I finally went to sleep, it was to the sweep of silence in my mind, not to the tap-tap-tapping of her nails.

Father is beside her, turning three times a minute to check on us – or rather, on Mary, his eyes ever so slightly concerned as they alight on me, pulling at her hair. *Gently though Father, gently.*

Our house is a two-up, two-down box with an open-plan living area and a garden roughly the size of a postage stamp, which leads on to the quiet street beyond. In the evenings, children and teenagers bundle on the kerb, kicking footballs, thinking themselves as good as George Best, skittering when a car honks its horn and goes on its way. Girls sit in groups, legs crossed, giving one another tutorials on the application of the latest make-up. Mothers slave away indoors, cooking chicken, cursing their husbands. Fathers combat the stress of their wives with a steady flow of alcohol down the pub, and the elderly residents of our street enjoy the comings and goings with watchful eyes, like owls

19

from a tree. The young yearn to be older and the elderly yearn to be younger. A strange sort of world we live in.

The neighbours complain that their similarly built houses are not big enough for the relatives who come and stay at Christmas and New Year. But we do not share their problem. I have never told you this although you have asked plenty of times. Eluding and sidestepping questions is easy once you have become practised at it. We are a family of three – the quandary that is me somewhere within it – and only three. Our relatives are dead. 'Nice and cosy in their graves,' as Mother likes to say, sarcasm lacing her words, as if they chose to die just to spite her and dodge babysitting duties.

At Christmas, as our neighbours celebrate, planting kisses, administering hugs, proffering gifts, we sit around Mary, me slightly back where Father has patted the floor. We watch her rip open her presents, Mother holding Father's hand. When it is time for them to exchange gifts, they tentatively pass them over. A laugh. A nervous smile. A kiss. An 'Oh, how lovely!' A pat on the arm or shoulder, all before the presents are silently nudged to the back.

Father swivels on his heels, penetrating eyes watching my hand as it brushes across Mary's cheek. 'Careful. Don't want to catch your sister now, do we?' He persuades a smile onto his twitching lips, brow furrowing. I look up at him and shake my head.

'No, Daddy.'

He gives a little nod and turns around to help Mother with the soup. Mary giggles as I twirl her braids round my finger. Her Zip-a-Dee-Doo-Dah braids, I call them. She grins up and squeals 'Hummy'. Her name for me. I nod and study her pink lips, pulled back to reveal her baby teeth.

That sweet smile slips as I lean back and pull her braids. And it keeps on slipping until tears shimmer down her skin and her cheeks bloom red as she screams. And even then, I keep on pulling.

Chapter 5

John

Tuesday 1 December, 2015

Two Weeks Later

He runs his finger across the photograph in what is nearly a caress. He scans the child's face, and it is as if a map has been drawn across it, the red lines navigating the black and blue bruises, traversing the blotchy skin and the swollen, bloodshot eyes as if to reach some unknown destination. He touches the girl's face, hovering over her parted lips where blood has dribbled down and dried on her chin. She peers up at him, a silent plea in her eyes.

He feels a body brush past him and then hears a muffled gasp somewhere off to his right. He catches Jules just as she slips to the ground and sits her on the staircase. She weeps into her hands, hiding her eyes from the photo, as if it will burn itself onto her retinas. She can't bear to see it and yet he can't take his eyes off it. He knows it will come; within minutes an avalanche of emotion, bearing an almost unimaginable force, comes crashing into him.

Turning the photo, he reads the inscription and his hand begins to tremble. His wife, sensing the change in the air, glances up at him, then down at the photo, hands falling to her swollen stomach as if to protect her baby from the photo and the assailant who has suddenly marched into their lives. She takes a ragged breath and stares at the typed message on the back, Bonnie's scrawl signing it off with her name.

Do you remember that day in 1992, John? Do you remember what happened?

John swipes his thumb across the six-year-old girl's writing and shuffles to the sideboard, feeling as if he is wading through mud. He grabs the phone and dials.

One… two… three…

Four… five… six…

He counts the seconds until the policewoman answers and he explains what's happened in dull tones.

And then it comes. He covers his weeping eyes as his legs give way and the photo of his daughter flutters to the ground.

John watches Detective Chief Inspector Alice Munroe gently deposit the photo in a clear bag, her gloved hands delicately touching its edges. She tells him it will be sent off and subjected to a forensic examination, as will the envelope, to see if any fingerprints or DNA (aside from their own) can be found. But he doubts it. He doubts this person would be so foolish.

Since the DCI's arrival and her cool, professional introduction, he has been bombarded with questions about his past. What happened to him in 1992? What does he remember? Does he have any idea who this person is? Has anyone ever expressed any ill feeling towards him? What was his childhood like? Who are his parents? Who were his close friends growing up? Has he ever had any enemies?

22

He answers all their questions patiently, a sickness in his stomach threatening to overpower him. Jules sits beside him during his interrogation, rubbing her bump with her left hand, her right entwined in John's. A silent support.

DCI Alice Munroe explains what will happen in the following days and the severity of their situation. But despite trying to digest every word, the flurry of useless sentences pass over his head. In one ear and out the other. Things like this don't happen. Not to him. His family. This kind of thing belongs on the television, on the radio, in the newspaper. Local girl missing. Police suspect kidnapping. John blanches at that word. Kidnapping. His daughter. His sweet, kind, funny little girl. Gone. Taken. He rubs his neck, a tick that has, despite his mother's incessant correction, followed him doggedly into his thirties. His neck turns red and blotchy as he rubs it, working the tension and panic through his fingers.

Munroe flicks her eyes to his hands, taking note. He doubts anything goes unnoticed. She runs her nail along the inside of her little finger – an exercise to help her concentrate perhaps – legs crossed, back straight, expression professionally cool. As if this sort of thing happens every day. It probably does, he supposes. For her. In his small lounge, on the tired, sagging sofa, two realities converge. One that walks on the periphery of loss and fear and devastation constantly; the other residing firmly in what was, until a few days ago, perfectly normal. Good. Happy. But any semblance of normal life has been washed away. Their lives are stripped bare now.

John looks at Munroe and wonders how she bears this every day. He can't tell if she has children but, judging from the pale skin peeping out from underneath her wedding band, he guesses she has been married for many years. He silently asks her questions in his mind. Do you have children? Do you have a daughter? How would you feel if she had been taken? What if it was your fault?

He pinches the bridge of his nose and squeezes his eyes shut to quell any more tears. The questions have penetrated and sieved through nearly every inch of his past. All his memories have been invaded and examined. Albums from his childhood, given to him by his parents, have been bagged and taken away; any letters, written or received, have met a similar fate. They have asked him who his friends are. For his agent's and publisher's details. If he has ever been involved in any fights, brushes with the law. No, he tells them. No, no, no. The longer the DCI and her colleagues sit in his lounge, the more personal the questions become. When did he and Jules meet? When were they married? Were there ever any jealous girlfriends? Boyfriends? Did he ever notice anyone watching him, studying him? Again, he answers in the negative. They seem surprised at how cooperative he is, and he wonders if they usually have to tease answers out of people, soothe their grief and trick them to get at the truth. But everything he remembers, he offers them. Every morsel of his past, he gives them to study. They are his only hope. Bonnie's only hope.

'You'll be provided with an FLO – Family Liaison Officer – to help in any way, support you, talk through the situation, and explain where we are with the investigation. But first, as there's a suggestion you and your wife might be in danger, we'd like to relocate you.' She looks at them both, studying their reactions.

They nod but neither one of them cares. John wraps his arm round Jules, wondering for the umpteenth time why anyone would target them, target Bonnie. 'Because of you,' a small voice in his mind whispers. 'Because of you.' But why? He'd had a normal childhood. Been a good boy. Done his chores, spent time with his friends, done well in school. Said please and thank you. Hadn't hurt or upset anyone. He'd never wanted to. He isn't a bad person. Or perhaps he is… His daughter is a 'hostage' – at least that's what the police are calling her. His little girl. Alone. Frightened. And he is helpless. Useless. It is his own fault.

Jules squeezes his hand. Suddenly he is overwhelmed by the

urge to hold her. When Munroe and her colleagues eventually leave, they climb the staircase, each step a hardship, each breath a toil, to their daughter's room. There isn't enough space for them to lie side by side on Bonnie's small bed so John leans back on the headrest and holds Jules to his chest, and she cradles their unborn baby. They count the stars they helped Bonnie glue to the ceiling over a month ago and bring forth her smiling face and the sound of her laughter as they danced beneath them.

Wednesday 2 December, 2015

John gazes at the photographs spread across the wall. Left to right, past to present, they follow Bonnie's life. From the day she was born, bundled up in a pink blanket in Jules's arms, to last week, when she lost her first tooth; in the picture she holds it proudly up to the camera, excitement written across her face. After the picture was taken she'd run to his study and deposited the tooth safely in the tin she kept under his desk. Throughout the day, she'd crept back to check her trophy was still there. He'd tried to tell her the fairy only came at night when she was asleep but curiosity consistently won out. The next day, she'd skipped around the house with her pound coin clutched tightly in her fist, showing them, then, moments later, showing them again.

He sits at his desk now and wonders why his daughter has been taken from them. Is it retribution for some wrongdoing? Is it a past mistake come back to haunt him? Is he being made to repent? Useless thoughts buzz around his head. Peering underneath his desk, he looks at the debris of a life Bonnie built one morning when she came down from her bedroom. A pile of blankets folded neatly where his feet are supposed to go (since she'd made the move into his study, he'd sat slightly sideways or with the laptop perched on his knee), Barbie dolls scattered across it, stuffed bears and boxes of puzzles stacked tidily to the side. Along with the tin she kept for 'special treasures' are a notebook, pencil case, the Nintendo DS she only played with when she was bored, and a small child's toy designed to look like a laptop. When he wrote longhand, she copied him, pencil finding its way to her mouth, eyes thoughtfully rolled up to the ceiling. When he typed out his novels on the laptop, she settled her pink one on her lap and typed out hers. The most recent being about a mole having a tea party with his friends.

John looks at her 'cosy corner', as he and Jules call it, leaning forward and snatching the tin from its perch. It was a sample tin they'd got when painting her room over two years ago. She'd insisted on keeping it, despite the dried paint running down the edges. He pops the lid off and fishes out its contents: three pebbles with heart-shaped marks on them, two neatly folded notes he'd given her that simply read 'I love you', and the necklace he and Jules presented to her on her fifth birthday. He runs his finger over the small pendant, which reads 'Protagonist'. She had been overjoyed when she unwrapped it. But unlike him at her age, she'd done so with care, folding, easing off the strips of tape, pulling out the black box with velvet trimming and slowly peering inside, as if each moment was one to savour.

He rips a sheet of paper from his notebook and carefully writes 'I love you' in his neatest handwriting, popping it in the tin for when she returns.

'We're going to find her. We're going to find her.' He repeats the mantra over and over, as he had to Jules last night before they eventually slipped away from visions of her torture to the murky nightmares of it instead. He repeats it until his mouth grows dry and his voice begins to catch in his throat.

A blanket, pencils, a sheaf of paper… Bonnie's was a world you'd never want to leave. Simple and easy. They'd spent hours in his study together. Sometimes they wrote to music, usually just to silence. When she was bursting with energy, he abandoned his laptop screen to dance round the room with her. When she was exhausted and fell asleep curled up under his desk, he gently pulled her onto his lap, a tiny pool of dribble marking his shirt. If she was upset, he read a suitable chapter from his novel and gradually her tears dried. And if that didn't work, he folded her in his arms and span them round on his chair until they were both laughing.

John turns and smiles at Jules as she walks into the room, carrying two plates of sandwiches. Her red cheeks are marred by tracks of pale skin marching down her face, eyes swollen and rimmed with black shadows. She puts the plates on the desk and sits on his lap, head resting in the exact same place Bonnie's had. He wraps his arms around her waist and kisses her. The hours will pass with them still in this position, the lethargy of shock and fear at this new tide of events making them feel as if they have been dunked in clay and left to slowly dry in the sun.

John swivels the chair round so they can look at the photos. Bonnie's Wall, he calls it. His eyes are drawn to a photo off to the side. Bonnie is being cradled in Don's arms, thumb stuck between her lips, face flushed from their day at the zoo. Don, wearing a Donald Duck cap, smiles tenderly down at her, eyes glued to her small face. The picture was taken two years ago, after John's novel had won an award for crime and thriller novel of the year. And now he wishes he'd never taken it, never put it on the wall, because it brings his thoughts full circle to his and Jules's failure, to the day Bonnie dropped out of their lives. She had been missing four days before they received that photo through the letterbox.

He and Jules were arguing in the kitchen at the time. He'd just received a text from his uncle about visiting in a few weeks. Jules was adamant he shouldn't come, shouting that he was a creep. John was stuck in the middle – wedged would be a better word – between his wife and his uncle, two halves of his family. He could faintly remember hearing Bonnie giggle in the other room over something Don said.

'Daddy, Mummy, Uncle Duck's on the telly! He's on the telly!' She squealed in excitement.

And then Don's voice. 'Guys, I'm famous. I'm famous—' He was cut off when Bonnie laughed – John assumed because Don tickled her. 'Quack! Quuuaaack!' Don, again, his usual sunny self, a sudden contrast to his and Jules's bleak dispute. 'Quaaaack!' They'd been watching a Donald Duck cartoon before he and Jules left for the kitchen. John couldn't remember when Bonnie had decided to call Don after her favourite character, his brain foggy with thoughts of what came next.

Don wandered into the kitchen, smile drooping as he took in their expressions. 'Oh, guys, come on! Bon's waddling round like a duck in there, you know! It's hilarious!' He patted John on the back and made his way to the bathroom. John barely even noticed him, frustrated as he was with Jules. When they returned to the lounge, moments later, with a plate of biscuits, the television was playing for an empty room. John called up the stairs and Jules rushed out to the garden. They screamed and cried her name but the voice they so hoped to hear didn't call back.

'What are you doing? She's in the lounge!' Don walked up to them, expression puzzled, hands spread in a question.

'She's gone! She's gone!' Jules cupped her face, eyes shooting back and forth across the room as if Bonnie was about to reappear suddenly and shout, 'Here I am! I'm good at hide and seek, aren't I, Mummy?'

Don wrapped a comforting arm around Jules. 'John, I'll take the car and have a scout round; you go on foot in case I miss her. Jules, go and ask the neighbours if they've seen her. She's only been gone a few minutes, she can't be far away!'

They jumped into action as if it was something they'd rehearsed. John rushed out of the door and down the street, making laps around their house, inching further away each time, scanning the area for her. For some reason, it was her shoes he kept hoping he'd see. Her sparkly red Dorothy shoes. They were getting too small for her but she insisted on wearing them, polishing them with a cloth twice a day, proud of the way they shone. Those shoes were lodged in his mind. Sometimes he thought he saw them, but when he looked back they weren't there. He spotted Don twice on his frantic laps but not Bonnie, never Bonnie.

They assumed at first that she had run away, but 'Bonnie wouldn't do that!' they told themselves and then repeated it to the police, to be met with looks of nonchalance and boredom. With nothing else to go on, they began to think she'd just wanted a walk and got lost. The police trawled the streets and neighbourhood. They checked the little village shop, the play area, rechecked where John had already looked. But it was all for nothing. She hadn't run away or got lost. She'd been taken.

John doesn't know how. It is one of the questions that bombard him; even when he is asleep it finds a way to dig its fingers into his subconscious and prey on his ever-befuddled mind. How was she taken? They were only in the kitchen for a few moments. Don was only in the bathroom for a few moments. Did this person lure her outside and kidnap her? Did he walk into the house they were supposed to be safe in and simply take her hand and walk right back out again? No, he couldn't have – Bonnie knew not to go with strangers. She knew the world was a scary place. She knew, she knew, she knew. But then, he asks himself, would he have heard her talk, shout? Don wouldn't have from inside the bathroom. All this person had to do was hold his hand over her mouth and leave. As simple as that.

And now they are sitting here, while their little girl is suffering God knows what. Over and over. Again and again.

Jules places his hand on her bump. He feels a slow, firm kick against his palm and smiles sadly. How are they supposed to care for a second baby when they've spoiled things so badly with their first? This is their fault. His fault. Their only job since the day she was born has been to protect her. And now they have failed, it seems they will surely fail with the next one as well. How can they not? How is this one going to fare any better in their care?

His eyes slowly begin to flutter closed, exhaustion creeping up on him. They sleep like this for hours. And he dreams that when he leaves their newborn in its crib to fetch a nappy, it has gone when he returns. And in its place is a photograph of *both* his children together, side by side, broken and bruised, tears and blood forming a pool at their feet.

Chapter 6

Maisie

Friday 15 January, 2016

She supposes he is a handsome man. With his attractive face and messy hair, she imagines him to be someone who draws eyes easily. But despite what the nurses say behind closed doors, how they gossip and prate about the poor man, she doesn't see him the way they do. She thinks he looks kind, sweet, honest. And when he smiles, she thinks he might be a funny man. With his teeth slightly crooked and the crow's feet beside his eyes nestling deeper into his skin when he frowns, she wants to know more about him. More about his life. More about the man beyond the chemical smell of the ward and the bleeping of the equipment. She looks at Heidi, sitting opposite her, and wonders whether she should ask. They washed his hair with warm water and shampoo moments before, carefully avoiding his stitches.

Heidi looks at her husband, silently. Thoughtfully. Maisie notices that if he smiles, she smiles too – like a reaction to a joke he's just told. Something only they are privy to. Holding his hand to her lips, she kisses it softly. 'It still feels like he's in there. You probably don't know what I mean, do you?'

Maisie shakes her head, leaning forward.

'We've been together for fifteen years. We know each other's sounds and signals, every inch of each other. Every single like and dislike even if we aren't familiar with it ourselves. I know that when he grits his teeth, he isn't angry, he's upset. I know that if our daughter jumps on his lap and falls asleep, he'll fall asleep too. When I'm stressed about something, he twirls me around the kitchen. If he fiddles with his keys, he's nervous. If he grins just before he has dessert, he's thinking about his mother's apple pie. Even if we're just watching a movie, he holds my hand until the end. Before we eat out, he checks the restaurant serves meals we like so my daughter and I won't be disappointed. He can't whistle and he hates broccoli. He loves books and hates comics. Loves the Rolling Stones, hates the Beatles. Loves life but isn't afraid of dying.'

Heidi glances at Maisie and her calm expression falters. But it isn't just sadness Maisie sees. It is something else. Something akin to dread. It blankets her face and shrouds the room in a thick haze. Maisie is reminded of the first time they met, when Heidi stood beside Tim, her hand flying from her chest to her bump, some unnameable emotion streaking through her eyes. It bothered Maisie then but it bothers her now even more. It is a quick flutter of concern in her chest, a creeping unease that settles across her skin. Mostly Heidi keeps calm, smiling and talking about their lives together. But then comes the shift in her behaviour and it taps out a restless rhythm in Maisie's mind.

Maisie wonders if Heidi is thinking about the attack. Is she afraid it will happen again? Does she think she is in danger? Maisie catches herself before she asks. Tim's presence has prompted a surge of twittering and clucking from the nurses. Gossip is currency. And in their breaks it flows freely, theories and suggestions shared hastily over homemade sandwiches and limp salad. The investigator they see plodding up the corridor and the article crushed into the corner of page six of the local newspaper tell them he was attacked and left for dead in the street. Maisie can't even begin to imagine what it must be like hearing your husband was attacked.

Heidi brushes a strand of hair from Tim's eyes, the dread in her own dissipating. 'I know how he feels. Even before I hear him, I feel him walk into the room. I've loved him for fifteen years. And—' she pauses and looks at Maisie '—he's still in there.'

'I think I know what you mean,' she whispers, taken aback.

'He's going to get better. I know he is.'

*

Maisie's thoughts inevitably find their way back to Heidi. They had spoken of their childhoods, their work and their parents to stave off grim topics. Maisie had told her she grew up in Cornwall with her mother. That she was given all the encouragement, help, support and freedom she'd ever needed, even with the tedious tests and studies she went through to become a nurse. Her mother was there every step of the way.

If Maisie closes her eyes she can see Janet's rust bucket of a car sitting dutifully outside her old home, sporting stickers all over the boot. One in particular always gave them a laugh, especially when people looked from the sticker to her mother's untameable hair, slapdash make-up and outrageously colourful clothes. The sticker announced to all who cared to stare, 'God Made Me Bespoke.' Her mother had come across it in a second-hand shop, her expression scrunching up the way it did when she found something funny. 'Well, indeed. Mae, my lovely, I think we might have found one for the collection,' she'd said in her strong Cornish accent, chuckling away under her breath.

Maisie smiles, kicking off her shoes and dashing to the bathroom to change out of her uniform. She flicks on the television, planting herself between the cushions on the sofa, nestling her feet into the Laura Ashley rug she and Ben had saved for. She glances at her watch. Ben will be back any minute. Even though they are both taking all the hours they can get – her at the ICU and Ben at the café – they refuse to budge on their Saturday evenings together. She prods the buttons on the remote, navigating her way through the soap operas neither of them has a taste for to the movies. She pauses the screen and drops the remote by her side. *Lord of the Rings*. Their favourite movie. Or rather movies – it is a trilogy, after all.

Their small flat isn't a fancy affair. Open-plan living area with three doors leading off to the two bedrooms and bathroom. Four walls with a few windows. A box, fish tank, crate, as her mother says. But it was all they could afford at the time. Since moving in together, they've decorated the flat with anything they can find to give it character, trying to gather together the essence of themselves and inject it into the atmosphere. And it's worked. Pictures and artwork bought from charity shops and car-boot sales adorn the walls, along with a bounty of other knick-knacks splashed across the units. The wooden furniture has been sprayed with woodworm killer. Maisie had said at the time that she hated the thought of all those tiny dead bodies inside her furniture, but if they wanted somewhere for their things to go, it was that or nothing. They've become experts at saving money. Better than that chap on telly, Martin Something, Ben once joked. They'd both laughed; that chap's advice had enabled them to save (what was to them) a small fortune.

Maisie looks at the frames lining the wall. Most were taken by professional photographers, but the rest are ones she and Ben snapped in Cornwall two years ago. It was a holiday for him but for her it was simply going home. A welcome break from the rush of traffic and noise and overbearing life in Oxford. Her eyes travel across the pictures and, like a child trying and failing to avoid the dark space beneath the bed, inevitably find the door to the spare bedroom. Most of the time she can block it from her thoughts, stop the tears and hide from the memories that reside in the corners of the walls and the cracks in the floors. When she is alone in the flat, like now, she finds it harder. Because her eyes are drawn to it and her thoughts back in time to a portion of her past she forced herself to abandon. A hope that was alive and bright and pulsing with fervour, only to be quashed and forgotten. But regardless of her best efforts, she can't stop it.

Shaking her head, Maisie pulls her knees to her chest and cups her hands over her face. When Ben opens the door, she is still sitting in that position, the tears dried onto her skin.

Chapter 7

Miller

Thursday 10 July, 1986

They tell me she is special. They stare in wide-eyed wonder at her face and coo and giggle when she mumbles. They look at me, then instantly, with a rising of the shoulders and a small, almost imperceptible shake of the head, look away, wishing they hadn't looked in the first place. They wonder why I'm with her, wonder how someone like me could be the brother of someone like her. And if they are in the mood, they lean forward and whisper, as if whispering to someone who won't understand, '*You* have a very *special* sister. Aren't *you* lucky?'

If she cries, a hundred hands fall to comfort her. If she laughs, they stop and turn, row upon row of strangers, expressions flickering from surprise, to joy, to envy. If she smiles at someone, that someone will look as if they have just been gifted with a miracle.

If someone is sad, she will waddle up to them on her chubby legs and pat their hand like a friend, not the toddler she is. And they will look at her in wonder, touched, mesmerised, wanting nothing more than to take her in their arms, to be as close as close can be. If someone laughs, she laughs with them and they stand a little taller, smile a little wider.

She possesses something nobody truly understands but everybody wants to share. A kindness, a gentleness, a lightness they're all fighting and tumbling and burning for in what is a bleak world. I think they sense it, you know. I think they feel how good she is. How pure. The honeyed, sweet, tempting child they all wish was theirs. Mother and Father lap it up, sucking in the attention and love for their daughter, revelling in the atmosphere she creates.

You're like her. You snatch people's attention, their ability to walk away, their minds, their love. There aren't many people like the two of you. I wonder if a part of you knows this? No, you probably don't. You are not arrogant. You are honest. I remember the time you used your mother's expensive hand lotion, sneaking into her room and quietly depositing a glob of the mango-scented stuff on your hand. I saw you. I watched from the window. You rubbed it into your skin, a smile turning up the corners of your mouth, nose grazing your hands. Later, when your mother asked if she could smell it, your face blazed with embarrassment and you scuffed your feet on the floor and stared down as you nodded and offered her your hands. But how could she be irritated? How could anyone ever be angry with you?

So honest. So sweet. So perfect.

They took her to the hairdresser yesterday, you know, probably so I can't pull her curls anymore. They stood back and watched as a gaggle of middle-aged women with rolled hair poked her stomach and squeezed her cheeks, eliciting moans of agony. Mother held her hands to her chin, proud of her sweet, rosy-cheeked daughter. Father stood by her side, nodding when a goose exercised her beak and asked if she liked mints. Yes, yes, she does, he said. The goose chuckled and popped one into her mouth. Because she couldn't do it herself, could she?

Mother saw me glaring and glared back. While Mary was having her hair cut, the women dispersed to their own chairs. I watched the snap of the scissors, wishing they would inch just a little further to the left. Snag the skin of her earlobe. Mary would cry and scream, and the geese would see how troublesome she could be.

I brushed away Mother's warning hand and shuffled to the chair. The hairdresser smiled at me, but I saw it was a false one, unlike the smile she sent Mary through the mirror every few seconds. I bent down and pushed my hand through the curls of blonde hair, smearing them across the floor. Then I stood back up, making sure I jolted the hairdresser's arm as I went.

'Oh!'

I turned and went back to my seat as Mary began to scream and the hairdresser cried, 'OH MY GOD! SOMEBODY GET THE FIRST-AID KIT! GET THE FIRST-AID KIT! GET IT!'

Mother and Father jumped up and rushed to her side, words soothing, fingers mollifying. I watched the scene play out, letting rip a torrent of apologies and false tears.

'I'm sorreeeee! I... I didn't mean it! It... it was an accident! I'm really sorry! Is... is she OK? Mummy, Daddy?'

I expected the geese to turn and throw dirty looks, angered by the disruption, but they didn't. They flocked to Mary like geese to a family throwing pieces of bread. They told her she 'must be brave' and 'oh, it's just a little cut'. They fondled her cheeks and kissed her forehead. And I thought, if those stupid women *were* geese, I would throw them shards of glass inside balled-up bread.

Mother said I meant to do it. I meant to jostle Christine, the hairdresser. I told her I didn't, of course, but nevertheless she made me clean the dirty dishes and sweep the floor. Then, when she ran out of ideas for punishment, she sent me away to my room.

Mary had a plaster on her ear. Mother said she could spend the rest of the day watching cartoons because she was such a brave girl. She sat on the sofa, calling my name, asking me to join her. I didn't, though. It was only when Mother ordered me to help her hang a frame that I went down. She was holding a nail to the wall, hammer in the other hand. I stood by her side, awaiting instructions, but she was utterly focused on what Mary was saying over her shoulder.

'Mamma, sheep, sheep!'

'Well done, Mary, sweetheart. That's right. It's a sheep.'

I glanced from Mary to Mother, my fingers prickling. Then I snatched the hammer from her hand and slammed it against the nail of her finger.

She screamed and spluttered. And when she looked up at my face, her mouth cracked open, just wide enough for a letter to slot through, and her eyes turned to angry blue discs.

'I'm sorry. I was just trying to help. I'm really, really, really sorry, Mummy.'

She gave me a tight nod. 'It's… OK. It's OK. Now, off you go, son.' No darling, no sweetheart, no honey. Nothing.

I went back upstairs then and laid my head back on the pillow and smiled.

*

I swing my legs back and forth under the dining table, pencil lolling between my fingers as I ponder my homework. Mother sat me down here and told me to 'be good' while she 'weeds the garden' with Father. I scratch the pencil across the paper as I listen to them outside. Through the window, they look up in unison when Mrs Taylor across the street hails them and wags her finger, the wart on her face jigging as she talks. How *is* Mary? How is that *delicious* daughter of yours? Oh my, I could just *eat* her up. She's just so *scrummy*! Her flow of words shoots across the street to the elated expressions of Mother and Father. They brush down their clothes and walk over, lured by the promise of conversation.

I drop the pencil onto the paper, an itch in the tips of my fingers inching its way up my palms. I look out of the window, then make my way to the stairs, hearing the bubbly sound of her laughter. It beckons me, as it beckons everyone. I take the stairs one at a time, wondering if Mother's long, lacquered fingernails will scratch me for what I am about to do. Or if Father will look at me with fury in his face. I wonder if the eyes that seek out Mary will turn to me and know. If Mrs Taylor will bolt her door and close her curtains should I walk past. If Mr Terry next door will turn the wheels on his wheelchair a little faster when he sees me. I wonder all of this as I go to her room, thoughts marking off the moments like the hands of a clock ticking by. Tick. Will they know? Tock. Will they smell what I have done on my skin like a dog? Tick. Will they be able to see it written into my hands? Tock. Will they feel it? Tick. I bet they will. Tock.

The sound of her laughter fills my ears, consuming my mind like the music Mother always turns off when it comes on the radio. When she does this I turn it back on, brushing her arm with my hand as I go by. It always makes her jump and always makes me smile. She'll watch me switch the dial back, my eyes glued to hers, unblinking as the song fills the room. She'll stare at me, biting her lip, then shrug and carry on. But I see the looks Mother and Father share afterwards. Looks of anger and denial. Then I will go back to my game with Mary and they'll study us, feet tapping the floor, eyes shooting from Mary to me. Mary to me. Back again, fingers fiddling with the sofa, legs prepped to pounce. I think they know I only play with her to worry them. I'm such a naughty little boy. *How* could they possibly have had such a *naughty* little boy?

I can hear the music now, the squeaky tone of the band she hates – what is it? The Bugs? The Flies? The Beetles?

Mary sits on the floor, braids pushed back, legs kicking, arms flying about the air. In her hands are the prince and princess dolls she lavishes with love. Her laughter penetrates the room and I wonder if the whole street can hear it.

'Mary?' I say, kneeling down and picking up the plastic carrier bag she keeps her toys in.

She turns and smiles, the biggest smile I have ever seen stretching across her lips. 'Hummy!' she squeals, dropping her dolls and grabbing me. I shake my head and put my finger to my lips. She nods and giggles, copying me, her sweet, trusting eyes peering up. Then, as that itch buries itself into my arms, I think that surely Mother and Father must hear me breathing. It comes out hard and hurried, as if I have been running. Surely they must know. Surely they will come flying up the stairs, feet hammering the floor in a frantic drum, and grab me by the hair and pull me away from her. Surely. But do you want to know something, Blue-Eyes?

They don't.

With a gentleness that could almost be love, I slip the bag over her head and squeeze it to a close. Her hands find my chest and her legs jump up and down like they are puppets dancing to their master's strings. But she doesn't fight. Her loyalty and love and trust in brother Hummy do not falter.

They don't falter as I pull her close and squeeze tighter. They don't falter as the last morsels of strength, which were only ever feeble to begin with, drift from her limbs. She trusts me as her lungs cry for air, as her fingers search for my face, as her eyes blink and blink behind the bag. She trusts me even as her body withers and slips to the floor, among the scattered shrapnel of a life suddenly departed.

They throng to the centre of the cemetery, the women clutching their husbands' arms, faces suitably aggrieved, and in return the husbands pat their wives' hands, like mothers mollifying their children. When the time comes, they stand round Mother and Father, a circle of black outfits and blacker expressions staring down at the mound of earth. A small mound for a small coffin. A small coffin for a small child. A child's death they believe was an accident. Just a game gone wrong. After all, how could she have known the danger in a bit of plastic?

They rub Father's shoulders and stroke Mother's hands, those who are more consumed with their façade, swiftly wiping a tear from her cheek or kissing her head. She doesn't seem to notice them. Her face is tear-stained and blank. She is hovering on the periphery of her grief, between shock and agony. But soon it will come. She will follow in Father's wake; she too will sob and scream into the comfort of her pillow at night. They will do it together.

The mourners cluster together and peck and prod at them, and I wonder how they bear it. Then they move to the mound of earth to lay down their flowers, closing their eyes, making their faces solemn, imparting a silent message they make sure is noticed by Mother and Father. How they act and deceive. It is almost natural. But the truth of the matter, Blue-Eyes, is that people are actors, the small roles they play applauded and replayed in their minds later on. They think to themselves, 'I hope I looked sad enough', 'I hope she didn't see me yawn', 'Oh, God, please don't let them have seen me get that bit of carrot out of my teeth'. Everyone does it, even if they don't realise it. Everyone except you. And Mary. You both are (were) special. You don't act. Your intentions and emotions are not something you have ever had to hide or modify for the sake of appearances. You are honest and true. You are both so good. I smile. The Good Ones.

Once the crowd finally disperses, retreating forms already visualising the cup of tea and tin of biscuits awaiting them at home, Mother and Father stand by her grave, unmoving. And then, as if they have shared the same thought, they look at me, heads turning sideways in unison to where I stand. They look at me; I smile. And suddenly a new flavour of grief finds its way into their eyes, like a thundercloud creeping across the gaze of the sun. Now they are no longer thinking of Mary. They are no longer mourning the loss of her; they are mourning the loss of one life and the beginning of another. A life with me. Only me.

Chapter 8

John

Thursday 3 December, 2015

John counts to five before he swings his legs over the bed and shuffles onto the landing. The screams grow in volume then and he ignores the urge to cover his ears. They penetrate the walls of the house and make his eardrums feel as if they are about to burst.

'Bonnie, sweetheart, it's OK. I'm here. Daddy's here.' He opens the door to see her sitting up in bed, hair askew, tears dripping down her face. She opens her arms, the scream dying in her throat. 'Daddy!' she mumbles through clenched teeth. He can see a glob of blood in the corner of her mouth. He grabs a tissue from the side of the bed and wipes it away, cradling her head with his hand. 'Did you bite your tongue again?'

She nods, small hands grabbing fistfuls of his PJs, sobbing quietly into his chest. John picks up the glass of water on her bedside cabinet and presses it to her lips. She sips reluctantly. 'That's it. Good girl. Wash the blood away.' He kisses the top of her head and rocks them from side to side. 'What did you dream about?'

She wraps her arms around his neck and mumbles through the snot and tears that coat her mouth, 'Under the bed!'

He nods. 'Smithy was under the bed again, was he?'

'He said he was going to eat my fingers!' Her hands begin to tremble.

'OK. Come here, sweetheart. It's just a dream.' He pries her arms from his neck and sits her in front of him. 'We're going to blow it away. Are you ready?'

She nods again, wiping her eyes. 'Yes, Daddy.'

He rubs his hands together until they're warm and cups her cheeks. He sucks in a breath and slowly blows on her forehead. Wisps of hair dance and sway on her skin. She closes her eyes and takes five deep breaths. He blows again, blowing the dream from her mind. He waits for her to sigh, something he has come to see as a good sign. He snaps his hands together. Her eyes ping open and she looks at him in surprise, as she always does. 'I've got it! It's in my hands! Shall we blow it away?'

'Count!'

'OK. On three, I'll open my hands! Ready?'

'Yes.'

'One…'

'Two…'

'Three!'

He opens his hands and they blow into his palms. Bonnie sinks back into his arms and he cuddles her until her eyes begin to flutter closed. After he's tucked her in bed, he makes his way to the door.

'Daddy?'

He sighs. 'Yes, Bonnie?'

'What if Smithy comes back?'

He turns and kisses her head. 'OK, sweetheart.' John crouches down and slips himself under the bed. 'Can I have one of your pillows, please, Bonnie?'

She drops one onto the floor and curls up on the edge of the mattress to be close to him. 'Thanks, Daddy.'

He smiles and rests his head on the pillow, his limbs already screaming in protest. 'He won't come back now because he won't fit under here with me.'

She giggles and dangles her hand over the bed. He reaches out and holds it until she falls asleep.

'Goodnight, sweetheart.'

Will there be more photographs? More messages typed out and signed by his daughter? He isn't sure which is worse: seeing the harm done to Bonnie or letting his imagination fill in the blanks. Both scenarios fill him with despair.

He looks round the small cottage they were relocated to that morning. With its orange sofa, inglenook fireplace, wooden floors and thick thatch, it isn't something he is used to. But it oozes comfort. Any other time, he would have relaxed here. He would have sat crossed-legged like a boy with Bonnie on the rug, piecing together a puzzle, Jules beside him reading her book. Lemonade and plates of food scattered across their little world on the floor. The image makes him dizzy. Or perhaps it isn't that. It probably has more to do with the fact he has hardly eaten for days. Jules on the other hand is overwhelmed with cravings. He often sits beside her, watching her eat, tears filling her eyes. Taking care of one baby while thinking of another. He dreads to think what the stress is doing to it. Him? Her? They don't know and it really doesn't matter.

How will they prevent this baby from being taken? What if Bonnie isn't enough? What if this one is wanted too?

John rubs his neck, fraught with worry. A small part of his brain thinks that, if he cut himself, he would bleed fear and panic and pain.

John pulls himself up from the sofa and forces himself to make a sandwich. When he finishes, he is surprised to find it is the peanut butter sort Bonnie adores and he hates. He eats it anyway, cramming it into his mouth, wishing he could sweep Bonnie up onto his lap and kiss her head as he has so often done in the past. Overcome with emotion, he leaves the kitchen and climbs the stairs to the bedroom. Jules's 'panic bag' sits on the bed, along with nappies, blankets, baby grows, towels, dummies and spare clothes for her. She took the panic bag out of their cupboard before they left for the cottage. Now all they have, aside from that, is a suitcase with toothbrushes, soap, aftershave, clothes and photographs of Bonnie. Their tablets, laptops and computers have been confiscated by the police. Their iPhones have been replaced with cheap pay-as-you-go mobiles for the time being.

DCI Alice Munroe had sat them down on the sofa as soon as she arrived that morning, Amy (their FLO) flanking her, and explained where they were with the investigation. He and Jules had sunk noticeably deeper into the sofa, clutched hands tightening until the blood drained away. Alice told them their examination of the photograph and envelope had turned up no DNA. They had nothing to go on but John's past. He was the only clue in an otherwise clueless investigation.

They proceeded to comb through every inch of his past once again. Facets of his world strewn out on the floor and picked and poked at. He proffered it all with a desperation only Jules understood. They looked at him with sympathy and determination, but they didn't know how it felt. How could they?

He gave Munroe his parents' address and numbers so she could contact them for more of an insight into his past, a place this person resided so prominently. It was almost like the monster – Smithy – that Bonnie used to be so frightened of. Except this wasn't Smithy, an imaginary creature they'd personified with a name. This was far worse. They had no face or name. Not a single modicum of knowledge. They were blind.

Munroe, delivering the onslaught of questions and information, had been tactful and almost gentle. John sometimes thought he glimpsed another side to her perfunctory manner. A soft middle to the hard edges. He looked at her and, before he could be completely sure, the humanity in her brown eyes slipped out faster than it had slipped in.

John wraps an arm around Jules's shoulder, looking at the items splayed across the bed. If the baby comes early at least they will be ready. But he hopes it won't. Where once he would have been eager to see his new child, now he wishes it could just remain where it is. Warm and protected. Safe from the torment of these long days.

Chapter 9

Maisie

Saturday 16 January, 2016

'Excuse me, is your name Maisie Green?'

'Yes. Can I help you?' The man is in his early thirties with wavy brown hair, bright-green eyes and a spattering of freckles across his face. He's wearing an Armani suit, black with silver cufflinks, which adds authenticity to the air of wealth and class surrounding him like a bubble.

'I'm here to see Tim. He's a friend. Heidi told me to ask for you.'

'Oh. OK. I just need to check it's OK for you to see him. Just bear with me while I give her a quick call.'

Maisie studies him out of the corner of her eye as she dials Heidi's number. When she is finished she gestures him forward. 'Great! He's in room 217. Follow me.' She walks with him through the door and down the corridor, dodging other staff members. 'So how do you know Tim?' She knows it isn't her place to ask but she can't help but wonder.

49

'We knew each other years ago. I… I read about the attack in the paper. I would have come sooner but I've got a big case going on at the minute.'

'I understand the nurse you talked to at reception explained the situation.'

'Yes. She explained everythi—' He stops mid-sentence. His expression turns blank, his eyes empty.

'Hello. I didn't expect to see you.' She sees Watson walking up to them.

'No… no, I didn't expect to see you either.' The man bites his lip and casts his eyes to the floor. What is that, Maisie wonders. Anger? Concern? Irritation? A change of atmosphere chokes the hall. The nurses – usually an insensitive bunch – turn and look, eyebrows raised. Lailah sends her a questioning glance. Maisie shrugs, putting her hands up as if to wave away the fug of tension. 'So you know each other too?'

Watson pats the man's back, a warm smile stretching across his lips. 'Yeah. We go way back, don't we, mate? Huh?'

He cringes, shuffling out from under Watson's arm. 'Yes. I suppose so. I've come to see Tim.'

'He'd be so glad you're here, mate.'

The man frowns, glancing at Watson. Glance. Glance. Glance. It's almost as if he is looking for something. Something he can't find.

'Follow me, please.'

The three of them stop outside room 217. 'I'll leave you both to catch up.' Maisie watches the man follow Watson into the room. They sit either side of Tim, Watson exuding warmth, his friend staring at the floor, cold and reticent. A sharp contrast to each other. Maisie wonders if they had a disagreement in the past. A tiff that has stretched long fingers into the present. She smiles, hoping they can resolve their issues, then turns and makes her way down the corridor to check on her other patient. When she returns the man is gone. Watson is leaning over Tim, holding his hand tenderly.

She watches thoughtfully, a smile playing across her face. Watson's lips are moving but Maisie can't tell what he is saying.

Chapter 10

Miller

Thursday 4 June, 1987

Mother holds the phone to her ear, nails tap-tap-tapping on the plastic. She preens her hair with the other hand, subconsciously flicking and twirling her dry and brittle locks. This is a habit that has withstood the derailment of everything else. The red varnish on her nails is chipped and cracked. Brown roots sit at the top of her head, a nasty contrast to the yellowy shade of blonde from copious amounts of Sun-In. Her face, once plastered with layer upon layer of make-up, is empty, the pores and blemishes she tried so hard to disguise there for all to see. A woman who was once confident in a beauty only she saw has sunk into a pool of disarray.

Father is much the same. I hear them in the bedroom next to mine. At night they take two deep breaths to steady themselves; in the morning they take four, bracing themselves for another day, needing strength to seep into their bodies. And for the rest of the time, a silence sits between them. Deep and unrelenting.

In the evening they watch television, flicking glances over to me. I know they are thinking about her. About their sweet angel, Mary, and wondering if perhaps it was not a game. I can see the question in their eyes. Did he have something to do with it? No, he couldn't have. No child of theirs could do something as wretched as that. No. He is a naughty boy but never, no, never. They look at me, wondering, denying their wild thoughts, their eyes unblinking, a mixture of confusion and disbelief blurring together. When they do this, a smile I find hard to contain flips onto my lips. They look away instantly, banishing those wild thoughts to the backs of their minds. And even though there is no love or even warmth between them now, their hands nevertheless seek each other's out.

The only enjoyment Mother sucks from life is to gossip with her friend Maggie. The silly, idle chatter they share reminds her of who she used to be. She performs with gusto, the blather blowing her up like a balloon. For a few hours she feels better, fuller, then, when she puts down the phone and looks at me, the air escapes her and she shuffles away. Poor, sad Mother.

I watch her now, tapping away with those nails. I grit my teeth and instead focus on the words falling one after the other out of her mouth.

'I know, Mags. I know. Well, why don't we take a cake round for her? Show her she has support. I know, she probably won't eat it. Well, she can take it with her to the hospital, can't she? Her husband's had a stroke, I'm sure he can still eat cake. Sugar might do him some good. I know, Mags.' She juts her lip out, brows knitting together, false sadness dancing across her features. 'I know. So sad. Yes, let's. She needs to know we're here for her.' Sympathy, if real in the first place, has a use-before date that prevents it lasting more than a few weeks. When the time is up, the avalanche of 'I think she needs to move on now' or 'This has been going on for weeks' pours in.

Mother puts a hand on her hip and begins tapping the cabinet instead.

I try, Blue-Eyes, I try so very hard. It is almost a game now, you know, holding down my anger, seeing how strong my reserve is. Sometimes, though, the sound of those nails is just too much to ignore.

She gasps as I pull her hand to my mouth and rip four fake nails off with my teeth. They taste chalky and sour in my mouth. She screams, shying away, eyes expanding into shocked saucers. I pull the last one away, feeling the varnish break up in my mouth as I so often imagine. She yanks her hand to her chest, cradling it, skin slick with saliva as I spit the nails into my cupped hand. I can hear rumbling in her throat, a combination of a groan and a whine. The phone skitters to the floor and I hear Maggie shriek, 'June, June? What is it? June!' I drop the mess onto the cabinet, stretch my arms around her weak little shoulders and kiss her cheek. 'I'msorryI'msorryI'mreallysorryMum.' Like a little naughty boy, I stare at my feet and force tears into my eyes, sniffing, wiping the snot from my nose because I know it will make her cringe.

She wriggles out from my arms and pats my head as if she is patting the back of a slug. Her nose wrinkles. 'That's... that's OK. Now off you go.'

She picks up the phone and continues her conversation with Maggie, finger poking the mess of spit and fake nail on the cabinet. She won't tell Maggie, not that I would be worried if she did. Her pride gets in her way: she could never admit to the oddity that is her son, to having a child as naughty and strange as me. I walk to the door, her gaze needling the back of my head as I go.

On the street, people cluster together in the sun, tongues wagging, hands waving, faces greasy with sunblock. It makes the wrinkles seem deeper on the old and the spots redder on the young. The middle-aged men, carrying paunches that bend their backs to the floor, stand and talk with their hips thrust out and their faces taut with arrogance. The women, stick-thin from attempts at keeping their husbands' attention, mill about like hens, clucking and swapping titbits of information, glancing at the men as the men glance at the girls across the street.

The elderly sit in their deckchairs, sipping tea despite the blistering heat, gazing sadly at the young, wishing they could still leap and jump and run with their friends. Wishing their skin was as smooth and their hair was as thick. They sip and they sip, drowning their sorrows in tea. The young flitter about, playing hopscotch and riding their bicycles, alive with freedom, the perils of adulthood something far removed from their small universe.

Do you know the arrogance makes me sick? It turns my stomach and makes me want to heave. The teenagers flick their hair and flaunt their bodies like salesmen showing off their wares on the market. They see themselves as gods and angels in a world of mortals. The way they walk, the way they stand and talk and believe they are entitled to everything. I dig my hands into my pockets and walk along the street to the centre of town. A school, a few shops and a town hall. A small place to grow up, a place where everyone knows everyone. A place where they all look at me and quickly look away. Being different is bad. They think I am a strange boy. A boy who will be a strange man. They don't like the look of me with my black hair and my black eyes. But I don't care because the feeling is mutual.

I only love you, I will only ever love you. With your blue eyes and unassuming personality, you are not arrogant or insolent like everyone else. You exude something special, something precious. You make others flock to you, want to be your friend. Want to please you and comfort you and make you laugh. But you don't see it. You are too good for that.

*

We sit in rows, waiting for Mr Philips to take us through our history lesson. A new teacher is going to take his place tomorrow. A girl

Mother says is as 'cute as a button'. I haven't seen her yet, only heard how everyone adores her and yet she has only just moved into town. Mr Philips saunters in, balding head slick with sweat, and greets us all in his droning voice. As he begins his tirade on the Roman Empire, the boys and girls slump in their seats. They try to look interested because Mr Philips talks to their parents over coffee in the café but I can see how they really feel. Micro expressions flit across their faces. Tiny truths unveiling the boredom or irritation or even awe that sits there. One girl, smaller than the rest, ugly, looks at the tall, beautiful girl to her left with something akin to love. Her feet dance under the table and I wonder if she wants to step on the tall girl's feet and spin round the room. The boy in front of me turns every few seconds to snatch a glimpse of a girl. Lust. Love. Hatred. Envy. Emotions are as transparent as glass. I see them all. And soon I will see you. Soon, you will crash into my life with more colour and sincerity than I have ever seen before.

Saturday 6 June, 1987

She stumbles into the classroom. Books fly out of her arms and land with a heavy thump on the floor. A strand of hair catches inside of her mouth. She swats it away and bends to pick up the books, blushing red. She gives a nervous smile to the pupils sniggering behind their hands. I can feel the embarrassment peeling off her in waves. It hits me in the chest and all of a sudden I want to scream at the girls and boys to stop it, stop it! Stop sniggering. I want to hurt them more than I have ever wanted to hurt anyone for making her feel this way. For making her feel small and silly. She is like you, Blue-Eyes. She is like Mary. She is special. A Good One.

She straightens her shirt and pushes her hair off her shoulders, standing a little taller, meeting the eyes of every pupil in the room; I sense Mr Philips has advised her to do this. A trick he uses when he wants our undivided attention.

'Hello, class. My name is Sarah Hardman. I'll be taking over from Mr Philips. Some of you might have seen me about – I've just moved into town.' A pause. 'I believe you've been learning about the Roman Empire and so we'll carry on with that today.' She folds her hands in front of her stomach; it is usually a gesture of self-satisfaction but with this woman I think it is a means of trying to make herself feel more confident. She smiles half-heartedly, snatches up a piece of chalk and fumbles with it for a moment before scratching across the blackboard. A girl behind me whispers to her friend, 'Think I might just start liking school now! We're not going to learn a thing.' The friend sniggers.

They think she is an imbecile but I can see she is not. She is nervous and embarrassed. She is also clever, engaging and sweet. It shows in the way she moves, the way she holds herself. And sure enough, when she gets into the flow of teaching, the boys and girls around me stop pulling faces and pointing and instead lean forward, eyes glued to her, faces taut with concentration. She has pulled them from their silly habits. She has got their attention.

Before the lesson is over, they are looking at her as if she is hope at the bottom of Pandora's Box; a light in their dark, boring lives. They stare up at her with big eyes, round with awe and amazement. And if she walks past them and smiles or praises them, they grin to themselves and look about the room, making sure others have noticed. It has only been one lesson and already they worship her. She is beautiful with her brown hair and hazel eyes but it is something sitting deeper than the surface. She emanates a quality that is irresistible. A sweetness and unassuming sincerity that makes her stand out from everyone else. The boys fancy her, the girls envy her. It is almost like a spell she has put them under. One she doesn't know she has the power to cast. It is one of the reasons I love you so much, Blue-Eyes: you don't realise how special you are.

She looks at me and I feel a flush of heat envelop my face. I count the seconds, one, two, before she looks away. And I know I want that look again. I crave it. I crave her attention and touch. I want it more than I have wanted anything ever before. I need it. It is a gasping, burning pull deep inside my gut. I won't be able to walk home unless I know I will come back tomorrow and have it again. I know how it seems, Blue-Eyes, I know I sound like all the other boys and girls, but it is different. It is stronger.

Much stronger.

I am the last to leave when she finishes her lesson. I walk past her, inhaling her vanilla scent, revelling in the proximity between us. She has her back to me, bending over a book on her desk. I mumble a goodbye.

'Bye, sweetheart.'

As I go, I reach out and touch her skirt. My fingers graze the fabric and make it sway. She doesn't notice and I leave. But my fingers are alive with the essence of her. Later, I run them down my face and I think I can feel her on my skin. I sleep with my hand tucked under my cheek, lips sucking on my fingers like a baby.

Chapter 11

John

Friday 4 December, 2015

The sonographer smears on the gel and runs the probe across Jules's bump. 'Ahh, here we are.' She smiles at the screen. 'All seems well. I know you asked for another scan because you were worried but this little one is a very healthy baby. Would you like to know the sex?'

John looks at Jules and she nods. There isn't much point in keeping it a surprise now. 'Yes.'

'A boy. A little boy.'

Jules puts her head against the headrest and stares at the screen, her face awash with emotion. She covers her eyes but he can see the glint of a tear under her little finger. He leans forward and kisses her head. The doctor jumps up from her seat and makes her way to the door. 'I'll give you a minute.'

'She… she secretly wanted a brother! She told us she didn't mind but I saw her mark the calendar with the date her baby brother would arrive. She… she wanted a brother.' Jules leans into his shoulder and sobs. John wraps his arms around her.

This is supposed to be a happy time. A time to treasure, but instead here they are like this. For a moment, John wonders if it is a dream. This can't actually be happening. When they return home, Bonnie will be sitting on the sofa with a book or playing a board game with Don. She'll look up at them and smile, running over, trying to look at the scan photo. That is the way things will be. Except they won't, will they?

Jules rummages through her bag for a tissue, pictures and make-up falling out. John pulls one from his pocket and hands it to her. This is their reality: who can get a tissue quickest. He knows he shouldn't be having these thoughts. He and Jules are healthy, their second child is on his way and they *will* find Bonnie. They have hope. Hope. Such a feeble thing, such a wavering, useless emotion. No. They must be positive, otherwise what's the point? Bonnie, if – when – they find her, will return home to a mum and dad who are no use to her. They have to be positive.

'Jules.' He wipes hair from her eyes and smiles. 'Jules, Bonnie would want us to enjoy this. She'd want to be here with us. Right now she'd probably be sitting here—' he pats the examination bed '—and staring at the screen with that look she gets when she's excited. She'd be jumping into my arms and telling me all the things she's going to do with him.' John wipes her cheek and holds her hand. 'She'd be telling us about the books she'll write for him, the jokes she'll tell him. She'd be happy. Excited. And when she comes back, when the police find her, we need to be ready. She needs to come home to a happy house, not to us as we are.'

Jules tucks her hair behind her ear and nods slowly, her face regaining some of its composure. 'You're right. I know you are.'

'What do you want to call him?' John gestures to the screen, mesmerised by their baby.

She runs her hand across her stomach, smiling. 'Bonnie wanted to call him Bertie.'

'Bertie it is.'

*

She pulls on his hand and points to the floor. *'Just a minute, Daddy. I dropped a penny.'* She leans down, chubby fingers reaching out. He stops her. *'Leave it, sweetheart. It will give someone good luck.'*

'Will it?'

'Yes.' John kneels down and squeezes her hand. *'In an hour or two, someone will see that penny. And they'll kneel down like you and I are doing now. They'll pick it up and for the rest of the day they'll have good luck. All because of you. Because you left it there for them to find.'*

She smiles and looks from him to the coin. *'Really?'*

'Really, really.'

She fumbles through her pink purse and gently drops another next to it. *'Now they'll have more luck.'*

John nods and grins. He takes her hand and they walk down the street. When they come back, the money is gone and Bonnie smiles all the way home.

Chapter 12

Maisie

Sunday 17 January, 2016

She looks at him as if she can't decide whether he is really asleep or playing a game and at any moment will jump up from his bed and pull her into his arms. Her eyes snag on the tubes and needles embedded in his skin and all of a sudden fear slips through the cracks. The girl looks at Maisie, then studies the machines, small hand guiding a clump of hair to her mouth. She chews, and Maisie can see a glob of spit in the corner. A thousand different emotions jump across her features and for a moment Maisie is fascinated by their depth. Confusion. Hope. Surprise. Worry. Love.

When she frowns, her face wrinkles just like Tim's, small creases appearing at the corners of her eyes and mouth. Chewing her hair, she takes three steps to the bed, guided by Heidi's hand. Maisie smiles at her, eyes drawn to the cast that looks oversized on her small hand.

'Hello.'

The girl looks at her and quickly looks away, gripping her

mother's hand as if she is worried Heidi might suddenly disappear. 'Can… can Daddy hear me?'

Heidi gives her a silent nod, twisting her scarf into a small ball, eyes darting from the door to her daughter. Today her dense curls are combed back into a hairband and her eyes accentuated by mascara. Waterproof, Maisie thinks to herself. She wonders if she has applied it to detract from the red patches under her nose or if it's just her way of feeling human again. Either way, the small act does nothing to assuage the fear that glistens in her eyes.

Maisie kneels down and smiles at the girl. 'We don't know, darling. Nobody knows. Your daddy is a little bit of a mystery. We like to think he can. Your mum and I talk to him all the time.'

She nods and leans over the bed, wincing as she catches her cast on the bedframe. Heidi jumps out of the seat and helps her, brow furrowing and creating a nest of wrinkles in her skin. She is on edge today; there is a tension in her movements that worries Maisie. A coiled spring. Maisie supposes she would feel the same in her position. She watches the girl carefully touch his hand, her fingers navigating the tubes. She is grateful Tim is asleep; even in a vegetative state, her patients have sleep cycles.

The girl cradles his hand, nestling her face into his palm. 'Hi, Daddy.' Tears spring to her eyes. Her voice rings through the room, sending a wave of sadness down Maisie's chest.

Heidi lowers herself into a chair and rubs her daughter's back. With the other hand she caresses her bump. Maisie watches her fingers make circular motions, hypnotised by the thought of a baby of her own. As a swift pang of agony stabs into her chest, she looks away, blinks three times, takes two deep breaths and then returns her gaze to Heidi. That usually does the trick.

Slowly the girl runs her fingers along Tim's cheek, a crackle of quiet sobs bouncing off the walls. Heidi gathers her up and cradles her to her chest, careful to avoid the cast, rocking them from side to side. Maisie eases herself from the chair and waits in the corridor. She counts out ten minutes, then returns to her spot beside Tim. Now the girl is perched on his bed, tears dried on her skin, words tumbling from her mouth. Heidi rubs her back, smiling despite the look of dread that clouds her face. Is she worrying her daughter will lose her father? No, it is more than that. Maisie sinks into the chair, pondering the possibilities. Is the girl ill? Is something wrong with the baby? Is Heidi ill herself? Is she afraid she or her daughter will be attacked? Is she concerned the person responsible is still out there?

'Me and Mummy watched *Moana* yesterday. I wish you could have been there, Daddy. You would have liked it. We had popcorn. And even when Mummy put it in my bowl, it popped and popped!' The girl fiddles with the hem of her shirt just as her mother fiddles with the fabric of her scarf, twisting it into a tiny ball. 'Daddy, can you hear me? I love you, Daddy. Don't forget.' A tear forms in the corner of her eye and trickles down her cheek. Maisie sits up and smiles, trying to lighten the atmosphere.

'Was it good? The movie?'

The girl looks up, surprised. 'Yes. I like Moana. She has nice hair.'

Maisie nods. 'Is she your favourite princess?'

'Yes.'

'Who's your second favourite princess?'

'Belle.'

'And third?'

'Cinderella.'

'I've always wanted glass slippers like her. Have you?'

She nods, staring up at Maisie with a guarded expression. 'I want a carriage. Mummy says I'm not old enough for one yet. Daddy says I can have one when I'm eighteen. He says he'll find me some slippers on eBay.'

'That sounds nice.'

'What's wrong with Daddy? Mummy says he's asleep.' She looks back at Tim, and Maisie is surprised how fast the subject has changed.

'Daddy's got a bump on his head. He's in a very, very deep sleep. We've put a plaster on it so it can heal.'

'That's what Mummy said.' She chews her hair again, hdf broken expression glued to her father. 'Daddy gave me a tape recorder for Christmas. I recorded myself reading his favourite book so he can hear me. I don't want him to forget me. Can you play it for him?'

'Of course! That's a lovely idea'

Heidi rummages in her bag and produces a small black device. Maisie hasn't seen one in years. Her mother let her borrow one to sing into as a child; a time when she wanted to be a singer instead of a nurse. When she was very young and the future was just a wisp of something blurry on the horizon.

'Thank you.' She takes it and holds it in her lap. 'What book is it?'

'*Jack and the Beanstalk.*'

'I used to read my brother that book. It was his favourite too.'

'You have a brother?' Heidi says, gently positioning her daughter on her lap and dropping the ruined scarf on the floor.

'I used to.'

She nods. 'I'm sorry.'

'Mummy, why are you sorry?'

'I… er…'

Maisie leaps in. 'I have an idea. Why don't you help me massage your daddy's feet?'

Her nose wrinkles and she glances to the foot of the bed. 'I don't want to do that!'

Heidi smiles sadly, kissing her head. 'OK. Well, monkey. Why don't you go and get a drink? She sees Watson. 'Look who's here.'

Maisie watches the little girl rush out into the corridor. Watson pulls her into his arms and kisses her nose. Then he nods at something she says and turns, making his way back down the hallway.

'She's sweet.'

Heidi repositions herself in the chair, taking up the scarf once again. 'Thanks.'

'So, how are you?'

'I'm fine. We're… we're coping.' She gestures to the door. 'She's sleeping in my bed now. And I'm glad because every time I close my eyes I'm afraid something will happen. It's a relief to know she's OK.'

'She coped with all of that really well. She's a strong girl.'

'I know.' She looks at Tim. 'That tape recorder was his. He gave it to her for Christmas. When she was a baby, she cried constantly if we left the room, so Tim recorded us both talking to her. Played it and she was fine.'

'Good idea. I wish my mum would have thought of that. I cried all the time.'

'Do you have children?'

'No, I don't.' Maisie shakes her head. She fiddles with the tape recorder, keeping her eyes low. She has worked so hard at building a wall up against the pain, each brick carefully laid with tears and effort. It frustrates her when she finds a breach. She doesn't tell Heidi how much it hurts just to see her touch her bump. Or how the pain makes her feel like balling up on the floor and crying. It knocks her sideways and leaves her breathless.

'When I was pregnant with my daughter, I was craving peanut butter constantly. We had the cupboards full of it. If I was upset or just fed up, Tim would stick a spoon in a tub, drop a dollop of ice cream on top and sprinkle it with jellybeans. He'd put a cheesy rom-com on the telly or stick the Rolling Stones on. He always knew what to do. He knew what I wanted even before I did.' She leans forward and takes his hand in hers. 'He's a kind person. Always has been.'

Maisie nods. 'One of the kindest things I've ever seen happened when I was twelve. Mum and I were sitting on this open-top bus, chatting about a movie we'd just seen at the cinema. Anyway, a girl in a wheelchair and her mother got on. She had special needs.

From what I gathered, it was her birthday – she must have been about twenty – and the open-top bus ride was her treat. You should have seen her face. I don't think I've ever seen anybody so happy. She had this… this smile, this huge smile that lit up her face. Her mum looked so stressed, flustered. When she realised she couldn't get her daughter up the stairs, the girl was heartbroken. She didn't cry, she didn't shout, she just sat there, staring at the floor. A man sitting at the back went over and talked to them. He picked her up – he was so gentle – and carried her up.'

'And then?'

'They came back down. Her hair was windswept, face flushed. She looked like she'd had the time of her life. The mother thanked the man over and over again. Before they got off, she hugged him. He returned to his seat and just sat there smiling away. That's one of the kindest things I've ever seen.'

Heidi smiles. 'That's lovely. That's the sort of thing Tim does.'

Maisie looks up as the door opens.

Watson peers round. 'Heidi, I've got you a cup of tea.'

'Oh, thanks.' She stands and walks out of the door. Maisie follows and smiles, watching Watson wrap an arm around Heidi's shoulder, struck by how lovingly he touches her.

Chapter 13

Miller

Friday 12 June, 1987

I hold the tangle of brown hair to my nose and inhale deeply. Closing my eyes, I envisage her standing before me and her smile fills me with joy. I'm not used to this type of emotion. It laces itself around my limbs, suffusing every inch of my body.

Her bedroom is small and stuffy, brimming with haphazardly placed knick-knacks, stacks and stacks of books shoved into the corners, and clothes – clean and dirty – thrown across the floor like one big, lumpy carpet. On the walls hang pictures of the sea, and I wonder if that is where she comes from. A home by the sea. Perhaps Cornwall? Mother and Father took me and Mary once. A long time ago. I can still remember feeling the water lap at my feet, the frigid temperature making me shiver as I stood and waited for the three of them to tire. It seemed like hours. They built sandcastles, splashed in the sea, chased each other and, when the sun disappeared behind the cliff, huddled inside the beach tent to keep warm, hands cupping steaming flasks of hot chocolate. After they'd sucked the last drops from the bottom, they sank into each other and smiled, content in one another's company.

I scrape more of her hair greedily from the brush, sniffing as I pull and stuff it into my pockets like a starving boy feasting on a banquet. The smell is intoxicating. Sweet and pure, like her. Her diary sits on the nightstand. I run my finger over the page, smiling at her small scrawl, at the way she dots her i's with hearts. Bad ones. She can't draw but that hasn't dissuaded her from doodling in the margins. Hearts and arrows. Wings and swirls. Pieces of her imagination laid out on a piece of paper; segments of her raw, beautiful mind encapsulated for evermore in ink. The indentations beneath the pads of my fingers cut deep into the grainy paper. Sunday she is having lunch with her mother. Monday she is meeting a man called Jack. His name is circled twice. Five exclamation marks stand off to the side. I absent-mindedly wonder if he is her brother. Her father? Her friend?

Sitting on the bed, I cradle her diary in my arms. A red stain catches my eye to the right. Small, nearly unnoticeable, but it is fresh, bold against the white sheet. Blood. A cut finger perhaps? From the page of a book? I touch the stain and smile. I am not repulsed but happy, fascinated. With the diary in my hand and my finger digging into the stain, I feel close to her. How many others would she allow to see something as private as this? The blood from her cut smeared across her bed, her sanctuary from the harshness of long days. Not many. I know she doesn't know I am here, Blue-Eyes. But later, when she is in bed, I wonder if she will smell me, if she'll look around and wonder, just for a moment, if someone has been in her room? And if that someone was me.

She doesn't know how I feel about her. I keep a lock on those emotions until I am away; I cannot risk her seeing something on my face, or catching my staring eyes as she floats about the classroom. She has only just moved here; the rumours will find her soon enough. The people of this town will fill her ears with poison and trick her into thinking I am an odd little boy. I can just hear you asking now, 'But are they rumours?' Yes and no. Yes, the things I say and do people find strange. But no, she need not be worried about the rumours. I won't bother her. She is the best thing I have ever seen. She is rich and raw, her personality innocent and sweet. A special kind of person. She is so good. Pure. Like you, Blue-Eyes, only not *as* good.

I close her diary and pat it gently into my satchel. Later, when I curl up on my bed and pour over its contents, I feel as if she is with me, her honeyed breath a fragrance that relaxes me, her skin cool, soft, a balm against the sunburn. If I concentrate hard enough, I can hear her whisper my name over and over and over into my ear. And when she smiles, I reach out and run my fingers across her lips, mesmerised by the emotion that bleeds into her face.

Thursday 18 June, 1987

My hand glides across the page, in a way you'd least expect from a person like me. It is almost artistic, creative. I twirl the pencil between my fingers, catching the sketch, striking a line through the middle. The face I have drawn is split in two. A creation undone.

I once saw a rat splayed out in the road. Its back was broken, raggedy fur clumped with blood, teeth poking through an open mouth. Its eyes were two large, unblinking black pools. I remember looking at it and being surprised by how calm it seemed. It didn't struggle, didn't whine. It just lay there, the look in its eyes something between shock and surprise, a combination of the two, and I thought how ignorant it must have been to step into the road.

Children and their parents clustered around me, disgustedly shrieking. Some were sympathetic, others repulsed. The children pinched their noses and shouted 'Ewww!' and the adults tutted and said, 'Someone should put that thing out of its misery.' A few shared looks, subtle shakes of the head, and that was it. They stood there, looking at me expectantly, then they pointed and said, 'Well, go on, then.'

But I didn't.

Eventually, the adults disbanded, tutting and muttering about me into their hands. The children soon followed, all but one. A girl – short, blonde – who sat beside me on the hot tarmac and watched for a few minutes longer, sympathetic to the rat. Her mother called her away and I was left alone. They watched from afar. But still I didn't kill it. Rats didn't bother me. It was fascination. It wasn't the passage *into* death, it was the passage *from* life. I've come to realise that even as the final seconds are filched from your grasp, emotions play across the face like scenes in a movie. So much emotion. And it occurred to me that the rat lived more in its last seconds than it had its whole life.

The people standing by didn't see that, though. They only saw a boy fascinated with death. But they were wrong. It isn't death that fascinates me. It is *life*.

Mother creeps into my room when I am at school. She takes my drawings to sit and look at. She expects the rat. She expects bodies and blood and gore from her oddity of a son. Snapped fingers and gushing wounds, a dark creation from a dark mind. Instead, I show her something which disturbs her even more. I show her our community.

The last bunch Mother stole included one of Maggie's husband, Joel. He was asleep in a deckchair on a sunny day. Above him, I'd drawn a smaller image, with puffs of smoke made to look like a dream rising from his head. The image was of him stuffing his wife's mouth with dirty socks and carrots. Neither of them notice me when I look through their window in the evenings. She reprimands him for not picking up his dirty socks and for not eating his carrots. 'I went to all the trouble of cooking you that dinner,' she says, pointing her finger at him like she would a naughty child. He bites his lip and frowns at the plate, cringing if she adds 'Mr' on the end, for that means he won't be allowed any of the apple crumble she made him buy on the way home.

I imagine Mother cupping her mouth and staring at the drawing with wide eyes. Maggie's treatment of Joel is something she likes to keep secret. But I flushed it out into the open.

The second was of Mrs Berry across the road. In the picture she was looking at her children with disdain. A shocking contrast to the adoring façade she conjures.

I was in a shop with Mother and Father, waiting in the queue, three weeks ago. In front of us were two women paying for their things. The first a humpbacked old lady with bumpy knuckles and deep wrinkles and the second an overweight, greasy-haired woman. The elderly lady was paying for a basketful of squeaky toys for her dogs. The younger woman was buying a packet of sweets for the child that bawled and cried in the pushchair at her side. The woman, flushed with anger, knelt down and snapped her hand round the child's, eyes blazing. 'If you don't shut up, you won't get any sweets!' The girl stopped and hugged her teddy bear close. When the mother let go of her hand, it was white, drained of blood. Crescent-shaped marks were cut into her skin. The girl nodded and the mother carried on paying, proud. Proud of her authority over her child. Proud of her control.

The third picture depicted this scene. And I imagine Mother being shocked because I saw something she missed.

I wipe away the line with as much care as I can muster, swiping the detritus of rubber off the paper. This one is of Sarah. She stands in front of the village hall, arms open, eyes wide. Behind her, the sun sets; the light sweeps around her, making her look as if she is an angel. Her hair has turned bronze in the sun and in her eyes dances a confidence that makes others seek out her guidance. She is an angel, a goddess among mortals. Something special in the plain. Light in the dark. Good against evil. And by her side, I stand proudly.

If you look closely, you can just see our hands clenched together through the folds of her dress.

Chapter 14

John

Saturday 5 December, 2015

Her fingers are snapped like breadsticks, jutting out at odd angles, shards of bone punching through bloodied scraps of skin. He can't see her face in the photograph, but when he closes his eyes he can conjure her expression. A combination of shock, agony and fear splashed on her face like the blood spattered across the back of her hand. He can hear her crying in his ears, a high-pitch wail that resonates through his mind and body. It makes his fingers twitch and his heart thump in his chest, as if someone is playing the drums.

Dum de dum de dum.

He absent-mindedly wonders if her heart was beating this fast when her little bones were snapped. Clever, though. Ruining the left hand of a right-handed girl. Oddly enough, it isn't the sight of her little fingers, but the words on the back of the photograph that make his body feel as if it is being pumped full of ice-cold water.

The first time you took her to Disneyland, Don had to take her round the park because you and Jules had a sickness bug.

We three had a wonderful time.

John studies the last six words and wonders if anybody is as safe as they believe. How is anyone to know if they are being watched when they take out the bins on a Sunday morning in their pyjamas, bleary-eyed and yawning; if they are being watched doing the weekly shop, guiltily adding ice cream to the trolley; if they are being watched when they scream at the TV in the evenings, cross with 'those blasted politicians'. John finds himself shuffling backwards, feet carrying him away from the picture in Alice's hands.

They'd been watched for years and hadn't been aware of it. He feels as if the rug has been pulled from beneath his feet. The private life he built with his wife and daughter was all just a mirage; their reality is a life watched and studied like germs under a microscope.

John's legs begin to shake. Inch by inch, he slips down to the floor, the strength leaching from his limbs. In the corner, where the floor and wall meet, a spider sits in the centre of its web, and John can't help but think he is the fly and Bonnie's kidnapper the spider: he is the one in the middle, helpless and afraid, haunted by something that has turned life into a misery.

Jules comes to his side and sinks down beside him. He wraps his arm around her shoulder, muffling the sobs.

Once, when they were watching a movie with Bonnie, he'd covered her eyes to prevent her seeing a violent scene, but he didn't want her to feel left out so he asked her to cover his own eyes. He wishes she could do it again now. He doesn't want to see or hear or feel any of this. It is his fault. He must have aggravated someone in the past. He must have been rude or unkind.

He must have hurt someone. He must have. And now they want revenge.

'I'll be honest; I'm not hopeful we'll find any DNA.' Alice tucks the bagged photo into her pocket. It was found under a sheaf of letters on Don's doormat. As it doesn't have a postal stamp, they assume it was dropped off by hand but the CCTV covering his house offers up no suspects. Whoever has Bonnie is bringing others into the mix. Alice has told them it is to galvanise John; to make him see that he or she knows who those closest to him are. To see that even the smallest corners of his life are being studied.

A clever system, she said.

A clever mind.

Yes, John thinks. Clever. What sort of person makes a child sign their cruel messages? John cringes. Bonnie is the victim but he is the target. He is the one this person wants to hurt. Bonnie is a piece of weaponry in the kidnapper's arsenal. That much is clear.

Don rubs his eyes, cheeks sore from dried tears. The tissue he holds in his hand is soaked through. 'Is… is there anything I can do?' Don had turned up on their doorstep that morning, shaking, words tumbling out of his mouth about fingers and bones and Disneyland.

They'd taken that trip as a family, to celebrate Bonnie's first birthday, but Don had tagged along too after a bad breakup. John and Jules had come down with a bug, the rest of their holiday taken up with vomiting, and Don had taken Bonnie round the park, keeping her in his room at night so she didn't catch the virus. The holiday had been one of the worst he and Jules ever had. But for Don and Bonnie it was the best. They watched the parades, met the characters – had a great time. Just a shame they weren't on their own. Unbeknownst to them, someone had been tagging along.

Don eventually let them guide him into the lounge. There he

76

explained that at no point had he seen anyone watching them. He would have told them straight away. He would never have left the hotel room. They patted him on the back and told him not to worry, none of it was his fault.

'No, there isn't anything you can do, I'm afraid,' says Munroe. 'Stay vigilant.' She slips her woollen coat on and leaves.

Amy passes round fresh tissues and makes them tea. They sit together on the sofa, hands twitching, toes tapping the floor, images of Bonnie's broken fingers filling their minds. The atmosphere is tense, as if at any moment someone will jump out at them. The miasma puts them on edge and makes their hearts flip. Amy tries to soothe them, to mollify the fear that creases their brows and makes them fidget in their seats, but nothing abates it. Their life together, once something as familiar as the backs of their hands, has morphed into something strange and horrifying. As unfamiliar as the future that now awaits them.

Later, when Jules is asleep, curled up in John's arms, his mind refuses to slow down. He can't stop himself thinking through how this will end. Will the police find this person, save Bonnie? Or will they be constantly chasing someone who evades their grasp?

The kidnapper is trying to hurt him, John knows that; what he doesn't know is how far he or she will take it. Will more and more photographs pour in from all directions, depicting their daughter's torture until her eventual death? What will be the outcome? John can't see a happy ending on the horizon. This is bound to end in only one way and even to think about it makes his body involuntarily flinch. He can't bear it. All he wants to do is scoop Bonnie up and hold her until the darkness of their lives is washed away by the arrival of a new day.

He looks at Jules, eyes flickering in her sleep, hands clenching and unclenching, wondering if she is dreaming. Has it occurred to her how this will end? He knows it has occurred to Alice; he saw it in her eyes, when the professional veneer cracked to reveal the human behind.

Jules turns, groaning, her hands spreading across the expanse of her bump. John brushes his hand across her wet face, visualising Bonnie's red Dorothy shoes. He was surprised how much she enjoyed *The Wizard of Oz* the first time she watched it. The red shoes were her most prized possession and whenever she got excited, she clicked her heels together. He can just imagine her sitting somewhere in the dark, in the outfit she wore the day she went missing, dirty, frayed. Her green shirt, pink skirt and orange tights covered in layers of grime. But most of all he can imagine, with a clarity that makes his chest ache, those red shoes splattered with blood, creating a pattern of bright and dark speckles.

Jules's eyes flutter open. A groan slips from her lips. John jumps as she throws back the duvet and sits bolt upright. She sucks in a breath. 'John! John! Oh my God! Oh God! Oh no! John!'

Blood soaks into the sheet and expands between her legs. He dials 999 as Jules begins to cry into her hands.

Chapter 15

Maisie

Monday 18 January, 2016

'And they lived happily ever after…' Maisie scoops up the tape recorder and presses the pause button, then gently begins to rub Tim's wrist with her fingers, soothing and relaxing the spastic muscles. Heidi watches her, lost in thought. They'd listened to *Jack and the Beanstalk* all the way through, smiling when the wrong word was mumbled or one missed out.

'I've got to go soon. My mother-in-law is moving in today. She takes care of my daughter while I'm here. She and her husband will be coming to see him soon. They're still in shock. I suppose, in a way, it must be worse for them. He's their baby.' She frowns, burrowing her face into her hands. 'You know, most of the time I just want to curl up and cry.'

'Most people do. I've cared for a lot of people here – and their families. You're doing well, Heidi. You're coping really well.'

She smiles softly. 'Thanks, Maisie. I'll let her know you played it for him today.' She gestures to the tape recorder.

'How is she?'

'OK. She cries herself to sleep at night but during the day she's mostly just quiet. Detached.'

'Have they found anything out about the person who attacked him?'

'No.' She sighs. 'No, and I don't think they will.'

'There is still hope, you know.'

'I know. I know. I feel like I'm in emotional limbo.' She drags a tissue from her bag and blows her nose. 'Some days are worse than others. Especially today. I miss him. It still feels like he's here. There's still that presence, you know? I miss him hugging me, making me laugh. I miss our conversations. We were always talking. About the day, weather, work, silly stuff. It made us stronger.'

'I'd miss that too, I think.'

Heidi motions to her face and tuts. 'He'd be making me laugh round about now. Poking fun at himself. "Well, at least you don't have to hear me eat dinner – enjoy it while it lasts, sweetheart."'

'Eat?'

Heidi nods. 'I've never heard anyone eat so loud. It used to really bug me. I actually miss it now. You poor thing, listening to me bang on. Go check on your other patients.'

'No, no. I like hearing about him. I only have one other patient and another nurse is covering her care today.'

'Is that Lailah?'

'Yes. That's her. ICU nurses usually only care for two patients at a time. She and I share the care of Tim and a lady down the hall.'

'She's nice. Jolly. She talks to Tim.'

'She's one of the few who do.' Maisie shouldn't have said that. She shouldn't have, but she can't deny her relationship with Heidi is something akin to a friendship now. They sit together for hours talking and it has cemented something in the way they are with one another. The small, knowing smile on the rare occasions they share a joke. The swift wave of the hand when they greet each other. Maisie just wishes she could ask the question she has been wanting to ask from the moment they met. But how can she?

'I'd better get going.' Heidi heaves herself up and adjusts her shirt. When she spots Maisie looking, she gestures to her bump. 'Big, aren't I?'

'Not for long now.'

'Not long at all.' She pulls a scan photo from her bag and passes it to Maisie. 'I'm secretly hoping he'll recover in time for the birth. I know it's not likely and I know he wouldn't be the same straight away. I've done so much research – it all says he'll need time to get back to his old self, if he ever does. Some people wake up missing some of their memories but I can't help hoping.

'That... that's right.' Maisie takes the ultrasound photo and nods. She runs her finger across the baby's nose, transfixed. When she gives it back, her legs are trembling. Heidi shakes her head. 'Can I leave it here? I want it to be with him.' She takes Tim's hand and kisses it.

'Of course.'

Maisie only notices her leave because a wave of calm passes over her. She realises now that whatever is affecting Heidi is beginning to affect her too. It is a weight that hangs over them constantly. It snaps at their heels and pokes at their clothes like fingers trying to pinch their skin. There is no escape from it. Maisie straightens Tim's sheet and checks his temperature. Stable. Good. She leans over his bedframe and looks into his eyes.

'She's scared it's going to happen again, isn't she, Tim?'

*

Maisie flops onto the sofa and rubs her feet. She pulls her book, *The Night Watch* by Sarah Waters, from the coffee table. Lailah recommended it on one of their short breaks. 'Powwows' as she calls them. Those chats have seen them through numerous upsetting days on the ward. Working in an ICU isn't easy. Despite the professionalism they exercise with patients and their families, they both share the belief that there must be an element of humanity in what they do. And at the end of the day it's an honour to support and care for people who are at their most vulnerable.

The easiest – and quickest – way for her to 'switch off', as Ben puts it, is by watching a movie curled up on the sofa or reading a book. After ten minutes, she feels a little more like herself, less like an amalgamation of five different people. Family members' emotions inevitably rub off on her and, by the time her shift ends, she feels as if she is floating in the air like a balloon, the string holding her down the thought of her quiet time in the evening with Ben.

She leans her head back on the cushion and closes her eyes. Thoughts of Heidi's baby leap, unbidden, into her mind. She tries to banish them but realises it is like clutching at straws. She feels the hairs on her arms rise up and opens her eyes, looking to the door across from her. She hasn't been in that spare bedroom for just under a year. And yet still she remembers the way it last felt to turn the handle and walk in, the sweet smell greeting her in the doorway, the memories clamouring about in her head. Faces and smells and feelings she locked away, finding her once again. But most of all she remembers the pain and the guilt. A pain so strong it made her want to pull her hair out and a guilt so overwhelming, she felt as if shreds of herself had been torn away.

Chapter 16

Miller

Wednesday 8 July, 1987

He says he saw me. Saw me standing by the road watching her through the window of the post office. I should have been more careful but I couldn't help staring, Blue-Eyes. She dropped her change on the floor and, as the redness bloomed in her cheeks, I found my eyes were glued to her face. The woman behind the counter saw it, the knee-high children buying Pez dispensers saw it, the man with the long eyebrows and goatee did too. She has that effect on people, even the adults. Probably even Father if he had been looking at her. But no. He wasn't. He tells me to stop 'mooning' over her. He says it's not healthy, the look in his eyes telling me he won't forget this, won't allow it to carry on. But he doesn't know I have followed him to work and seen him grope the woman he likes to wink at when others aren't looking. Tanya, her name is. A name to make Mother cringe if she ever heard it. And hear it she will. Father must go. He must go so I can have Sarah.

Mother likes to 'take a moment' in the morning, sitting at the dining table with a mug of tea and her book. She says it is her time to relax. More often than not, the latest romance she is reading will slip from between her fingers and land with a thump on the floor as her eyes flutter to a close. Father wakes her with unloving hands when he comes down for his newspaper. She jumps up, hands reaching for her book. 'Oh, oh, I must have nodded off.'

Father nods, muttering something under his breath.

'What did you say, dear?'

'Nothing, nothing. I'll get off. Don't want to be late.' These are the words he says every morning when he is sick of Mother.

'OK. Have a good day.'

He bangs the door as he goes. Mother sits back down and continues to read; after three seconds, she gets up again to make herself another cup of tea. No milk, four sugars. She hums as she does this, and I know it is to block out her thoughts. She reads between sipping her tea and glancing at the clock. This lasts for half an hour. When she is finished, she closes her book, runs her hand along the cover and sighs. The morning ritual is complete.

I have watched her do this hundreds of times, peering through the banister of the stairs, both irritated by her mannerisms and fascinated by the way the ritual does not alter. Not even in the slightest. A part of me wonders if it is because this was the ritual she kept when Mary was alive. As if by repeating it she finds a form of solace in her sea of grief. I wonder if the ritual makes her feel close to Mary, to the past she so yearns for.

As she puts her mug in the sink, I make my way out of the door. I do not speak and she does not look at me. Our own small ritual, it seems.

I follow close behind Father, knowing he is already having thoughts about the quick half an hour before his colleagues arrive for work, his time with Tanya, a spotty thirty-year-old. He goes into the reception, closes the curtains and locks the door. But I can see through a gap in the fabric. I aim the camera, a Nikon, into the room and take snaps, one after the other, as the first garments of clothing fall to the floor like confetti.

Saturday 11 July, 1987

I could have left them for her yesterday but doing it while she takes one of her 'moments' is just too appealing. Father hasn't come down yet and Mother's book is slowly edging out of her hands. When it lands on the floor and her eyes close, I slip the four photographs onto the table, directly under her chin. I go back to my room and later, when I follow Father down the stairs, his aftershave making me gag, his face cleanly shaven and fresh for Tanya, she is still sitting there. Only this time, the book is still on the floor and in her trembling hands are the four photographs.

Father looks at them over her shoulder and his expression of contentment caves in. She turns, sensing him, and for a moment they just watch each other. It is almost like a silent conversation. Then Father mutters, 'Who gave them to you?'

She doesn't respond, only tears them in half, lip quivering. 'Get your things and leave.'

'Sweetheart—'

'Leave!'

He sighs and makes his way to the door. As he passes me, I look at him and smile. His eyes widen to an almost comical extreme. The door bangs shut in his wake. Out of the window, I see his shoulders loosen, and I wonder if now he finally feels free. He will no longer have to bear the hassle of a nagging wife and strange son. He makes his way down the street, and I can't help but laugh. That's right, Daddy, leave. Leave June and her little oddity behind.

Chapter 17

John

Sunday 6 December, 2015

The grief comes in ebbs and flows. If he lets his mind wander for a few precious moments he forgets, his mind releasing its hold on memories of the past two weeks and offering him some relief from the pain. But then it returns as it always does and, once again, he feels as if he is drowning, lungs burning, chest aching with an inconsolable pain. Once more, the rug has been pulled out from under his feet and he is standing on a bed of nails, each sharp point a reminder of his daughter's absence.

Jules feels the same. She eventually fell asleep on his lap, the hospital smell clinging to their clothes, tissues clutched tight in her hand, cheeks swollen with tears. When she woke, her eyes were clear, bright; then it caught up with her as it caught up with him. He didn't say a word as she began to cry again. No words would remedy the pain, so he pulled her close to his chest and kissed her head, the rocking of her body moving in time with the sound of their agony.

When Jules was pregnant with Bonnie, he was so frightened of being a bad father. What if he didn't check the temperature of the milk before he gave it to the baby? What if he just forgot to feed her or change her? What if he lost her in the supermarket? What if he didn't show her enough love? What if he didn't make her feel safe and wanted? What if? What if? But it seemed to come naturally. He did all he could as soon as Bonnie was born. He pulled himself from the bed before Jules had the chance, rubbing the sleep from his eyes; burped and hugged and rocked her until she quietened, milk dripping down her chin; mopped up sick from her mouth and poo from her bum, grimacing at the smell of both, sometimes at the same time; made sure she knew she was loved. So why had this happened?

*

John wipes tears from his eyes and sighs. Perhaps this is a sign that he is a bad person. Can it be that? John doesn't believe in God but he knows for a fact He is not kind. He is a sadistic bastard.

Jules sits up, tearing away from his hug, cupping her bump in her hands. 'Empty' was a word she'd mentioned earlier. Empty is how he feels, devoid of everything but grief.

He eases himself from the sofa and goes to the cottage bedroom. Photos are tacked to the wall. A smaller version of his wall at home. Bonnie smiles at him, gap-toothed and messy-haired. In the centre is a black and white photo from their scan.

Bertie.

*

He pulls three small cards from his pocket. In each, a one-pound coin is taped to the paper. The first card bears the words 'I love you', the second 'I love you more', the third 'And more'. He'd given them to Bonnie for her fourth birthday. She'd been saving up for an expensive dress from Debenhams. Three pounds was all she needed but then she couldn't bear to ruin the cards. Five days passed before she got her pocket money and only then did she buy the dress, cards safely tucked away in her bedroom at home.

John had grabbed the cards just before the relocation. The thought of leaving them behind had made him cringe. He swipes a finger over the bundle in his hands, remembering the day she ran into his study, red-faced, clutching the money high in the air. 'Daddy, I have enough! I have enough!'

'That's good, sweetheart! Shall we go and buy your dress after lunch?'

She nodded, dancing on the spot and swinging her arms from side to side, face alight with joy.

'Yes! Mummy's making us fake bacon sandwiches!'

'Yummy!' The nickname had come about from a joke Jules made about Quorn one morning. Bonnie overheard and it stuck.

When Bonnie was frightened of spiders, he'd asked her to name them, saying that, by doing so, they would have less of a hold on her. Hence, all the small black ones were Daniel and the spindly ones were Big Bertha. An unusual thing to do, he knows. But it worked nonetheless. When Don heard about their little 'naming game' he burst into hysterics.

John smiles. When he hears a knock, he rushes down the stairs, two at a time. Jules is already there; this is their reaction every time the phone rings or someone knocks on the door.

Don's eyes mirror their own pain when they open the door. He hugs them both, muttering how sorry he is. 'Your mum rang me. I… I can't believe it. Is Bertie OK? Is he going to be all right? What did the doctor say?'

He guides Jules to the sofa and holds her close to his chest. 'He said it was a cervical polyp. Bertie's fine.'

'Jesus.' Don rubs a hand over his face. 'That must have been terrifying.'

John sits beside them, cupping his face in his hands. He can feel Don looking at him. And, as if reading his mind, he says, 'Bertie's OK, John. He's going to be fine. Don't worry.' John is no longer surprised by how perceptive Don is. They've known each other since they were children, endless days laughing until their sides ached. Don hasn't changed much in that time. He is still jovial, funny, daft Don. If he had to describe his friend in a word, he thinks it would be loyal. He can still remember the time he and Jules were involved in a car crash. Don was on a date with a girl but he came running as soon as they called.

Since then, he's been in a relationship with a woman called Kim. As his assistant at the paediatric unit, she shares his love of children.

'We're going to find Bonnie, you guys. We're going to find her.' He says it like a mantra, muttering under his breath to Jules.

John looks at him and is grateful for his presence. He is trying to be positive but in truth he is nearly as heartbroken as they are. The telltale signs jump out at John: the bumps in his jeans pockets where tissues have been hastily stuffed, the stains on his shirt, the puffiness to his eyes and the soreness under his nose. Don kisses Jules on the head, as much a friend to her as he is to John, and jumps up. He claps his hands together and forces a smile onto his lips. 'Right, I know you probably don't feel like it but you guys need to eat. I'm going to make one of my specials – you're both as thin as I wanted to be when I did that diet a hundred years ago.' He clicks his heels and walks to the kitchen, albeit not with his habitual bounce.

John finds himself wondering if he too sees Bonnie's face when he goes to sleep. He and Jules do, every single night. Sometimes he even sees her in the day, his imagination sculpting her features from thin air. And he has no doubt that when they eventually fall into bed in a few hours, Bertie will join her in their nightmares because, for a moment, they really believed their son had been taken as well.

Chapter 18

Maisie

Tuesday 19 January, 2016

'You know, when he proposed, there wasn't a candle in sight.' Heidi pushes a curl off her cheek and sighs. 'It was beautiful, but not in the way you'd expect. There was no meal, no roses, no fancy speeches beforehand. It was just him, kneeling in front of me, smiling like he knew we were meant to be, in a room with some of the most beautiful art I had ever seen. It was simple. But it was beautiful. I wouldn't have had it any other way.

'I wasn't like most children growing up – I didn't envisage meeting my husband or getting married in a big white dress, none of that. We got married in a field, surrounded by cows and sheep. My dress was ruined by the end.' She laughs. 'The wildflowers stained it so badly it looked like I'd tie-dyed it. But it was perfect. Friends and family stood around us, John wore a shirt and a pair of jeans, my dress was a beautiful bright-yellow number. We didn't have the 'Wedding March'; instead Watson hooked his iPhone up to a speaker and played 'Clair de Lune'. It was perfect.'

'That sounds wonderful.' Maisie visualises Heidi at her

wedding, who she would be, what she would be like if she was removed from this terrible situation. Maisie watches her twist the scarf between her fingers and wonders if she is talking simply to drive her emotions away. To distract herself from the atmosphere. Maisie's concern for her grows more every day. She wishes she could ask, she wishes she could help. She read last night that the families of crime victims often suffered terrible stress disorders, nightmares and a reluctance to step out of their own homes for fear of being attacked. Is Heidi scared she or her daughter will be mugged? That the person who hurt Tim will hurt them? Does she feel responsible for Tim? Does she feel guilty? Did she say something she regrets? Did they argue before it happened?

'You know, when he proposed, my first thought was of him folding a map.' She runs her fingers down Tim's cheek, the depth of her despair filling the room. 'Whenever we're on a journey, he always folds the map the wrong way. It drives me mad. I don't know why, it just does. And when he asked me, I wondered how many times I'd see him do it. Then I thought, "That's the only thing about him that really bothers me," and I said yes on the spot. Of course, he's not perfect – he'd be laughing right now, you know, hearing me talk about him and that silly map; he's stubborn and forgets to turn off the lights at night when he comes to bed. He's lazy at times and gets easily frustrated if his work isn't going well, but they're such tiny things.'

'My partner's the same.'

'How long have you been together?'

'Three years. We got a place together quite early on.' She leaves out the other side of their relationship. 'He puts his feet on the coffee table, which drives me mad. And he's terrible with technology – I have to do everything at home when it comes down to it.'

'What's his name?'

'Ben. But like you said a minute ago, they're such tiny things. I love that he always remembers to water my sunflower.'

'You have a sunflower? Don't you live in a flat?'

'Yes, but we keep it next to the window so it gets lots of light. My mum gave it to me, told me that sunflowers always face the sun, follow it across the sky. I love it but I forget to water it – Ben does it for me. And he hasn't forgotten once.'

*

Stacked haphazardly in the corner is the plethora of CDs she and Ben have collected over the years. A combination of Rod Stewart, Otis Redding, Paolo Nutini, Sam Cooke, Stevie Wonder and the Rolling Stones. She swipes the duster across the cases, dancing across the floor, singing with wild abandon, just like she did as a child.

As soon as they moved into this flat, they stuck on some music and danced through the rooms, banishing the cold silence. Afterwards, exhausted, they splayed out on the floor, laying out the furniture in their minds.

Maisie digs through the fridge and snaps the lid off a jar of gherkins. She's been craving them all day. Popping one into her mouth, she sighs, savouring the taste under her tongue, then throws a jumper over her shirt. Despite the blood pumping through her body, the cold bites at her skin like a dog at her heels. She has always been one to feel the cold easily.

At night, when the temperature plummets, she sometimes lies awake for hours, too cold to drift off, remembering how she used to lie shivering under the duvet at her mother's cottage, a fine layer of ice building on the fabric. They didn't have enough money to pay for heating and so they gathered every duvet and blanket in their house and curled up together on the sofa. They lit candles to kick off some heat and played music or read books. It wasn't always easy but she remembers those times with her mother – squashed up under blankets, feet ensconced in five pairs of socks, two scarves wound around her neck – with fondness. Of course, she and Ben have enough money to pay for the heating now, but they try to keep it off. Every penny is set on a course for the bank.

If the weather forecast says the temperature is set to drop overnight, she always finds two hot-water bottles on her side of the bed. One at the bottom, one at the top, Ben curled up, waiting for her. It is such a small thing but she appreciates it more than she can ever put into words.

Chapter 19

Miller

Thursday 16 July, 1987

Do you know, late at night I can hear her talking to me. That oh-so-soft, melodic tone of voice. She isn't aware of the spell she puts people under. I spend as much time as I can with her; if she lingers at her desk in class, I linger too, pretending I am scribbling something on my paper, deep in thought; when she walks to the shops from the old cottage she has rented just outside the village, I walk ten steps behind her, matching her pace, marvelling at the way her body sways; if she runs a hand across a chest of drawers she wants to buy but cannot afford, I caress the piece of wood with my fingers, feeling her beneath them.

Lately she has glanced at me and something strange has been in her eyes, something I haven't seen before. Confusion, is it? It only ever appears when I am in the classroom, my eyes trained on her chest. Sometimes, when she takes a breath, I take one too, and for a moment I feel as if we are one, joined. I am her and she is me.

That is how I feel now. I feel close to her. Closer than I have felt before. Just a piece of fabric keeps us apart.

It is the middle of the night and she is tucked up under a duvet reading, the light of her torch illuminating the inside of the tent. It is a school project. She is trying to imbue a sense of adventure and excitement for nature in her pupils and thinks by doing this they will follow her lead. But they will not.

We are in a field behind her home, a crumbling, mouldy cottage filled to the brim with furniture she scrounged for free. I can see her silhouette but she can't see mine. I blend with the darkness. A cacophony of nocturnal life makes the air buzz and pulse: the scuffling in the hedges, the flapping of wings in the trees, the scuttling of insects and rabbits. I wonder if she is scared in there, in her small tent, with only a weak partition to keep the nocturnal world from pouring in. She told us she had never camped before, and I wonder if the darkness scares her as it would a child, if the noise unsettles her. I feel a thrill chase through my bones at the thought of her shuffling a little deeper under her duvet.

I hear the rustle of a page turning in her book. *Sarah*, I want to whisper, *Sarah, are you afraid?* Persuaded by an undeniable pull, my legs carry me closer to the tent. Only a few steps, but if I wanted to, I could touch it. I could touch something she is touching. I could touch her. Before I can stop myself, her name slips from between my teeth and my mouth waters with the sound of it. 'Sarah…'

A gasp breaks through the still air. I smile, seeing her silhouette pull the duvet over her head. She has dropped the torch and book on the floor. Her head reappears and it is as if she is a terrified rabbit peering out of its hole, weary of the hungry fox. And it occurs to me then that I am the fox. I draw in a deep breath to still my shaking hands; I am not shaking for the same reason she is, though.

She reaches out of the cocoon and takes up her book, shining the light onto its pages, thinking her imagination is playing tricks on her. I say her name again and this time a terrified noise works its way up her throat and into the air. She dives under the duvet again, and I think I can hear crying. She is hiding. The rabbit is hiding. I can still see you, though, Sarah. I can still hear you. Fear emanates from the tent like heat from the sun, a strong, impenetrable force.

Guided by that irresistible pull, I reach out and run my fingers across the tent. The fabric is soft, ingrained with the smell of damp and the honeyed scent of the woman shivering inside. My body ripples with pleasure, it burns through my veins like adrenalin, it makes my bones buzz with excitement. A new, fascinating, beautiful emotion she is feeling and it is all because of me.

I sigh, loud enough for her to hear, quiet enough so she isn't sure. Her hand whips out of the duvet and snaps off the torch. She thinks if she turns off the light, I will forget she is there. But would a fox forget the rabbit if it tunnelled into its burrow? No. I can smell you, Sarah, I want to say. I can hear you.

An hour later she turns the torch on again, head peeping out from under the duvet. I force my hand into the fabric of the tent. The impression makes the poles fold inward. When she looks round and sees, she screams. Oh, Blue-Eyes, it is the most wonderful scream.

'Leave me alone!'

We look at each other, her and I. I feel close to her. So close. When morning comes, she unzips the tent and runs as fast as her legs will carry her. The rabbit is fleeing the fox. But the fox is close behind.

Friday 17 July, 1987

She rubs her stomach, eyes swivelling around the room, fear lingering in her system like a bad smell. Sarah's hair, normally neat and moulded into place, is dishevelled. And black bags hang under her eyes; from afar, it looks like she has covered the skin in black make-up. She hasn't told anyone about what happened to her. Instead she keeps it secret, locked within, thinking if she hides it away she will forget. But she won't. I can see it by the way she stumbles around, a once-graceful creature turned into a clumsy one. If a pupil asks her a question, it takes her a moment to find him in the small room, as if she is hearing his voice from a distance. When we look at her, her gaze only meets ours for a few seconds before it is scanning the room again for signs of a person who does not belong there – as if a hand might suddenly make an impression in the wall.

The pupils notice. They look at her as if she has lost her mind, and I want to scream at them, hurt them. How dare they think so. How dare they think she is anything but perfect.

Sarah touches her stomach, gently, tenderly, and I wonder if I have made her ill. If pain cripples her body. I don't want to make her ill but something about the emotion pervading her face is intoxicating.

I rest my chin in my hand. I'm still sitting there as she walks out of the door, the first to leave in a line of pupils, casting her eyes round the room one last time, then checking before she goes into the hall.

Sunday 19 July, 1987

The lights inside her cottage illuminate my path. The gravel crunches underfoot and adds a new note to the nocturnal cacophony that is beginning to play. I pluck a rose from the flower patch by her front door, twirling it in my fingers, avoiding the sharp thorns. A car sits next to hers. In the dull light, I think I can just make out the colour blue. I run through the possibilities in my mind. Her mother? Father? Brother? Friend? I haven't seen that colour car before.

The curtains are flung back letting the darkness stare in; whoever is with her makes her feel safe. Since that night she has shut them tightly, even before the last light has fallen. Her mother, I think to myself. It must be her mother.

I crouch by the window – one hand on the sill, other hand clutching the rose – and peer into the lounge. She is splayed back on the sofa, a soppy smile upturning the corners of her lips, hands squeezing the arms of the sofa. A man is on top of her, kissing her lips, saying something I can't make out. She laughs, wrapping her arms around his neck, legs around his waist.

I stare, both fascinated and repulsed. Not by her. By him. His touch. She requires more care, more tenderness. She is special, beyond her class of women. Beyond all others.

He runs his mouth down her neck, leaving a line of kisses in its wake. Her lips part and she tips her head back, the ghost of a smile lingering on her face. I can't take my eyes away. I am addicted to the sight of her. I have never seen so much emotion displayed on her face. Even when she was frightened in the tent, the emotion was nothing compared to this.

The man runs his hand down her skin into the waistband of her trousers. When she arches her back, his hand changes direction. Instead of digging further down, it rises, pushing up the fabric of her shirt as it goes, revealing a swell of stomach.

I stare, unblinking. Suddenly the sense of time abandons me and I am unsure of how long I have been standing here. The noise has evaporated, leaving the air parched of life, devoid of everything but the emotions that swirl and scatter in my chest. She touches her stomach, and I feel a wave of sickness pass over me. My feet stumble. Beads of sweat appear under my clothes, making my skin prickle with heat. And yet, despite that, despite the warm air, my body feels cold. It feels as if my bones have been dunked in water and left to ice over in the freezer. Small gasps leap from my mouth until I am panting.

And yet, even as this happens, my eyes are trained on her stomach. The man and Sarah fight their way out of their clothing, taken by a fervour of emotion, careful of the space between them where a new life grows.

As I turn and walk away, I look down into my shaking hand. In it, the rose is crumpled, dying.

Monday 20 July, 1987

I wait for the steam to escape through the open window and rise into the darkness. Then I know she will have lowered herself into the bathtub and closed her eyes. I can still remember the first time I climbed the pipe and peered into the bathroom, when she was still just lovely Sarah, not a combination of herself and the man. When she was special and untainted by the life of another. A life that is going to end before it begins.

She rubs her hands across her bump, a tender smile I want to beat from her lips slowly materialising. She leans her head back and sighs. I know soon she will be asleep, unable to avoid the call of pleasant dreams.

I pull a matchbox from my pocket, fiddling with the red strip on the side, thinking of the way she was before. Such a waste. Such a shame. She was so beautiful, so honest and perfect. Why did she have to be lured away from her old life – away from me?

I don't blame the man, I blame her. I saw by the look on her face last night that she wants this pregnancy. Well, her wish has been granted. Now she is corrupt. Once a perfect person, a special one, a *good one*, now just a skin full of bones like everyone else in the world, the life, the genes of that man diluting the purity in her body like a disease.

I swipe the match across the strip and hold it up to the eave of the thatch roof. It splutters and dies. I light another and repeat. This one takes and a long ribbon of smoke streaks through the air. When it begins to burn, I take a long look at her, remembering who she was before, then I climb back down, stand in front of the window and wait.

The left side of the roof is blazing before she wakes up. Her face is blackened and she is coughing. She flings open the window and sucks in breath after breath. She doesn't have the energy to scream, even as a section of the roof caves in.

I shuffle to my right, moving just enough to catch her eye. When she looks at me, I think she knows. I think she realises it was me that night outside the tent. Our eyes meet and I smile.

Hello, my darling.

Chapter 20

John

Monday 7 December, 2015

The red shoes are the first thing he sees. He wasn't supposed to come into town but after the third photo, he felt he had to escape the house. He needed to be somewhere he could tap into other lives and escape his own.

But now he sees the shoes.

The high street buzzes with noise, the flurry of bodies blurring into one huge form, elbows and bags whipping out and jabbing him in the chest and back. A siren rings through the air and all eyes turn in a collective gaze. All except John's.

He stares at the little girl's shoes through the tangle of legs and feet. His heart thrums in his chest and his legs begin to shake. He stumbles forward, forcing a path through the crowd, ignoring the cries of anger and frustration, even the pangs of pain. Through a gap in the bodies, he can just make out the back of the girl's head. Brown hair. Wavy brown hair.

'Bonnie! Bonnie!'

People turn and look at him, eyebrows raised.

'BONNIE!' He shouts her name over and over again until his lungs are burning. He pushes people out of his way and runs to the girl's side. He grips her arm, unaware of the woman next to her beginning to scream. The girl swivels on her heel and stares up at him with big amber eyes. Amber. John looks at her, his heart breaking all over again. The woman shoves him away. He stumbles and falls to the ground muttering apologies through a veil of tears.

He doesn't know how long he sits in the middle of the crowd and he doesn't care. It is only when he feels a pair of hands helping him to his feet that he realises it has been a few seconds.

'John? John? It's me.' He tries to match the face to someone familiar but he can't; his mind is swarming with thoughts of Bonnie. 'John. It's OK. Come on. Come with me.'

The woman takes his hand and guides him through the crowd, her hands gentle and kind, like the hands of a mother on her child. They break through the hordes of people. John recognises her. Alice. DCI Alice Munroe.

She pats his back and leads him into the Dog and Duck Inn. The heavy darkness and smell of beer and sausages wallop him as soon as he steps through the door. Middle-aged men prop up the bar, their calloused hands nursing half-pints, their greasy hair and dirty fingers blending in well with the grime. The barman looks to be the cleanest person there. He smiles, revealing rotten teeth that ooze the smell of infection. Not the cleanest person on the inside then.

The middle-aged men turn on their stools, buttocks sagging over the wood, to get a good look at them. Alice waves and leads John to a booth at the back, its seats plastered in red fabric, the dark-wood table as scuffed as the floor. Light from a nearby window pours onto hundreds of tiny marks and stains scattered across it.

John slumps in the seat, burying his face in his hands. But it is not because he is ashamed; it is because he is blocking out this world in favour of another, one in which he ran up to that girl in the street and looked into the face of his daughter. The face of a girl with green eyes. His Bonnie. He savours every last vestige of that image before it begins to slip out of his frazzled mind.

'John?'

He looks at Alice and leans back, daring her to tell him what a fool he is. But she doesn't. 'I saw you. I watched it all happen. I can see why you thought that was her.'

He takes a shaky breath. 'I terrified her. That poor girl. The mum… she… she thought I was going to hurt her. I… I thought… it was her… she had red shoes on.' He runs a hand across his face, distraught. 'Bonnie… she had red shoes on when she went missing.'

'I know.' She leans forward and holds his hand, her fingers warm and comforting. He looks at her and notices she isn't wearing her customary blue three-piece. Instead, a woollen sweater and dark-blue jeans hug her petite form. Her hair is down, framing her face. The hard, professional version of herself has vanished, the softer side he suspected was underneath laid bare for all to see.

'Where's Jules?'

'At home. With Don. She needed some space to think – she still hadn't come out of the bathroom by the time I left.'

'I can see why. I won't ask how you're holding up because it always seems like a stupid thing to ask someone. John, we will find her.'

'This is my fault.' He tucks his trembling hands under his legs, hot tears running down his cheeks. 'This person is obsessed with me.'

'Yes, he or she is. But it isn't your fault, John.' She wraps an arm around his shoulder, and he absent-mindedly wonders if police protocol allows her to be so unprofessional. 'How's Mrs Graham been since this morning?'

'Not good. She's broken up. Dad said she couldn't stop shaking when she found it.' John can still hear his mother's voice on the phone, screaming through a veil of tears about an envelope on her doormat and a picture of Bonnie inside. He has never heard his mother so terrified. She has always been the strong one.

The third picture is a shot of Bonnie's leg. Of a bloodied, swollen gash streaked across her skin. It is four inches long and clumped with blood, the skin raw and inflamed. In the corner of the photo, next to Bonnie's foot, sits a long nail, its point rimmed with gore. Something in him tells John this person intended to catch the nail in the picture.

On the back of the photo is a typed message once again signed off with his daughter's signature:

When you were young, you fell off your bike – Molly picked you up, rubbed you down and sent you on your way. I would have done more. I would have looked after you, cradled you in my arms and kissed away your pain.

He remembers where and when it happened, even the way he felt as his mother wrapped her arms around him. He'd felt safe, better, the pain dulled by the strength of her love. But what was a sweet memory is tainted now because all he can see is a person standing on the periphery of his life, peering in. Watching him. A person who types out messages with a disturbingly loving voice.

Don wondered if it was a woman. An ex-girlfriend with a grudge. But he knows as well as John that it couldn't possibly be.

'Who do you think is doing this? A man or a woman? You heard what Don said this morning.'

Alice takes a moment to ponder his question. 'I don't know.'

'I keep trying to remember someone – anyone – when I was growing up who could be doing this but no one would.' He sighs. 'Don and Mum and Dad can't remember anyone either.'

'I know. I questioned them all again this morning.'

'When you say we're going to find Bonnie, is that your professional opinion or a hope?'

'It's both, John. It's a hope because, on a personal level, I want more than anything to find your daughter. You're not like some of the creeps I've seen over the years. You haven't killed your daughter and buried her body in the back garden. You're a good chap and she should be playing dress-up and enjoying her childhood, not suffering at the hands of a psycho. Bonnie is my priority. It's a professional opinion because the creeps who are clever always slip up in the end. They get cocky, arrogant. I've seen it a lot over the years, John. I've been doing this job a long time.'

He nods. 'Do you have kids?'

She shifts in her seat, debating whether to answer his question. Eventually she shrugs. 'Yes. A daughter. And if you tell anyone any of this, I'll arrest you.'

John smiles sadly, wondering why she risks it on him. 'How old?'

'Fifteen. Her name's Rosie.' Alice waves over the barman and orders them two cottage pies; then she rummages in her bag and withdraws a small photograph. She is posing beside a girl with thick blonde hair and a face full of dense freckles. John takes the picture and, in what has become a habit, turns it over. There is no writing. No message. 'She's sweet.'

Alice takes the photo back. 'I always wanted a daughter. Since I was a little girl. I promised myself if I ever had one, I'd call her Rosie. When I was pregnant with her, I just sat on the sofa for what seemed like hours wondering how I ever got so lucky.' She smiles, running her finger across the photo. 'And then when she was born, I didn't feel lucky anymore. I felt afraid. Afraid I might drop her, afraid I might not be able to prevent her getting poorly, afraid I might not be able to keep her safe from the creeps out there. I was just a ball of fear rolling through the days.'

John smiles. He'd felt the same when Bonnie was born, when even just a chill in the air was a dangerous foe. 'Go on.'

'I think what I was most afraid of, though, was her getting cancer.' She tucks the photo back in her bag and rubs her little finger. 'My father passed away when I was little, and a year after Rosie was born my husband died. Lung cancer and prostate cancer. It runs in the family. I got so suspicious of every little thing it became a bit of a problem for me. I watched her so closely for signs. If she coughed, I was afraid. If she got a stomachache, I was afraid. I took her to hospital for check-ups when I didn't need to. I only ever fed her healthy food. She didn't consume any chemicals when she was young – I was that careful. I know that probably sounds a little bit over-the-top but when the sound of people saying "they fought valiantly" is ringing in your ears and you can still remember your husband coughing up blood… well, believe me, it didn't seem like it at the time.'

'I hate it when people say someone has lost their battle with cancer. I think it implies that the person was weak. No one who dies from cancer is ever weak.'

Alice looks at him, surprised. 'You're the only one who's ever said that to me. And you can imagine how many people I've had unwanted remarks from over the years.'

He nods. 'Your daughter hasn't had cancer, has she?'

'No. Thank God. I had counselling after Jerry passed away and it helped, but even now, I go to bed every night praying she never will.'

'What about you?'

'No. I'm not so worried about me, though. The only reason I'd be upset about dying is because I wouldn't be able to take care of Rosie. That's all.'

'You know, when I first met you I thought you were really cold. Professional but lacking on the humanity side.'

She laughs, a big, rumbling laugh deep in her chest. 'I have to be, John. If I got caught up in the emotional side of it, I wouldn't be able to think clearly.'

'I can understand that.'

'So, you're an author. If you ask me, what you do – projecting yourself into your characters' heads – is a little like what I do. I try to get into the heads of creeps, try to predict their next move and catch them out before they can do it. So, tell me, John, from what you know about this person, what would your next move be if you were them?'

'They're obviously wanting to hurt me, get a reaction, so I'd probably draw this out for as long as I could. I'd send photo after photo, the injuries bloodier each time, building suspense for the climax.'

She leans forward, eyes concerned, lips pursed. 'What would the climax be, John?'

He looks at his feet. 'I'd kill her.'

Chapter 21

Maisie

Wednesday 20 January, 2016

Grief is a peculiar thing. When you least expect it, having been lulled into believing it was gone and that you could move on, it announces its arrival back into your life, out of the blue, with a sickening punch to your gut. A throe that makes your chest ache and your eyes smart. Maisie has been through the tedious cat and mouse game of it for months. She has tried to fight it, failed miserably, then decided to give herself a set amount of time to give rein to what lurked in the back of her mind. She has learnt that ten minutes is the perfect measure. Five is too short and she inevitably slips over, but twenty is too long because the lure of the darkness grew too strong. Ten is perfect.

She remembers sitting on the floor and crossing her legs, one hand resting on the door of the spare bedroom as if trying to feel movement on the other side. She wouldn't have been surprised if she had felt something. Maybe the memories and emotions tucked away in that room would start knocking on the door, wanting to be let out. And she wonders if she will ever be strong enough to open the door and face her demons head-on. Face the blood-splattered clothes and heartbreaking mistakes that set her teeth on edge. She has never been a liar, someone who hurt others, but now she wonders if perhaps this new version of herself has lurked beneath for years. Her mother always told her that to be good you had to be a little bit bad. After all, how would anyone be able to differentiate good from bad if there wasn't a contrast? But now she wonders if there is *only* bad in her.

Her mother is the only one she has ever told. Not Ben, not Lailah. Only her mother. If she closes her eyes, she can feel Janet's soft, warm fingers on her hair, brushing it off her face, making her laugh with tales of myths and legends, safe, worry-free. But above all happy.

*

Tim sighs deeply, his eyes drooping to a close. She gathers up the cotton wool and bunches it up in her hand. Bathing the inside of his mouth to prevent sores is one of the nicer things to do. Especially in comparison to checking his catheter.

'He's always done that.'

'What?'

'Sighed before he goes to sleep.'

'Oh.'

Heidi nods and kisses Tim's knuckles. Today she clutches her bag to her chest, fiddling with the strap until Maisie thinks it might break. Fear and dread pulse through Heidi. Her eyes flick from Tim to her hands, which are just beginning to shake. She stuffs them under her legs and bites her lip. Maisie pretends not to have noticed, then walks out into the corridor, rubbing her eyes. Her mind flits from thoughts of her mother to thoughts of Ben.

She's kept it from him for over a year now, hiding her mistake

110

and guarding it with lie after lie. Now she is beginning to wonder if she should tell him. Heidi would tell Tim if it was her. They tell each other everything. There are no lies between them. But can she? He will never forgive her. He'll look at her with disgust and hatred and she will have to relive it all over again. But isn't that what she's doing every day anyway?

*

His hand trails a line down Tim's arm, carefully, delicately, as if Tim is a china doll and his touch could shuttle a web of cracks down his skin. You won't hurt him, Maisie wants to say to the man in the Armani suit, but she doesn't because somehow this moment means something for him. For them. She sensed an atmosphere in the way he and Watson reacted to one another. A disagreement, perhaps? An argument in the past? Friction that has left behind a smudge of something poisonous. But it has not affected the friendship he has with Tim; this she can see in the way he touches his hand.

'So how did you and Tim meet?' Maisie offers him a chair, then gently holds Tim's eyelids apart as she administers his drops. A clear film coats his eyes and he blinks rapidly.

Maisie sinks into a chair herself, glancing at his Armani suit.

The man smiles at her, jumping when Tim moans through clenched teeth. 'Er… is he OK?'

'He's fine, I promise. It's natural for someone in this condition.'

'OK.' He nods, tapping his head with his finger as if filing away the information to study later on. 'Our mothers arranged a bit of a playdate when we were two years old, I think. That's the first time we met, I suppose. It wasn't a friendship straight away. Mainly, I just wanted Tim's packet of crisps…' He smiles at this, shooting a glance at Tim, as if he expects him to smile back. 'But in no time at all we were inseparable.' He sits deeper into the

111

chair, a patch of skin peeping through the buttons on his shirt, his suit jacket creasing into a fine map of lines on his lap.

'You've known each other a long time then.'

'We have.' He smiles, and Maisie can see the past sitting like smoke in his eyes. Something that still clouds his days, even as an adult. She wonders what it is, but shoves her questions to the back of her mind. Their past is private.

'It must have come as a shock to read about the attack in the newspaper. I can't even imagine what that must have been like.'

'It was… I almost thought someone was playing some sort of trick on me. How could this have happened to Tim?'

'Have you talked to Heidi yet?'

'No, not yet. I need to speak to her. How does she seem to you?'

'She's coping really well. Were the two of you friends when you were youngsters as well?'

He smiles fondly. 'Yes, we were all really close. But especially Tim and I. You know, when I was about eight I fell off my bike and broke my leg. It hurt like hell. I think I must have blacked out because when I opened my eyes again, I was back at my house and my dad was carrying me up the garden. And when I looked over his shoulder I saw Tim standing by this massive piece of cardboard. His hands were shaking really badly and his whole body was soaked in sweat. It didn't hit me until the next day that he'd pulled me all the way home. This was the Eighties; kids didn't have mobiles like they do now. And most of the neighbourhood was on holiday or at the shops so he couldn't use a landline. I just remember thinking, wow, I wish I was as brave as him. I never would have thought of doing that.'

'It must have been frightening for you, though.'

'It was. It was. But you know what? I quite enjoyed it in the end.' He chuckles. 'Tim came round every day and he always brought something new with him to cheer me up. A game, a book, a snack we hadn't tried before. Sometimes we did experiments in the kitchen, or Tim did while I watched from the chair. Other times we challenged each other to come up with stories and characters like the ones in our books. On a Friday one week we decided we were both going to be bestselling authors of fantasy and science fiction. Saturday we were both going to be like Buzz Aldrin and fly to the stars in a rocket. Sunday we rubbished those ideas like leftover pizza and made up our minds to become international spies.'

'I dread to think what Monday brought!' Maisie says, and he laughs, his crow's feet curling like squashed bookends beside his eyes. His presence is a tonic to Maisie, a welcome break from thinking about the lies she has told.

'By Monday we wanted to be Batman and Robin. And Tim made me be Batman because he said he would have the most battle scars. My broken leg became the subject of many conversations, as you can probably imagine.'

'How long did it take to heal?'

'It took all summer. But it wasn't as bad as you probably think. Tim was great company. And he made sure he was with me every day to help me along.'

'Had you not met Watson yet?' As soon as the words are out of her mouth, she wishes she could take them back.

He bites his lip and shakes his head, worrying the fabric of his jacket with his middle finger. His nail digs deep into the stitching, burrowing a hole into the thick cloth. 'No... no, he came later.'

Chapter 22

Miller

Tuesday 21 July, 1987

We look at one another across the street, and I feel this is more of an ending than the night she was meant to die. Perhaps it is because she no longer looks at me with the fondness she does the other girls and boys. Perhaps it is because now her house is a pile of charred rubble, smoke billowing across the sky, filling the town with a stomach-churning smell.

People press handkerchiefs to their noses, walking as quickly as their legs can carry them, heads bowed, following a path to and from the shops. They don't look up and they don't see us stop and face each other across the street. They don't see me smile, or her hands begin to shake. They don't see me glance at her bump and slowly run my fingers down to my stomach, lingering, as if I am caressing something precious. They do see her run.

Sarah leaves our small town, shooting across the road like an animal being chased away – a rabbit. I take pride in the fact that I am the fox.

The man leaves with her. I hear through the town grapevine that she is going to stay with her mother and father. And I think how clever she is still, despite her no longer being the special person she was before. I wonder if she has told the man – Jack – about me. About my visits to her in the night. I doubt it. He wouldn't believe her. I'm not angry she didn't die that night. I nearly find it funny. Funny that she has to run from me.

When she is gone, I go home to find letters strewn across the dining table, Mother staring at them with glazed eyes. I peer over her head and grin. Divorce papers.

Father hasn't returned since I gave Mother those photos. Nobody knows where he is but I've seen him sneaking in and out of Tanya's house, hands stuck deep into his pockets, eyes cast to the ground. He isn't ashamed, though. Or guilty. He's embarrassed his wife kicked him out of his own home, regardless of his betrayal.

There isn't even a flicker of love between my parents now, only love of the memories they have of Mary. I pick up the letters, proud of my feat. Mother will be so much easier to mould now Father is gone. The backbone in the relationship has splintered and turned to dust.

I put the letter on the table and rest my hand on Mother's bare shoulder. A soft tremble meets my touch, as if my finger is a bug running across her skin. She bites her lip as I squeeze. And when her lip begins to bleed, I squeeze harder. Just like when I pulled and pulled Angel Mary's hair and she had to rip me from her head like a plaster from a cut.

She cringes. And I say, 'Oh, sorry, Mummy. Didn't mean to catch you.' I kneel down and kiss the coldness of her cheek.

Chapter 23

John

Tuesday 8 December, 2015

She loops the laces between her fingers, brow furrowing in concentration, muttering under her breath, 'The jet plane does a loop the loop, then flies under the bridge and out the other side.' She pulls the laces tight and smiles up at him. 'Ta dah! I did it, Daddy!'

He bundles her into his arms and bounces her up and down. 'You definitely did. Well done! Do you want to try again?'

She nods determinedly. He unravels the laces and sits back for her to retie them.

'Bon-Bon? John?'

'In here!'

John rushes to Don's aid and quickly snatches the takeaway bags before he drops them, tripping over his laces as he goes. 'Are you showing her Molly's way?'

He nods. 'I think it's starting to stick.'

Don grins. 'Bon-Bon, you know Grandma Molly taught me to tie my laces too when I was your age?'

'Really?'

'Yep!'

'I don't know what you mean by "taught you", mate. You still can't tie your laces.'

Don glares at him, sweeping Bonnie into his arms. 'Cover your ears, Bon! It's a lie. A lie, I tell you!' He swings her onto his back and spreads his arms, positioning his feet apart. 'OK. Are you ready?'

'Ready.' Bonnie wraps her arms round his neck and giggles.

'Set?'

'Go!'

Don peels through the room, rocking the furniture and making the pictures wobble on the walls, a deep rumble bubbling up his throat.

'Careful! I don't want any broken vases! Or bones for that matter!'

Don comes to a grinding halt in front of him and tuts, rolling his eyes theatrically. 'We're jet planes, John. We can't help it if we lose control and crash into things.' He whips his head round, grinning at Bonnie. 'Can you believe this guy?!' Bonnie laughs, tears streaking down her face. 'I think Daddy's a bit jealous, Bon. I think he wishes he was a jet plane too.'

Bonnie hops off Don's back. 'Daddy, can we watch cartoons, please?'

'OK, then.' John smiles, watching her speed off upstairs. When it comes to watching cartoons, Don is her companion. The daft voices he can conjure are a constant source of amusement to her.

Don follows him into the kitchen, smoothing down his shirt. 'I've lost count of the times I've watched those cartoons.' He groans. 'Oh, and that one where Donald Duck gets stuck in that hot-air balloon…' He puts his head in his hands.

'Don, you love that cartoon.'

He sits a little straighter, pursing his lips. 'No, I don't.'

'You do. More so than Bonnie.'

Don flicks his head to the side, clutching his heart. 'Sometimes it's like you don't know me at all.'

John laughs, throwing a packet of crisps into his hands. 'Catch.'

'Thanks.' Don shuffles round to the cupboard and distributes plates on the worktop. 'So, anyway, is Jules on her way yet?'

'Should be back from the gallery in a few minutes. Busy day today apparently. She sold the cottage painting she did, remember? Said on the phone some tall guy bought it.'

'Oh, that was Marcus. We got chatting and I recommended Jules's gallery to him. I told you, didn't I?'

'Oh, yeah! I forgot. Thanks for that. Tell her when she gets home. She'll be delighted.'

Don pushes the chicken chow mein onto the plates. 'So how's the new book coming? Figured the plot flaw out yet?'

'It's getting there. I worked out the kinks this morning. Fingers crossed Penny likes it.' He cringes at the thought of his revision letter. Edit after edit after edit.

'Bonnie learnt a new word today. Inevitable. She's been going round saying it all day. Inevitable this, inevitable that. It's really sweet. Oh, hold on, here she comes. Brace yourself.'

She skips into the kitchen, waving the DVD in the air. 'Got one!'

'What have we got today?'

'Donald and the Hot-Air Balloon.'

'My favourite.' Don grins at John.

'It was in-ev-it-able.' Bonnie draws out the word.

John nudges Don in the ribs. 'OK, then. Go and put it on.' Don pats her on the head and smiles. 'God, that's adorable.'

'I know.'

'I may have to teach her the word tremendous.'

'Don't you dare!'

Don follows Bonnie into the lounge, sits her on his lap and weaves her arms through the air in time with the music. 'QUACK!'

John smiles as Bonnie takes up the chant of 'Duck Duck Duck'. He throws the empty containers into the bin and dishes out the onion rings.

Jules walks through the door as he is carrying the plates into the lounge. He kisses her on the cheek. She drops her bag on the sofa,

*kicks off her shoes and flops onto the floor next to Don and Bonnie.
'Oooh, I love this one. Good choice, sweetheart.'*

*Don spoons chow mein into his mouth, holding his plate to the
side, careful not to catch Bonnie's head.*

*Bonnie takes a slow bite of an onion ring and smiles up at Don.
'Oh, that's tremendous.'*

John buries his face in his hands, wishing he could wipe the
memory from his own mind. Jules pulls him into her arms and
kisses his cheek. They cry together.

Chapter 24

Maisie

Thursday 21 January, 2016

The sweet smell of peppermint pours from the open door and fills Market Jew Street, simultaneously drawing smiles and grimaces. This scent she remembers very clearly after spilling a bottle of the oil on her school uniform when she was a girl. She never did get the greasy stain out, even after her mother washed it.

Maisie breathes in the salty air and smiles, every fibre of her relaxing. An influx of memories invades her mind: her mother skipping along the path to St Michael's Mount, dragging her along, arousing dirty looks from other parents; her mother laughing as she splashed in the frigid sea, promises of hot chocolate floating in the air; her mother twirling her round the shopfloor, sprinkling confetti over her head, telling her she was a fairy like Tinker Bell; their trips to The Edge of the World Bookshop, tales of adventure and heroism heavy in their arms as they wandered home; those wintry nights they sat up listening to swing music, nibbling biscuits, giggling at the sweet dog they found by their door one morning; she and her mother sitting at their dining table in the cramped kitchen doing shots on her eighteenth birthday; her mother helping her prepare for the tests to become a nurse; sharing one last pan_of hot chocolate before she left for a new life in Oxford.

Maisie breathes in a mouthful of fresh air before stepping through the shop door with its red shutters and cracked wooden floors, awash with memories that make her feel as if she is a child again.

Her mother stands behind the counter – bright, big-haired, expressive, chatting to a customer, gesturing to the corner of the shop with a ringed finger. 'Yes, yes. That was where she was born. My Maisie Prae. She was such a small baby, you know. You can just about see the stain where my waters broke. Yes, that's it. Oh, she's a lovely girl. A nurse, you know. Very talented. Cares for people in big ol' Oxford. Yes, such a special girl. She's got her own flat with her partner – nice boy, Ben. Bit dim when it comes to technology. Bit dim. But lovely all the same. My Maisie's not like that. Very clever. Very clever.'

The customer wipes her sweaty forehead, eyes bulging, foot tapping the floor. 'Well, that's nice. I'd better let you go.'

'I hate it when people say that. "Oh, I'll let you go." My ex-husband used to say that. Just another way of saying "I'm bored of you now". But never mind. See you later, Morwenna.'

The woman nods and scarpers through the door. Janet watches her go, then her eyes widen as she looks at Maisie. 'Oh my…'

Maisie drops her bag as her mother wraps her in a hug. 'Hi, Mum. I think you just scared away another customer.'

'Oh, course I haven't. That's Morwenna. She loves having a chat. Now, now, let me have a look at you.' She steps back and studies her. 'You're looking a little bigger. Pudgy round the face. That's what I like to see. Don't want a daughter of mine being stick-thin. What's nice about hugging that?'

Maisie laughs. 'Good to see you, Mum. How are things with the shop?'

121

'You asked me that just the other day. Are you OK, poppet? How'd you get the time off work? I didn't even know you were coming. Is Ben with you?' She peers round her shoulder, puzzled.

'Nope. Just me. Ben's back in Oxford. Work's fine – I've been due some time off for ages. I just needed to see you.'

Janet looks at her daughter closely. 'What you not telling me?'

'Can we close the shop? Have a chat?'

Janet shuts the shop door with a thump and flips the sign, taking her hand. 'Come on then. I'll make us a pan of hot chocolate.' Maisie follows her through the door and up the stairs to their small kitchen. It hasn't changed much in the time she's been away. Jars of pasta and rice line the worktop, spice packets are dotted about the ceiling, hanging down on pieces of string – her mother's invention, designed for ease when cooking. The old cooker they've had since she was a child is still going strong, plus a few new marks and scratches. The table and dining chairs are the same except for a sticker in the middle.

'You got another one? This isn't the one from the car, is it?' Maisie smoothes the 'God Made Me Bespoke' sticker down, moving the air bubbles underneath with the tip of her finger.

'No, it's a new one. Mick found it for me. Thought I told you that on the phone.' Mick is a local fisherman, one of the few still eking out a living on the quiet waters. She can remember him popping her on his shoulders when she was young.

'How is Mick?'

'He's fine, he's fine.' Janet pats a chair and whips around the kitchen, plucking mugs from their hooks and flicking spoonfuls of sugar and cinnamon into a pan of milk already starting to boil on the hob. They used to joke she could muster enough force to create a tornado, twirling round their kitchen and grabbing cutlery.

Her mother pours two mugs of hot chocolate and drops marshmallows on top. 'You used to love those.' She smiles, her big blue eyes softening.

'I still do.' Maisie watches her mum lower herself into a chair, harrumphing as she goes. 'Are you OK, Mum?'

'Oh, I'm fine. Fine. Just getting old, poppet.' She takes her hand and squeezes it. 'It's so good to see you. I've missed you, poppet.'

'I've missed you too, Mum. And these hot chocs. Ben and I tried to make them once – failed miserably.' She laughs. 'We couldn't figure out how you do it.'

Janet shuffles down in her seat, grinning, more than a little smug. 'I'll leave the secret in a letter for you after I die. Until then, I want to keep it to myself – makes me special.'

'How's the business?'

'Maisie, I feel this is a prelude to something. Tell me what? What's wrong?'

Maisie sighs, the energy draining from her sore body, like sap from a tree.

When she speaks, the words feel as if they are sticking to the roof of her mouth. 'I think I need to tell Ben. About what I did.'

'I thought you decided not to. It will only be worse now you've left it so long.'

'I know.' Maisie takes a sip, worrying at the chip on her mug, panic rising in her stomach. 'There's this couple I know from Oxford and they have no secrets, no skeletons in the closet. They know each other through and through. And the way things are now, Ben doesn't know me. Not properly.'

'Oh, poppet. What do you feel you should do?'

'Tell him.'

'Then that's what you must do.'

Maisie nods, tears burning the backs of her eyes. Even now, she can still feel the warm blood on her fingers. Even after she showered, watched it pour down the drain, she could feel it on her skin, penetrating her thoughts with so much force it began to feel as if she was losing her mind. For the first few minutes afterwards, she'd thought that if she closed her eyes, the bloodied clothes and stench of tragedy in the air would have evaporated by the time she opened them. But they didn't. Instead she just stared – shocked, guilty, frightened – at the mess. At what she had done. At what she couldn't undo.

Friday 22 January, 2016

A cluster of photo frames sits on the scuffed pine sideboard. In one she and her mother stand by their small Christmas tree, which is swathed in tinsel and fairy lights. On the coffee table behind them is a plate with cookies, carrots and a glass of milk. Her mother had tried to tell her Rudolph didn't need five carrots, and that he stayed home for Santa's trip to Penzance in any case, but she insisted, saying Santa could take the carrots back with him and that Rudolph might want to share them with the other reindeer. Her mother couldn't argue with that logic.

She could remember the first time her mother told her the story of Santa coming to Penzance in a dinghy, the sack of presents for her and the other children propped against the side, his white beard blowing in the breeze. It was a sweet tale, one most of the children in their town were led to believe. Not a sleigh but a dinghy – very coastal-oriented.

Maisie kneels down and opens the doors of the sideboard, pulling out blankets infused with the scent of Rich Tea biscuits from their midnight feasts. She pushes her hand to the back. She can't remember the last time she thought about the doll. Funny how important a bundle of fabric and stuffing can be at a young age, and how easily forgotten later on. She pulls it out and runs her fingers across the doll's hair, which is really only a piece of fabric cut into a V shape at the end and sewn to the head. The eyes are drawn with black marker pen and the mouth is red felt-tip. She remembers cutting her curtains to pieces, declaring she was making a dress like the lady in *The Sound of Music*. Her mother should have told her off but instead she made her a doll from the remnants.

124

She'd treasured it for years but now she couldn't even remember its name. She holds it to her nose and inhales deeply: the aroma of biscuits, scented candles, and the faint smell of dried saliva from when she'd dribbled on it as a girl. She'd tried to get her mother to wash it but was told it would get torn to pieces in the washer.

'You've found Polly, then?'

'Polly! I forgot her name.'

'You used to love that doll. You always wanted a baby called Polly. That doll is a very ugly baby, though.'

Maisie smiles. 'Well, she's a lot better than the dolls you can buy in the shops, Mum. You did a good job.'

Janet laughs. 'Those things are terrifying. I was in Asda the other day and came across this hideous doll. Why do they give them such big eyes? I think it was a Disney one – a princess. I bet it gives children nightmares. Would me.'

Maisie stands. 'Do you mind if I take her?'

'She's yours, poppet.'

Maisie nods and follows her mother into the kitchen. Her bag is packed, sitting near the door. She has to leave in a few hours; the thought of going back to Ben makes her stomach churn.

Her mother is right. She needs to tell him. She needs to be open and lay down her secrets. Why couldn't she have broken that hideous vase his mother gave him? Or cheated on him? Anything was better than the shadow of death.

She slumps into the chair, propping her chin up, holding the doll close as if to instil in herself the strength she had as a girl. In a way she hadn't only killed *him*; she'd killed a part of herself too, lost it the moment she saw blood pooling on the floor. A light-hearted, carefree strength whose absence was like a constant punch to the gut.

For the first few months, she piled make-up onto her face to hide the crusty skin under her nose and the black rings beneath her eyes. She sprayed dry shampoo on her greasy hair and forced herself to get out of bed. The only consolation she found was in the routines of work. Where she cared for her patients and wiped away the slime of the monster. Even if it was just for a few moments, she felt human.

Her mother was the only person she told. After it happened, she drove down to Cornwall, escaping her life, much as she was doing now. She wonders if people look at her and think: murderer. If they're thinking that just over a year ago there was blood underneath her fingernails. Can they sense it? Can they tell? She doesn't think so but that doesn't mean it isn't true.

Janet kisses her head and holds her hand. 'Just tell him, sweetheart.'

'What will he do?'

'I don't know.'

*

He is light in her arms, featherweight. Such a small boy. She wonders whether, if she holds him close enough, she can breathe some life back into his body, just enough for him to open his eyes and wiggle his fingers. Just enough for him to look at her and for her to look at him. Just to say hello.

She opens the door and carries him inside with a care she did not know she possessed. The curtains are drawn, a partition to keep the world from invading their moment of time together. The candles she lit hours earlier are burnt down to the nub, tears of wax weeping over the edges. The book she was reading him lies on the floor, open in the middle, pausing the story – pausing the life she had that morning. Soon she will have to walk back out and stop that life completely. But for now, the moment is hers, and if she closes her eyes she can imagine a different version of this scene. One in which warm fingers reach out to touch her face and bright eyes peer up at her.

She walks to the middle of the lounge, slowly turning, as if to show him the room, her eyes fixed on the soft brown lashes sitting across his skin, at the pink nails and small fingers. She breathes in the smell of him, every detail of him. So that, when the moment ends, she can revisit it in her mind.

She kisses his forehead, the cold skin sending a shiver down her spine. It makes her feel unsteady on her feet. She tells him how much she loves him over and over again. He can't hear her but she likes to think that if he could, he'd look up at her now and know. And that if she hadn't taken his life, right now she would be singing him her favourite songs and welcoming him into a life she was going to make perfect.

'You look like your daddy, little one. You have his nose and his lips and you have my funny-shaped eyes and your grandma's ears. She loves you. She'll make you her famous hot chocolate and tell you stories about giants and fairies. And then Daddy and I will read you books and dance around the lounge with you.'

She strokes his head and smiles. 'Shall we have a dance now? Your first dance with Mummy. You know, when you grow up, even when you think you're too cool for it, we'll have to do it again. Then, when you get married, I want you to save me a dance at the reception. I want you to dance with me even when I get old, even when my back hurts and I'm struggling to see. Then you'll be twirling me round like I'm doing with you now.'

She rocks him in her arms, singing under her breath, hoping wherever he is he can feel her loving him. She nestles her face into his neck as tears roll down her cheeks, fingers seeking out his own. She squeezes her eyes closed and, when she kisses Billy's hand, thinks she sees him smile at her.

When the moment ends and life catches up with her, she leaves the room and takes his body away, a small part of her believing that, for those few seconds, when she poured all of her love into him, he really did open his eyes and look at her. And then she was no longer holding a bundle of blankets with a cold body inside, but a little boy called Billy, whose life extended far into the future and was filled with love and happiness and lots and lots of dancing.

She tells him and feels as if she has been set free. For the first time in a long time she feels weightless. And her memories of Billy are no longer tinged with guilt and lies. They are pure and beautiful. Hers to keep and to treasure until the day she dies.

He looks at his hands as they hover over the mug but his eyes are blank and it is as if his personality has been stripped from his body; she knows she has just destroyed something inside him.

The seconds stretch into one another, each one longer than the last, making her feel as if the moment will last for ever. Finally, with a slowness to his movements that makes her worry, he puts down the carton of milk and stares at the floor. When he meets her gaze, she doesn't see even an ounce of love. She doesn't blame him – she would feel the same.

When he eventually speaks, it makes her jump. 'Why didn't you tell me?'

'I felt guilty. I didn't want you to know what I'd done to him.'

'You are guilty.'

She flinches. He walks towards her, hands shaking. If she didn't know Ben through and through, she'd think he was about to hit her. But he doesn't. Instead, he looks at her, tears in his eyes. 'You should have told me! He was my son! My son! I loved him too!'

'I know! I know that, Ben.'

'What were you even doing? Why would you be rushing like that, when you were so heavily pregnant?'

'I fell asleep. It was my last chance to get your birthday present so I grabbed my bag and ran into the hall. I wasn't concentrating. I didn't realise I'd left my lace undone.' Maisie sinks onto the sofa, a place she always feels so relaxed but which now offers her no comfort. 'When I tripped, I tried to grab the handrail but I couldn't. It all happened so fast and yet so slowly at the same time. I can remember praying he'd be all right. I put my hands out, tried to protect him – that's why they were so bruised. When I got to the bottom of the staircase, I was already bleeding.'

Ben's hand goes from his mouth to his eyes, an amalgamation of shock and horror flicking like a reel of film across his face. His legs slip out from under him and he flops to the floor, a broken crackle of sobs escaping through his lips. He doesn't look at her – this is what she notices more than anything.

'When I opened my eyes, I think I knew he'd gone. I just felt alone, empty. I pulled myself up and called an ambulance. They took me to the hospital, performed a C-section, as you know. I already knew he was dead. I felt it. I felt him go.' Maisie grits her teeth, trying to stanch a fresh flow of tears. This is his time to grieve. Not hers. He deserves that.

'The doctor heard me telling him about us. Telling him about our life and our home. She shouldn't have but she pulled a few strings and let me bring his body home. I showed him the lounge, twirled him round where you're standing now, told him how much he looked like you and that, even when I got old, I wanted him to dance with me. Like we did together when we moved in. I told him how his grandma would make him hot chocolate and tell him stories about giants and fairies. I told him how much we loved him.'

Ben wipes his eyes, but he misses a tear, and Maisie watches it drip into his mouth. She reaches out to take his hand but stops herself in time. Ben stands and dashes to the door, and she watches it swing to in his wake.

His footsteps beat out a hateful rhythm on the staircase, and when he reaches the bottom – where she had lain in a pool of blood a year ago, crying over her little boy – she finally lets the tears fall into her hands. There is nothing holding her back now.

Chapter 25

They sit side by side, two little boys with the palest of hair and the brightest of eyes. One sits patiently, smiling at a bird in the sky; the other wails and grits his teeth, clawing, giggling when he scratches someone walking past.

The mother stands to the side, gossiping to a woman in her forties. The woman's teenage daughter and husband flank her, waiting for her to finish. The husband is looking at the teenager and the teenager is looking at the ground, thin body clad in silk shorts and a shirt advertising a football team. The mother looks at them, and I wonder how she doesn't see what stares her in the face. The man wanted a son and instead got a daughter, who he beats for punishment and lusts after for pleasure. The teenager stands quietly, sad, withdrawn. The clues to their family dynamic are as clear as the sun in the sky. But only to me.

When the bad boy begins to scream at the top of his lungs, they turn and stare. The mother rolls her eyes and kneels in front of him. 'Listen, Angus, if you don't stop you won't be having a lollipop at the shop. Look at Toby, as good as gold.'

The bad boy stops, ponders his choices and then begins to scream again, angrily rocking himself from side to side. The good boy shifts farther along the bench, away from his brother. The mother shakes her head. 'He's so naughty at times. I'm not giving him a lolly now.'

And she doesn't. Later, when they go to the shop, Toby has his and Angus goes without. And I realise, Blue-Eyes, you get what you want when you are good. You go further in life when you are well-behaved and sweet and kind. Watching those two little boys, similar in looks but so different in temperament, it becomes clear that if *I* am a good boy, I can have everything *I* want.

This realisation is one brick in the bridge that carries me to you because now I need to leave this place. The people in this town know who I am. They have watched me since I was a baby. I've had my fair share of 'tellings off' over the years. For being naughty, for being odd. Now, though, seeing those two little boys, I wonder if I have been wrong to let myself be seen. If perhaps I should have – what does Mother say? – put on an act. Like the apologies I let fly when I bother her.

A woman walks down the road, tottering along on heels that are too high for her. I walk up and push her to the ground. Her head grazes the tarmac. Her fingers come away with blood. She sees my face then crawls a few inches, pulls herself up and rushes down the street, as fast as her heels will permit, not daring to look back at me. What a weird little kid, she will think.

Another lady walks down the street, her nose pressed against the pages of a magazine. She isn't looking where she is going and when she trips on the bike I have left in her path, I am by her side, holding her up, righting her. I smile again. She brushes my cheek with her finger. Thank you, she says. You're my angel. She rummages in her pocket and hands me a five-pound note. Treat yourself to some sweets, love, she says, then pats my arm and

131

carries on down the street as I wipe my cheek, removing the smell of her skin.

And as simple as that, with two tourists, I have set my life on a new course.

Mother is easy to lie to. All it takes is a few choice words from me and a well-placed property paper to plant the seed in her mind. I tell her people are whispering behind her back. Saying how terrible it must be to have had a cheating husband. I tell her they pity her, talk about her at the WI every Sunday. She has been the topic of conversation for five sessions, beating the 'big-fire-at-that-old-schoolteacher's-house'. I tell her they are like archaeologists, raking over the facts of her divorce, studying the anatomy of her marriage. And – the final push for Mother – saying that the root of the divorce probably goes back to the death of their little girl. Mary's name is what does it. She picks up the property paper without thinking where it has come from and finds us our new home within minutes. Want to know where it is?

Right next door to you.

Tuesday 4 September, 1990

The day we meet is a day I will remember for the rest of my life. What makes it special isn't what you might expect. It isn't when I walk up to you, introduce myself as your new neighbour, ask if I can play ball with you and your friend. I smile and laugh and project an air of sweet, humorous sincerity. I tell you I like your bike because I can tell you are proud of it. I tell you I don't like your jumper because I see you scratch at the red skin on your arms. I say your mother makes nice cookies because the pleasure on your face when they crumble in your mouth makes my heart quiver and my hands clammy. I ask how old you are. What is your favourite food? What do you like to do for fun? Just *how* many pins did you say you got down bowling? Ten. That's impressive. I even ask your friend with his spindly legs, fat middle and full lips what his favourite games are because I know it will please you. You you you. I am instilling pieces of myself in your life and in your memory. So the next time you go bowling, when you knock down ten pins, you will think of me. When you play with your dolls – because that is what they are, your action figures – you will smile at the thought of me. And when you have your mother's cookies, I will be there at the edge of your thoughts, reminding you that you are mine now, even if you don't know it. Mine mine mine.

My treasured moment isn't even the eleven seconds my hand touches your skin. Your mother, pleased with her son for making friends with the new neighbour, takes our picture, asking us to bunch together and pose. I wrap my arm around your shoulder, fingers grazing your sore, sweaty neck, the smell of it sinking deep into my flesh. Exactly where I want it. By the time she has finished, my hand is shaking and I have to tuck it in my pocket. Later, when I am in my room, that will be the hand I caress my face with, imagining my hand is yours.

No, what makes it really special is the moment I first see you. I am standing in our new lounge, looking out of the window at our new garden, when you rush out, wheeling your bike, laughing at something your friend has said.

With your blue eyes and blond hair, you are everything my life has been leading up to. Happiness pours from you and fills our neighbourhood with a force that makes people smile. You are a vision. And finally I have you. A special one. A good one. Like Mary, like Sarah, but better. Far better.

Your name is John Graham. You are four-foot-six. You love Angel Delight and riding your bike. Every Sunday morning you take your little sister to the sweetshop for acid drops. You are a brave boy, wise boy. Good boy. And you are my boy now.

Chapter 26

John

Wednesday 9 December, 2015

'They've found her. They've found Bonnie.' John repeats it to himself. The fifth time it finally sinks in.

Amy sits them down and tells them Detective Inspector Alice Munroe just contacted her to say they'd had a sighting of a little girl meeting Bonnie's description. She is with a man in his late forties. They are at the airport.

John jumps up and grabs his car keys, a small part of him stung that Alice, after their conversation last Monday, didn't tell them – him – herself. 'We need to go! Which airport?'

'I suggest staying here until further news, John. We don't know it's Bonnie. It could just as easily not be. DCI Munroe is there. She'll call me as soon they've identified her.'

'Amy, we need to be there.' He gestures to Jules, who is by his side in an instant. 'If that's her, we need to be with her.'

'And what if it isn't?'

'It is. There haven't been any other potential sightings. This is her. It has to be.' He drums his fingers on his leg, impatiently.

How can she be so slow? This is his daughter. This is Bonnie. Frustrated, he takes Jules's hand and leads her to the hall. Amy shoots out in front of him, arms out, placating.

'John, you could turn up there, all guns blazing and ruin any chance of getting her back. The guy could flee and we might not find her again. And if it's not her, you'll just terrify a little girl and her father. Don't. Let us deal with this.'

'Amy, we can't just do nothing!' Jules is moving from foot to foot, twirling a piece of hair round her finger. A recent development. John thinks it is a stress reliever.

'I know, Jules. I know how you feel.'

'You don't! YOU WILL NEVER KNOW HOW I FEEL!'

John jumps, surprised. Amy looks as if she has been slapped across the face, and if he weren't angry with her for keeping them there, he would feel sorry for her.

Jules drags a ragged breath through her lips, balling her fists, fighting tears in her eyes. John can feel her frustration and desperation like a fog in the room. Amy nods, eyes cast to the floor. 'OK. I don't but I know you could jeopardise any chance of getting her back if you leave now. Don't do it. Let us deal with it.'

John's mobile buzzes in his pocket. He ignores it, glaring at Amy. He knows she is right. They should let the police deal with it. If anyone is going to find Bonnie it is them. But he feels so helpless. His daughter is about to leave the country, a future of God knows what awaiting her. He can't do nothing. He squeezes Jules's hand, then walks past Amy to the door. They'll go to the airport and wait outside. At least then they can be close.

The mobile buzzes in his pocket again. He pulls it out and stares at the words across the screen. A message from Alice. He shows Jules, and they turn and wrap their arms around each other, hope splintering like glass at their feet.

Not her.

I'm sorry.

He feels as if the crux of who he is has been stripped away. And like a shell, like a box, now there is nothing.

John sits with the sun on his skin amid the bubbling joy of young children, either playing tag, taking turns to push each other on the swings, or sitting cross-legged on the grass, sweet smiles of contentment smoothed across their lips. He'd brought Bonnie to Florence Park hundreds of times, watched her small form blend into the crowd of others and flopped onto the bench where he sits now with an audible sigh. He can spot some of her friends, blissfully unaware of Bonnie's struggle and his own silent fight to keep desperate fingers holding these feeble shreds of hope.

He watches a young girl with blonde ringlets and green-tipped fingers skipping across the grass, her mother watching from the sidelines, and ponders how old she is. Six? Seven? If Bonnie was with him, she'd initiate a friendship on a single smile, the offer of a toy or the sharing of a chocolate bar. And in that instant they'd be the centre of one another's world. Children cluster to Bonnie for her easy smiles, humour and generosity. Perhaps John is biased. But then he is allowed to be. She is his daughter, after all. Pulling his mobile from his pocket, he rereads Alice's message and feels a lump settle like a rock in his throat.

Not her.

I'm sorry.

'What'ya looking at?'

John jumps in his seat, turning to see seven-year-old Rachel peering over his shoulder, leaning forward on the bench and swinging her legs. 'Hi, sweetheart. I didn't realise you were there. Where's your mum?'

She shrugs and smiles. 'Talking on the phone. Where's Bonnie? I want to show her my new book. I haven't seen her in ages.'

John adopts a smile to disguise the clinch in his gut, feeling a flush of guilt at lying. But what is the alternative? Tell a seven-year-old her friend has been kidnapped? 'Sorry, Rachel. She's got a bug. In bed at home. I just needed a bit of fresh air so I thought I'd come here.'

Her expression fizzles into a frown. 'Oh. OK. Mum says to drink a lot of lemon tea when I'm poorly. I can make her some, if you want?'

'That's OK, sweetheart. She'll be better in no time.'

Rachel nods and skips back to her mother, who sends John a smile and a wave. He nods and looks back at the little girl with blonde ringlets. She is pulling against the hand of a man in a baggy shirt and tracksuit bottoms, her bright-red face a sharp contrast to the white crescents the man's fingernails have cut in her skin. John frowns, a niggling concern embedding itself into his side, like a splinter into the soft pad of his finger. Where is the girl's mother? Why isn't she helping her daughter? John sweeps his eyes across the play area, hunting for her perfectly permed hair and red lips. Nowhere.

Baggy Shirt shoots a glare at the girl and pulls her in the direction of the car park. John pushes down a torrent of fear and looks to see if anyone else has noticed. They haven't. But then, did he notice when his own daughter was taken? Did he sense a disturbance in their lives? No, he was arguing with his wife in the kitchen.

The girl lets out a thin wail under her breath, scratching the man's hand, batting away his glares with ones of her own.

John watches all of this happen but now a scene is playing out in his mind: a man is creeping into his house and creeping back out with Bonnie in his arms, her fingers stretched towards him and Jules. And she is afraid and confused at the absence of her parents. The ones who vowed to protect her.

'No! I don't want to! Let go!' the girl cries, tears streaking her cheeks. Baggy Shirt grunts and sweeps her into his arms. And at that moment John jumps up and rushes across the grass, dodging children and leaping over the bags and coats discarded on the floor, his head throbbing with panic. He is taking her! He is taking her like *He* took Bonnie!

'Hey! Let go of her! Don't touch her! I said, let go of her!'

Baggy Shirt pauses, eyebrows popping up into his forehead like miniature jack-in-the-boxes. 'What did you say, mate?'

John prises the girl from his grip and folds her into his chest, hands swift and gentle. Baggy Shirt glances down as if he can't believe the girl has vanished. Fear marks her face with twin blotches of red. She cries, drawing the eyes of children and parents alike. But John can no longer hear them; he can no longer hear the girl's wails and he can barely even hear Baggy Shirt's barrage of threats because Bonnie's voice is crying out for him and in his mind's eye he can see spittle flying from her gaping mouth, hair falling into her frightened eyes as she is pulled away.

She's calling for him. His Bonnie's calling for him.

'Daaaaaddyyyy!'

'Let go of her!'

'Daaaaaddyyyy!'

'LET GO OF HER!'

John grits his teeth and backs away, cradling the girl. She sits in the crook of his arm just like Bonnie did, and he feels a flush of anger. He won't let another girl be taken away from her parents. He won't let another man be the undoing of another little girl. 'No!' he shouts. 'If you come any closer, I'll call the police! I mean it! You're not taking her!'

Baggy Shirt creeps towards them, lunging on the last step. 'GET OFF HER, YOU FUCKING PSYCHO!'

John blocks his hands and sidesteps. Baggy Shirt grapples against his chest, prising the girl from his hold. John hears the girl's wails blend with the cries of a woman to his right.

'Oh my God! Oh my God! Pippa! PIPPA!' The woman with red lips and permed hair shoots forward and screams. John rushes towards her and gently slips the girl called Pippa into her waiting arms. 'She's OK! She's OK! She's OK!' John repeats the words not only to her but himself also.

The woman weeps into Pippa's hair. Between sobs, she strokes her daughter's head and looks at him. 'He wasn't kidnapping her, you idiot! He's her father!'

Her father.

Her.

Father.

The words skitter like stones in his mind, jolting him from his reverie.

Her father.

F

A

T

H

E

R.

'Oh my…'

It is then John feels the strength leach from his body and the blood drain from his lips. The man wraps an arm round the woman and delicately strokes Pippa's cheek, panting between two prominent middle teeth. 'Are you OK, Pips?' He nestles his cheek into her head and kisses her hair. John stumbles back, holding his stomach in the hope of delaying the sickness. 'I… I thought… he was… he was taking her away. I… I'm so sorry! Oh God, I'm so sorry.' John sucks in breath after breath, the words pouring from his mouth faster and faster as the realisation meets his heart like a ton of bricks. 'I'msosorryIdidn'trealiseIthoughthewastakin gherI'msosorryohGodI'msosorry!'

The woman looks at him, patting Pippa's back. 'You're lucky we're not calling the police!'

'I… I can't apologise enough! I was trying to help her! I'm sorry!'

The woman glares at him, turning away. 'Fine. Just leave us alone, please.'

139

John backs away, palms turned upwards. Guilt clenches a crippling fist in his chest. 'John, darling. Are you OK?' He is faintly aware of a pair of hands cupping his shoulders. Sally. It is Sally, Rachel's mum. John stares at her. 'Sal, I thought he was—'

'I know, darling, I saw. Come on. Pippa's OK. You were just trying to help. It's fine. Everyone's OK. Jean – Pip's mum – would have done the exact same thing.'

John turns and makes his way back under Sally's soothing wing. Pippa's mask of fear is imprinted on his mind. His legs buckle and he slips onto the bench. He lowers his head into his hands and cries. Squeezing his eyes shut, John feels a small hand tentatively take his. When he looks up he sees Rachel, but for a moment, just a moment, he is sure it is Bonnie.

Chapter 27

Maisie

Friday 22 January, 2016

The blue fabric is soft in her hands. She can tell they are the same ones because of a mark on the sole. Now, though, they are at the reduced rate. A cheap price for old stock. No one bought them because blue wasn't the 'in' thing. Purple was. That was all she saw: purple coats, purple shirts, purple trousers. She would have. She planned to. They were to be the first pair of booties Billy ever had. She and Ben were going to make a special trip into town to buy them. They didn't have much money then – even less after everything they had already bought for the baby – but these booties they left for last. Ben even went as far as to ask his boss for a raise. When that didn't happen, her mother posted the remaining money for the booties as a treat for her grandchild.

That was a few days before Billy died.

She holds them to her cheek and closes her eyes. She knows she must look strange to the security men standing by but she doesn't care.

She'd tried her best to avoid Mothercare in the past year. But

141

there was a store on her way to work she couldn't detour from. Every day she turned her head and looked away, pretending it didn't exist, and for the most part it worked. She did well, keeping calm, not letting the pain get to her. But when she saw a mother bend down to her child in the street or another wipe her baby's mouth or even just touch its head, her inner strength crumbled. She rushed in the opposite direction, cupping her mouth to stop herself being sick, tears streaming down her cheeks. One man asked if she was OK but she ignored him, dodging families everywhere, feet pounding the floor in a bid to escape. She garnered a clutch of dirty looks from people and, along with them, eye-rolls, tuts and hushed words mocking her. It was nearly laughable that they thought she cared enough to be bothered by it.

Maisie runs her finger along the golden stitching. She likes them because they remind her of Cornwall, the way the waves toss and turn and how the wind whips the spray into your face when you least expect it. Little sailor booties for her boy, like the little sailor her brother had hoped to be when he grew up.

Moisture gathers in the corners of her eyes. She lowers the booties and sees the fabric is wet. A woman walks up to the reduction stand, a toddler propped on her hip, his hair falling into his eyes. He puts the toy dinosaur he is holding into his mouth. When his mother pulls it out, a soft pop ensues. The boy laughs at the noise and the mother laughs with him, planting a kiss on his head.

Maisie turns and makes her way through the shop. Why did she have to lose her child? Why did it have to be her Billy? Every day mothers gave birth to healthy babies, girls and boys they didn't want and certainly wouldn't love. But she would have loved her son. She would have protected and cared for him. She would have given him a good life, striving for perfection every day. She would have been firm but kind. Tough but loving. She would have wiped away the tears and stuck a plaster on the cuts. She would have given him everything.

She moves through the sea of children, heart pounding, tears now streaming down her cheeks like they have done so many times before. She hears a scuffle and shouts behind her and wonders if a child is having a tantrum over a toy.

It is only when she runs out of the shop and the alarms begin to wail that she realises the booties are still clutched in her shaking hands. When the security guards come, she is quietly sobbing into the shoes her son should have worn.

Chapter 28

Miller

Wednesday 5 September, 1990

She tells me you were born early, two months before you were due. You get it from your father, that undeniable thirst for life. When she returns from the trip to see your parents this morning, Mother tells me what she learnt about you, word for word. I make her write it down in her neatest handwriting so I can come back to it later. I won't forget, I will never forget even a single detail of you, but I like the thought of hanging you over my bed at night. Watching over me as I sleep.

I also keep a photo of you I stole under my pillow so you are above and beneath me. Surrounding me. In the picture you pose with your mother and father, your sister, Bessie, sitting on your shoulders. All smiling, all happy. Already your face is beginning to smudge where my finger has run over it. I almost do it now but I stop myself.

*

I can't resist a special trip upstairs when I sneak into your house. The lure of your room is just too strong. You keep things tidy, bed made, floors clear, toys sitting neatly in the corner. All except the ten action figures – dolls – you have stood on your dresser. An honorary place in your life. I open your wardrobe and pull out the red jumper you wore the day we met. It smells of wool and sweat. A combination that takes me right back to that moment in the garden when I first touched you. I run my fingers down to the cuffs. A clump of fibres are stuck together in a dried substance. Blood.

Your blood.

I hold the cuff to my lips and rub it across my cheek. Holding the jumper to my chest like a baby with its comforter, I wander round the room. When I sit on your bed, I sink into the impression your body has made. A perfect fit.

Underneath the bed is a Monopoly board game. You have scrawled a J onto the blue car. Beside it are a deck of cards and a piggy bank. Your hidden treasures, perhaps? I tip over the piggy bank and watch money fall into my lap. Mixed up in the coins is a lollipop, half-eaten. I pull the wrapper off and stick it into my mouth.

I can taste you, John.

I rub my tongue over it until it begins to bleed. Only then do I reseal it in the wrapper and put it back in the piggy bank for you to find. When you next sneak a treat, you'll be sneaking it with me.

I stuff the jumper into my rucksack and leave, my fingers brushing your bedcover as I go. I am careful to avoid detection as I skip over your fence into my garden. I can't have anyone seeing me. If they do and rumours start to spread, you won't want to be my friend. But I want to be yours, John. I want to be so *very* close to you.

*

Mother wants to tell me to stay away from you like Father did with Sarah, but I don't think she will. She will bite her bottom lip and nod tentatively like a child after a few seconds, like this morning when I told her to go round to your house and introduce herself to Molly, chat about life with children, find out all she could about you. I think she knows how I feel about you already. She can probably sense it. I exist for you now, my beautiful Blue-Eyes.

Saturday 8 September, 1990

I tag along when you and your friend head to the river to play. It faces our houses and is only a short walk from our doors. We flop on the ground and throw rocks into the water, laughing. I don't understand what is funny but you obviously do as you are the one who laughs loudest. Your friend, a chubby boy whose jovial, silly personality makes you clutch your sides, sits next to you, twirling a strand of grass between thick fingers. You pluck a strand and copy him. When I do the same, cup my hands and blow through a gap in my fingers, both your faces burn with awe. You try and try but you cannot do it. I ask you to cup your hands and when I blow for you your skin makes my lips tingle.

The chubby boy pulls a notepad from his pocket and begins to sketch a robin. You watch him, brow furrowed. Then with a gasp you pat us on the back and say, 'Why don't we sign our names with sketches? Different types of birds? Then, when we're at school, we can pass notes back and forth to each other, and if Mr Donaldson finds one, he won't know whose it is.'

Chubby Boy grins, clapping his hands – an imitation of your sister when she gets excited. I feel a thread of jealousy being sewn through my skin at the thought of him knowing what will make you smile. I want to know these things. I want everything. I drop the grass onto my knee, lean forward and laugh. 'That's a good idea!'

You nod. 'Yeah! I'm going to be a woodpecker. What do you two want to be?'

'A robin!' I gather it is Chubby Boy's favourite bird. You both look at me and I struggle to hide my smile. 'A raven,' I say. When you both frown, I add quickly, 'I like the black feathers. They're shiny.' That does it. You both smile.

We practise our drawings on Chubby's notebook. He is the most skilled of our trio but that is only because I am pretending to be bad. I could make you both look at me in awe if I tried hard enough but I don't want that. Instead I grumble under my breath and say, 'Aw, I'm rubbish.'

'No, you're not! This is great!' You pat me on the back and I smile. The reaction I wanted. You are actually the worst. Your skill at drawing is practically non-existent.

'What do you want to be when you grow up?' I ask.

You reply, 'A writer.'

Chubby says, 'A paed… paediatrician. Like my Dad!'

When you both look at me, I shrug. 'Not sure. My dad used to fix cars – maybe that.'

Chubby throws another rock and it passes through a spider's cobweb. We cheer, as if this is suddenly the aim of the game. When you are both bored, we play rock-paper-scissors. You win five times in a row with scissors. I am letting you win and Chubby is too dim to understand the rules. You wave your arms in the air and squeal, kicking your feet out. Chubby laughs, rolling himself along the grass, and I have to stop myself from rolling my eyes, telling myself this is the behaviour of ten-year-olds. I am not used to it. But I soon will be.

Chubby has been your friend for a long time. This much I can see. It is in the way he casually asks you something personal and the way you casually reply when you don't to me. It is in the way you share a sneaky look, comrades-in-arms. The way you fall into each other laughing when you are too weak to stand. It is the small things. And they make me want to break them. I want what Chubby has with you.

When I look at him, I force away the hatred and anger rising in my chest and focus on the space near Chubby's waist where I imagine a piece of string tethering him to the ground.

When neither of you is looking, I reach out and snip the string with my fingers like you snipped the paper in our game.

Sunday 9 September, 1990

I saw you sneak into your mother's room, tiptoeing across the floor like that grey cat – Tom – you love so much in that cartoon. You sat on her bed and unscrewed the top of her hand cream, head whipping around like an owl, lips curling at the corners. You slipped a finger inside and rubbed the cream into your skin. Smiled. It's the scent of mangos; I know because I frequently smell it on you.

When your mother caught a whiff later, your cheeks burnished red and you embarrassedly nodded when she asked if that was her hand cream. I watched from behind a bush, enamoured of the sweet emotion running across your features. It is the same when you are watching your cartoons with Bessie, curled up together in front of the television, giggling, like a cat chasing a mouse is the funniest thing in the world. I pretend I enjoy them too, on the occasions you invite me in for breakfast, when in actual fact I am watching you.

It is taking time to build the 'friendship' between us but I can see it growing stronger each day, brick by brick, cementing our joint future.

*

Every Sunday you take Bessie to the sweetshop for acid drops. It is your special time with your sister, and as you begin the walk down the street, gloved hands clutched together, I see for the first time just how much you love her. It is beyond what you feel for

148

Chubby, even your parents. It is something without restriction. Something unparalleled. And it is something which even now, as I follow you step for step, keeping myself hidden, I already know I want.

Chapter 29

John

Friday 11 December, 2015

Amy had told them the little girl they mistook for Bonnie was on her way to Disneyland with her father for a special treat. Apparently he'd surprised her with tickets a few days before, saying it had been a hard couple of years since her mother died and they deserved a trip away. The girl's name was Penny and she was distraught because they'd missed their flight.

John's throat had closed up and his chest begun to ache. Jules had sighed and he knew she felt just as guilty as he did. They had done that. Broken that little girl's heart. He had asked Amy if they got the next flight. When she said no, he felt even worse.

He has received no further texts from Alice and assumes it is because she doesn't want to take any more risks. It must go against the rules. He is grateful, though. Her gesture hasn't gone unnoticed by him and Jules. Neither has the way she helped him in town.

After he and Jules crawled into bed the day they heard about

Penny at the airport, John stared at the text for hours, unable to sleep, imagining 'it's her'. They would have arrested the bastard and brought Bonnie home. She would have been safe and loved. They would have been able to resume their lives and move on, albeit as parents a thousand times more protective.

John's life has become a series of what ifs. What if they find her tomorrow? What if they never find her? What if this person kills her? What if he or she doesn't kill her?

He takes the mobile from his pocket and stares at the text now, running his fingers across the screen, wishing he could smudge the words into a happier dialogue.

*

John slips into the water as easily as if he is slipping into a dream. The first fingers of panic slice through his reserves of strength as the water rises over his waist, his chest, his neck, flicking across his cheeks. He feels droplets settle on his eyelashes and the cold punch a hole through his chest. But he doesn't care. He has found her. He has found his Bonnie. He remembers coming here as a family months ago, to this beautiful spot in Florence Park, away from the tornado of life at the play area. But the happiness he felt then is leagues away from the joy he feels now. The nightmare is over. The world has been put back to rights.

Her hair floats across the surface of the pond, like seaweed carried on the restless tide. Lily pads and cigarette stubs bump and poke at the top of her head. Glimmering just beneath the water, he can see her pale skin, like the moon in the murky depths of the sky. Her lips are frozen in a translucent smile: a ghost teetering between the edge of this world and the beginning of the next. And her eyes.

Her eyes...

They send a pulse of shock down his spine, turning his arms limp and his heart rigid. There is no love, not even an ounce of familiarity. She is looking at him as if he is a stranger. 'You should have protected me,' she seems to be saying. 'You should have saved me. You should have done better.'

John beats against the water, legs kicking in a desperate bid to reach his daughter. He hears an agonised wail, and it cripples him, the strands of horror weaving through it like a stitch sewn through the fabric of his mind. He looks at Bonnie. But it isn't her.

It's him.

The noise pours from his lips until it dips away into a long rasp.

'Hey, mister! What are you doing? Jesus. Get out! You'll freeze to death!'

The voice comes from behind him, ringing with a note of shock. John ignores it and dives under the water, his chest tightening, fingers tangling with reeds and plastic bags. He reaches out, his fingertips inches from his daughter. And in his mind he counts the seconds until he can touch and hold her again.

One.

'Mister! Jesus Christ! I'm coming!'

Two.

He can hear splashing behind him and for a moment worries that the man will pull him out before he can reach her. John breaks through the surface and glances at the man. When he turns back round, the mirage he thought was Bonnie is gone. And in her absence is a place where the sun shimmers on the water, reflecting his bloodshot eyes and tear-stained skin. In the depths of his confusion is a spark of realisation.

She was never there at all.

Three.

Jules sits at the dining table with vacant eyes and pale lips. 'John, can you fetch me some painkillers, please?'

He rummages through the cupboards and hands her the blister packet. He doesn't mention earlier. He doesn't mention how he thought he saw their missing daughter floating in the middle of the water. He doesn't admit to the way his mind is playing tricks on him because then he will have to admit it to himself.

She tips two into her palm and gulps them down. 'Headache?' he asks.

'A bad one.'

'Why don't you try and sleep?'

'I can't, John. Every time I close my eyes, I see Bonnie.' She runs a hand over her face, greasy hair slicked across her head.

'Do you think that girl – Penny – was frightened?'

'I don't know – I hope not. Alice probably would have handled it well. She obviously has a compassionate side.'

'I keep going over things in my head, trying to remember anyone strange from my childhood, but I can't. I didn't have any enemies. Do you remember anyone?'

'I've told you I don't, John. There was no one. Maybe… maybe this person hasn't been following you. Maybe he or she has met someone you knew when you were younger and is getting information from them.'

'Can't be. I didn't know anyone aside from you, my parents and a few friends. And none of you are missing.'

Jules closes her eyes and presses her fingers into her temples. 'I need her back, John. I need her back now.'

He holds her hand and nods. He can't offer any words of comfort because that well has dried up. The first few days, they took turns reassuring one another that Bonnie would be OK, they'd find her, they really would. But now she has been missing for fifteen days, and hope is just a pile of scattered glass under their feet, each new cut reminding them of her absence.

Jules looks up as Don walks into the dining room. 'Hi, guys. Any more news?' He deposits a bag of groceries on the table and smiles weakly.

'No.'

Don sighs. 'Right. OK. Erm, so, I… I brought some food round with me because I didn't see much in the cupboards last time I was here. I know you don't want to – God knows, I don't feel like it – but you need to eat, OK?'

'Are you making *yourself* eat?' Jules challenges him.

'Love, I can afford to starve a little bit. Have you seen me?' He prods his belly, grinning.

A smile flickers onto Jules's face. A sad smile but a smile all the same. John could kiss Don. He's been popping by constantly, keeping them fed, chivvying them along.

'OK. So I'll go make us some lunch.' He grabs the bag and marches into the kitchen, kicking his heels as he goes. Jules laughs. Bonnie used to beg him to do that all the time.

As soon as the smell of eggs wafts over to them, their stomachs begin to rumble. Don dishes out plates heaped with greasy food, then sits opposite Jules and smiles, chirpy, trying to keep the atmosphere light. 'Bon appetit.'

John pushes his food around the plate. The thought of eating even a morsel of it makes him feel sick to his stomach. He doesn't tell Don this.

'Do you remember that time we had chicken chow mein and Bonnie said it was tremendous?' Jules's fork pauses halfway to her mouth. She drops it with a clatter, tears springing to her haunted eyes.

Don leans forward, resting his hand on her cheek, forefinger by her right eye, little finger by the corner of her lip. 'Jules, we're going to find her. And you know what, she'll probably still be wearing those red shoes.'

'Probably…'

Don runs his nail across her eyelashes, slowly, tenderly, as if he is memorising the web of perfect lines in her skin.

And for some reason, John cannot pull his eyes away.

Chapter 30

Maisie

Saturday 23 January, 2016

'I feel like I've known you for years. That probably sounds really strange, doesn't it? It's just like I'm chatting to a friend right now.' Maisie straightens his bedsheet, wondering if perhaps they met in a past life. She isn't averse to unusual beliefs. Her mother encouraged her to have her own mind growing up, especially as she lived above a holistic shop. 'You probably think I'm daft saying that, but you know, I've worked on this ward for a while now and, aside from Lailah, the nurses don't know a thing about me. You know more. I've always found that talking is the best thing to do in these situations so I'll just talk about my life, like it's a story. It's not an adventurous one, not even a particularly exciting one, but it's better than nothing. And it's the story I know best.'

She begins the process of giving him a bedbath, peeling back his sheets and removing his patient gown before running her gloved hands through a bowl of water to check its temperature. She automatically assesses Tim's appearance, behaviour and condition as soon as she enters the room. A sort of spot check.

When she started work in the ICU, it took her a while to become accustomed to this procedure but now it is as easy and simple as taking a breath.

'I was born Maisie Prae Green. My mother runs a holistic shop in Penzance and my father was a mechanic when he was around. He left after my little brother was born – apparently he just couldn't cope. Funny, though, because later he started a family with a woman half his age, so he obviously could cope, just not with us. My brother, Danny, died when he was five and I was seven. He hit his head when he was riding his bike, suffered terrible bleeding on his brain. He was eventually transferred to an ICU much like this to be cared for. He was in a persistent vegetative state. A few months later he died, had a seizure. Mum and I were heartbroken. For a long time we were like ghosts, shuffling through life. My father wasn't bothered, said it was a shame. That was it. "A shame." Nothing else. You can imagine how angry Mum and I were with him. He didn't care, though. We'd just lost one of the people we loved most in the world and he got to carry on with his new family.'

She pauses. As a child, she'd spent hours pondering her father. Why didn't he love her and her mother? Why wasn't he upset about Danny dying? Why weren't they good enough? When she asked her mother, she was met with a blank expression.

'While my brother was in the ICU, we had a nurse – Jennie – who supported us through it all. She was amazing. And in the rare moments I thought about my future, I decided I wanted to do what she did. I wanted to help other people. A little clichéd maybe, but that was that.

'When I was eighteen I started by studying healthcare. And a lot of tests and a few sleazy boyfriends later, I moved here and began work as an ICU nurse. Then I met Ben, my partner. We've been together ever since.' She doesn't mention the fact that they might not be for much longer. The last few days with Ben have been agony. An uncomfortable few moments in the morning

157

before he left for work and a few in the evening before he went to sleep on the sofa. He doesn't ignore her but she can see he needs some space to get his thoughts in order and she hasn't interfered with that. She reminded him she was sorry, sorrier than she had ever been in her life, and that she loved him, but other than that, she feels she needs to leave him be.

'We're having a few problems at the moment. I haven't told anyone this before but whenever the weather is forecast to get cold overnight, he always makes me two hot-water bottles. One for the top, one for the bottom. I can't sleep when I'm cold.' She rubs the tiredness from her eyes and sighs. 'The forecast says it's going to be a chilly one tonight. And I'm worried when I go to bed it will be empty. I know then we'll be done. Our relationship will be over.'

She looks at Tim, eyes vacantly scanning the room, face twitching. 'Sorry. I'm blathering on about all the bad things. Er… I promise this little story has a happy ending but bear with me. OK, when I was about eight, four girls came into our shop. They threw my mother's bottles of essential oils on the floor, even threw them at me, said I was weird, my mother was weird. Of course, I understand now they were probably just insecure but at the time I was gutted. My mother, when she came downstairs, was furious as she cleaned up the mess. It's funny really. When my mother gets angry, she looks like a cartoon character. Her face goes all red, her eyes get big. We've had a few laughs over the years about that. Ben says I'm the same.' She smiles. 'Anyway, later on, my mother printed out a school photograph of the four girls posing together. She drew moustaches on their faces and pinned it to the door of the shop. That stopped them coming in next time. It's a little bit childish but it worked. And it made me feel better. She's always been good at doing that. I went to see her recently – in Cornwall – and she hasn't changed a bit. Neither has the shop. It's like walking back into my childhood.'

Maisie tentatively puts her hand in Tim's. She imagines he

would hold it if he was able. She bathes Tim's body gently, brushing warm water over his skin. It is a lengthy process and, when she is finished, she rolls surgical stockings up his feet and ankles to keep the circulation moving. 'It's strange, isn't it? Heidi not being here, talking to us. She had to take your daughter for a check-up but she's coming in tomorrow.'

Maisie wishes Al – the eighty-year-old husband of her second patient – had family who would support him. His children haven't visited their mother once since she was transferred to the ICU. It is only ever Al who comes to see her and that is every day without fail. With no signs of Agnes recovering, Maisie suspects he will be doing so for a long time. She sees him hobbling down the corridor every morning, walking stick in either hand, back hunched over in a permanent stare at the floor, making his way to Agnes's room. She can't help but wish she could do more for him.

'Anyway, Tim. That's a little bit about me. Can't be very interesting but it's got to be better than listening to the equipment hum and beep. It gets on my pip sometimes.'

She pulls off her gloves with a soft clap of noise and gathers up her equipment. 'I'll be back to check on you soon.'

*

She thrusts open the door and heads straight to the fridge, pulling out the jar of mini gherkins and popping the lid off. She tips her head back and drops one into her mouth; Danny used to love it when she did this. She often wonders if perhaps Billy might have looked like him. If they might have shared the same freckled skin or the same dark-blond hair. She keeps those thoughts to herself, though.

She fishes out another and closes her eyes, savouring the taste of it in her mouth – she's been craving them all day. Maisie turns and stops in her tracks. Ben is splayed out on the sofa, mouth partially open, eyes flickering behind closed lids. She smiles, wishing she could curl up beside him. Instead, she takes the jar into their bedroom and changes into her pyjamas. Just before she rolls into bed, she pulls back the duvet.

One at the top, one at the bottom.

She sighs, the relief audible, then walks into the lounge and tucks one of the hot-water bottles underneath Ben's arm. It is going to be a cold night, after all.

Chapter 31

Miller

Thursday 13 September, 1990

Rock.

Paper.

Scissors.

We play this game as if our lives depend on it. I have studied your face so much that, just by the way your lips sit, I can tell which you will pick: pursed lips for rock, flat for paper, lips parted for scissors. I let you win, time and again. You smile like you have achieved something monumental, high-fiving Chubby, but in actual fact it is me who has achieved something great. I get to watch the emotions slide like a reel across your face, the pure, devastatingly beautiful happiness shining like a torch in your eyes. Chubby looks on, trying to pre-empt what you will do. But he does not know you like I do. He has the advantage of years but I have the depth of feeling for you. I can see what makes you tick.

*

Your cropped hair falls into your eyes and you brush it away with a flick of your wrist. Your arm shoots out and you smack the white ball back to your father. Chubby and I watch from the sidelines. Chubby's eyes are watching the ball ping back and forth, applauding, cheering you both on. You are not as skilled at table tennis as your father but I can see you are trying with all your might to keep up with him. It is sweet, how you have him on a pedestal, how you look at him in awe, how you stick your chest out to make yourself taller.

I follow at a distance as you take your father-son trip to the river to play Poohsticks. You chatter about your bike, and Chubby, and even me sometimes. I must admit how my heart flutters when you say my name. Taking my camera from my pocket I point it at you and your father from behind the bushes and press record. When you say it again, I stop recording and clutch the camera to my chest, imagining your body is pressed against me instead. And oh, how good it feels, John.

Saturday 15 September, 1990

I don't think you realise how sweet you sound when you are lying on your bed, passing a ball from hand to hand, singing along to the music blasting from the radio. When you come across a lyric you've forgotten, you fill in the blank with the first word that comes to mind.

Or when, in the middle of the night, you go into the kitchen, push a chair over to the sink and stick a hand in the jar your mother keeps high up on the cupboard. You look at the clutch of yellow wrappers in your hand and giggle like a toddler. Acid drops. Your favourite. After you've pushed back the chair, covered all the evidence and slipped beneath the covers again, you dig into the sweets, fingers fumbling over the wrappers. But you always save one, don't you, John? You always save one to give to Bessie in the morning as you walk to school, asking about the dream she had last night. You slip it into her hand, put a finger to your lips. Bessie chuckles and pushes the sweet into her mouth. And when you smile at her with adoration, I want to kiss your hand and tell you how much I love you. But that would ruin my 'act'.

Or even when you invite Chubby and me round for dinner and you shovel the lasagne into your mouth, leaving the pieces of carrot on the plate. I tell you I heard a man say he ate five carrots every day for a month and it made him grow another five inches. That does the trick. You stuff them into your mouth three at a time. I see a look of pleasure flit across your mother's face; but I did not do it for her, I did it for you. I want to see you grow big and strong, into a healthy young man.

Once Mother has shuffled off to bed, moving sideways like a crab, keeping one eye on me as she goes, I pull out my camera and play the video to myself for what seems like hours. To the sound of your musical voice saying my name, I pull over a sheet of paper, cut it into the shape I want, colour it in red pen and write John across the middle. Then I hold your heart pressed against mine, bring it back and forth and mumble, ba boom ba boom ba boom. Our rhythms matching. Connected. Bonded. Like we are family, like brothers. Like we are one.

Chapter 32

John

Monday 14 December, 2015

'What is that?'

'What is what?'

'That sound. Didn't you hear it?'

John puts his cup of tea down and walks into Don's lounge. A muffled bang fills the room.

'Oh, that.' Don smiles. 'Kim's down in the basement – she's on this fitness regime thing. She's trying out those weights I got when I was on that diet. I said, "Kimmy, they don't work. I went down there every Sunday, pumped some lead, and look at me. Nothing. Nothing to show for it." She laughed and said she bet I had a bag of chocolate bars down there. Can you believe that? The cheek of it.'

John smiles, sitting on the plush sofa. He slips into the impression Don's rear end has made in the cushion. 'How is she?'

'Good, good. She's decided to do a course in creative writing. I think she's feeling a bit useless and wanting to branch out a bit. Her sister's just got this fancy shmancy job at this law firm. Er…

it's the really posh one. You know it? Anyway, so, yeah, she's trying to lose some weight and add another bow to her quiver or however the saying goes. I said to her, I said, "Kimmy, you're as thin as a twig, you don't need to lose weight." She just looked at me with that funny look she ha—'

Another bang rumbles through the house.

'I hope she's not dropped the dumbbell on her foot again.' Don frowns, biting his lip, looking at the floor as if he can see through to the basement. 'She blasts out music when she's down there – can't hear a thing I say when I bring her a cuppa. The singer who's wanting a guy to put a ring on her finger. You know her.'

'Beyonce.'

He snaps his fingers. 'That's the one!'

'I didn't know she liked her.'

'Yeah. She's a big fan. I'm getting her the new album for Christmas. Anyway, I'm banging on again. How's Jules?'

John feels a fluttering of surprise at the mention of Christmas. He and Jules will not be celebrating this year. 'As well as can be expected. Actually it's nice to chat about other things. Our brains have gone to mush. We keep going over the same things again and again. Sometimes, I drive round for no reason, hoping I'm going to spot Bonnie's red shoes. The Dorothy ones. Sometimes I even think I see her.'

Don pats him on the back. 'I know. When a little girl comes into the waiting room, for a split second I think it's her and we're about to start chatting about those cartoons. We'll see her soon, John. We will. We'll find her. I promise.'

John smiles to show he appreciates the optimism but all he wants to say is 'Don't make promises you can't keep'. He stands up, hugs Don, then makes his way to the door. 'I'd better get back. Mum's with Jules at the minute.'

'OK, mate. I'll come over tomorrow.'

John dons his jacket and laughs as another bang makes the

floor quiver under his feet. Don shakes his head. 'Honestly, she's not going to have any toes left by the end of the day.'

John smiles, hearing Bonnie's strident voice in his ears. As he turns down the street he sees her being carried away in the crowd, hand turned up in a final farewell.

Chapter 33

Maisie

Sunday 24 January, 2016

'Hello, Heidi.'

She turns to face him, lips parting to form an 'O' shape, eyebrows rising like crescent moons into the curls of her fringe. Words tumble haphazardly out of her mouth and her hand seeks out her lips in a bid to stem the words, before dropping back down to her chest, then her stomach, then starting the cycle again. Maisie organises two chairs for them to sit in and gently turns Tim in his bed, shifting his arms and legs with as much care as a mother would a newborn.

'I… I… I can't believe you're really here. Maisie said you visited but I just… I don't know what I thought.' She lassoes her words into order and tentatively wraps her arms around his shoulders, fingers making small pockets in his Armani suit. Maisie wonders how much a suit like that costs and promises to Google it later. Ben will need to have the smelling salts on hand, though.

'I hope you don't mind me coming. I wanted to see him again.'

'Oh God, of course I don't mind!' She squeezes his hands,

kissing him on the cheek. 'Tim would be over the moon right now!' She laughs, a thin, gasping sound that curls his lips into a smile. They pull each other into another hug, this one lasting a few seconds longer.

'Have the police found who did this yet?' He guides her to the chair and sits down beside her, their fingers refusing to part.

'No, no, I don't think they will either. Every time I walk out the door, I feel like I'm being watched. It's horrible.' She shakes her head, and Maisie feels the first tendrils of dread spiral round the room. Does the man know what she's hiding? Does Watson?

'Do they have any leads? Do they have any suspects?'

'No. There was no CCTV where he was attacked. No witnesses. Nothing.'

'I hope they catch him.' He nods, slumping into his chair. 'Congratulations by the way. Is this little one your first?' He grins at Heidi's bump, and Maisie notices the swift change in subject.

'No, our second. We have a little girl at home. What about you? Any children?'

'I have three. William, Dolly and Jess. Complete monsters but I couldn't live without them. My wife and I spoil them rotten.' He laughs, pulling a wallet from his pocket and offering her a picture folded in two, proudly pointing out his children.

'Oh, they're gorgeous. We'll have to get them together some-time.'

He nods. 'I think they'd love that.' A pause. 'How are you doing?'

Heidi smiles sadly, her fingers twitching against the fabric of her handbag. 'We're… we're doing OK. As well as can be expected, I suppose. It's… it's a lot to take in.'

'I bet. If there's anything I can do, let me know. I can't even imagine how you must feel right now.'

Heidi catches his eye and something passes between them. He wraps his arms around her and she tucks her hand into his shoulder. Maisie leaves the room as Heidi quietly begins to cry.

Chapter 34

Tuesday 25 September, 1990

Tufts of hair float to the floor, forming a circle round the chair. You stare intently at the Etch A Sketch, towel draped round your shoulders as your mother gives you a trim. I like it long on you, the way you push it out of your eyes and blow it away with your lips, but no matter. 'Look, Mum. It's an elephant!' You proffer your creation for her examination. She nods and smiles. 'Well done, John! Very good.'

I struggle with her lack of enthusiasm; it makes my skin crawl, as if thousands of ants are marching across me. Doesn't she see how hard you worked on that? Doesn't she see how proud you are of it? All she can manage is a 'well done'. If you were to show me, I'd shower you in praise, make you feel special. I'd give you more love than you could possibly know what to do with. I'd give you everything.

You erase the drawing and start again, fidgeting on the chair. You are too skinny, that is why your bum hurts. You need to eat more. More veg, John, I want to say.

I glance at the tufts of hair on the floor, my muscles bunching up in a yearning to scoop it up in my fingers. Your mother trims the last section, smiling. 'There you go, sweetheart. All done!'

'Thanks, Mum.' You jump off the chair and wipe up the hair. When you're finished, you grin at me and walk into the lounge. 'Mum might do yours too if you want?'

'Nah, I think I want to keep mine long.'

You shrug. I glance over at your mother, grit my teeth, curl my toes. If she came anywhere near me after what she just said, I know I'd want to stick the scissors in her hand. *Sweetheart*. She has the nerve to call you that after how she just reacted.

Chubby is sitting in front of your TV, munching on a bowl of crisps, Bessie beside him. Sleeping bags are laid across the floor, a pile of books, games, cards, comics scattered across them. You sit behind Bessie and pull her onto your lap; she curls up and rests her head across your chest, sucking her thumb. I sit beside you, smiling at her. You notice and look pleased.

'OK, Bess, come on. It's bedtime.' Your mother gathers her up and carries her from the room. You shout a goodnight, then roll across the duvets, laughing. 'What shall we do first? Play a game? Read?'

'A game! A game!' says Chubby. My dad got me a new one yesterday. Do you want to play that? I brought it with me.'

'Oh, yeah! Let's do that! What's it called?'

Chubby drags his rucksack over and withdraws it, lovingly, delicately, as if it can be broken with a single touch. 'It's called Buckaroo!'

While we play, I see what a difference the smile I directed at Bessie has made. You lean over to me, your shoulder brushing my leg, your head swivelling when I laugh. You like that I am making an effort with your little sister. I'll make lots more if it makes you happy.

You are turned away from me, snoring quietly, foot pressing against mine through the duvet. I am in the middle, separating you from Chubby, head propped up on my hand. I can't sleep, not when this is one of the best nights of my life. I study the back of your head, marvelling at its perfection, imagining the cogs turning over and over. This is the closest I have been for the longest time. A shiver goes down my back as I think how I could reach out and touch your head. I could touch you and not have to worry that I will destroy my 'act'. I have given you this boy, your neighbour, and now I have to stick to it. I cannot afford any slip-ups.

My fingers quiver as I run them across your downy hair. So soft, like a baby. I lean forward and press my nose against your head, breathing in the scent of you, holding my breath so I can lock it in my lungs. I wonder if you can feel me, if reality is converging with where you are and who you are within your dream. If perhaps now you are talking to me, playing rock-paper-scissors with me. You so love that game. It is one of your favourites.

You turn over and tuck your left hand under your cheek, right hand swinging across my waist. I wonder if you now think I am Bessie or your mother and in a moment you will nestle into me. I hope so. I'll be ready. I study your features, thinking you are not only special on the inside, you are on the outside too. I brush your fringe out of your eyes and caress your cheek.

My beautiful baby boy.

Sleeping, dreaming. My waist burns with heat. I pull your hand to my lips and kiss it, running the nails over my chin, closing my eyes, savouring this moment. Confident you won't wake up, I push your thumb into my mouth, pretending I am Bessie and that you love me with all your heart. I am your little sister and you are my big brother.

Family.

You mumble something in your sleep, brows knitting together. I release your hand and kiss your nose. I would kiss you all over if I could.

I know you don't love me as much as you do Bessie. But one day you will. One day, I will matter more to you than your mother, your father, Chubby, everyone. You were wary when I moved next door; I was a stranger from a strange town invading your close-knit community. But now I am growing into something else. I am becoming a friend. A close friend. I'm cementing a future.

Our future.

Together.

Chapter 35

John

Wednesday 16 December, 2015

You once told Bonnie that a fairy visited her in the night and touched her shoulder. I think you're right, John. Her birthmark is the shape of fairy's hand.

Just.

Like.

Tinker Bell's.

He turns the photograph over and stares at the cleft in his daughter's shoulder. Jules gasps, hand reaching for her mouth. Alice, flanked by two other detectives, stands in front of them. All of their expressions are hard, professional. John's hand shakes.

'Who… who was this sent to?'

'Me.' Alice catches his eye, and he thinks he can see the outline of fear across her face. 'My daughter found it on our doormat this morning.'

'Oh my God.' Jules looks from him to Alice, panicked. 'They know where you live?'

'Yes. We must assume we're being watched constantly. The investigation will proceed as normal. We've examined the photo and envelope for prints and DNA but there was nothing to find.'

John gestures to Alice and walks into the lounge. She follows him, her layer of professionalism cracking. She throws a glance at her colleagues, then says, 'I've sent Rosie to stay with my brother in France until we find this creep. God, I was so scared.'

'How is Rosie? Did she know what it was?'

'No. Just thought it was a prank. This is getting worse and worse. It means whoever's doing this is gathering momentum, trying to make us feel trapped. Make us wonder who will be next.'

'No new leads? There must be something we can do, Alice? He wants me – wants to hurt me – and he's using Bonnie to do it. Can't we use me as, I don't know, bait or something?'

She shakes her head. 'No. This isn't some crime drama, John. You're probably the only reason Bonnie is still alive. Think about it: they'll just keep on sending these photographs to try and get under your skin. If they didn't have you, Bonnie would already be dead. They'd have no reason to keep her.'

John cringes, the image of Bonnie's mutilated shoulder filling his mind. 'How do they know about the fairy? It was just Bonnie and I in her bedroom. Unless they were standing outside the door, but that's impossible. How could they know? Did they force Bonnie to tell them?'

'I don't know, John. I just don't know. We've asked my neighbours if they saw anyone suspicious-looking. If they saw someone come to my door between nine and ten this morning – nothing. No one saw anyone. No CCTV footage either.'

'If I'm right, Alice, if they are just drawing this thing out for as long as possible, how long do we have before he or she kills her?'

She sighs, shrugs, defeated. 'I haven't a clue. Not long, I'd guess.'

'And how long until these photographs get boring? They're clever; they're going to tire of it eventually.'

Alice's mobile buzzes in her pocket. She pulls it out and holds it to her ear. After a few moments, she sighs, a look of relief settling across her face. 'That was Rosie. She's OK. She's with my brother at the airport.'

'What makes you think she'll be safe there?'

'I don't think this creep wants to leave the country. They want to be close to you, John.'

'I wonder if they'll repeat themselves. They've sent photos to my parents, us, you, Don. Who else is there?'

'Friends?'

'Just Don. Jules is friends with Alison. She's an employee at the gallery but that's it mainly.'

'I'll get in touch with Alison. Get some uniforms over to her house. Anyone else?'

'No.'

She nods, squeezes his hand. 'I'll be in touch soon.'

Once they leave, he sits beside Jules and replays their conversation. She leans into him, head burrowing into his chest, eyes flicking up at the windows. He knows what she is thinking. Are they being watched now? Is this person outside, looking in on them? Or in the house maybe? He'd thought he was alone when he told Bonnie about the fairy. He counts using his fingers. Four photographs. Four messages. How many more before they begin to receive pictures of Bonnie's dead body?

175

Chapter 36

Maisie

Monday 25 January, 2016

She holds the fabric to her nose, inhaling the smell of blood. Old blood. The tunic is soft against her skin, and she can remember putting it on that morning, smiling at her reflection in the mirror, thinking she looked good despite being enormous. A beached whale but a well-dressed one. A world far removed from the one she inhabits now.

The guest bedroom was going to be the nursery. While she was pregnant, she and Ben decorated it with a fervour she hadn't known they possessed. They papered the walls, hung frames and garlands. Dotted about bags of lavender because she read it was soothing. She even bought a fluffy blue rug because she remembered loving things like that when she was young. The room was ready, a representation of their excitement and enthusiasm for the beginning of a new life with Billy. Something that reflected the hours they spent reading baby books, the countless times Ben massaged her feet and shoulders, the times he ran to the twenty-four-hour shop and bought her mini gherkins, the times she spent daydreaming, planning their lives, thinking how she would make birthdays and Christmases magical for Billy. The room was everything they planned and hoped for… then it was folded up and left to the dust.

She smiles at the toy she'd positioned in the cot. It was Ben's as a child. Toodles, it was called. She'd hoped Billy would love it as much as Ben. She runs her finger across its oversized ears, thinking back to yesterday evening and Ben sitting her down and explaining how hurt he was, how she shouldn't have kept it from him and how, despite what she thought, Billy's death was not her fault. It was then she realised they would be all right. They would restart, replenish their relationship, remembering their Billy with happiness.

It took a few hours but gradually she began to see it wasn't all her fault. Perhaps it *was* just a twist of fate, an accident. Perhaps she didn't kill their child. Perhaps now she can move on.

They can't have any more children in the future, of course. The life she and Ben want is an impossibility. In theory she shouldn't have been able to have Billy. He was their miracle. She doubts miracles happen more than once.

She'd picked up an infection after Billy's death and learnt she had PCOS. A syndrome that prevented her ovulating. The doctor told them it was hereditary and that, although there was no cure, surgery increased the chances of pregnancy. They could have had the treatment but at the time Billy's death was still too raw.

Maisie opens the wardrobe and pulls out a box brimming with photographs. Most are of her and Ben during the pregnancy but a few are of the nursery, documenting the different phases of its redecoration. She pushes her hand in and pulls out three. In one she is standing in front of the fridge, spooning a gherkin out of the jar with her fingers, a look of surprise on her face. The next is of Ben sitting on the sofa, head back, mouth open, snoring, a baby book in his hands. The final one is of them together, dancing round the lounge, laughing. She smiles, holding it close to her eyes. She can just see a slight bump underneath her jumper. Billy had been dancing with them.

Maisie heaves the box out of the wardrobe, carrying it into the lounge. She goes back and forth, transporting parts of the past back into their lives. And when she is finished, she leaves the door of the nursery wide open.

Chapter 37

Miller

Tuesday 3 March, 1992

I rub my hand across your back, smearing the sun cream onto your skin, careful not to miss a single inch. When I am finished, I squirt more into the palm of my hand and add another layer. Our neighbours make the most of this early heatwave with water fights, glasses of pina colada and newly bought shorts and skirts.

'Sorry to ask, but I can't reach back there.' You smile sheepishly, and I want to snap a picture and hang it on my wall.

'It's OK. I don't mind. Can you do mine too? Mum would but I think she's making lunch.'

'Sure.' You take the sun cream and smother it over my shoulders. You are gentle but firm, and you have no idea how much pleasure I garner from that touch. I close my eyes and sigh, my muscles relaxing. I could sit here like this all day, the sun shining on my face, the smell of raw eggs filling the air as Chubby tries to fry one on the pavement even though we've told him it's not *that* hot, your sweet breath blowing into my face. A small slice of paradise.

'Hey, guys! I think it's working!' Chubby excitedly hops on one leg.

You drop the bottle of sun cream in my lap and run over to him, hair flopping over your eyes. In the two years it's been since your mother cut it, it has grown down to your chin. I like it like this; I like that if I am walking behind you and a breeze blows it back, I will feel it. I like it when we have our sleepovers and I run my fingers through it. I cut some of it once, you know. A bit at the back so you didn't notice. I keep it in my pillow so I can smell you at night. Our houses are within jumping distance but even that seems too far sometimes.

'No, it's not!' you say, laughing, pointing. 'It's still runny! Look, Chubs. It hasn't even cooked round the edges.'

'Oh. Daisy Williams said it worked for her.'

'I think Daisy might have told a lie.' I smile down at the egg, patting Chubby on the back.

You nod. 'Yeah. Don't worry, though, Chubs. I'll go and get something to clean it up with.' You rush into your house, helpful as always.

Chubby sinks to the ground, legs crossed, cheeks squashed by his hands. 'I really thought it would work.'

I grit my teeth, stopper the words I've been wanting to scream at him all day. 'Never mind, old chap.' He smiles at me.

'Guess what? Mum's made us some ice lollies.' You run up to us, tissues clutched in your hand. I want to tell you to let Chubby clean it up himself but I know you want to help, want to make him feel better about his failed experiment.

'There we go! All done!' I smile as you wipe up the egg, wondering if you realise you are talking like your mother. You lead the way to the kitchen, Chubby second in the line and me at the rear. I can sense it coming even before he begins to sing. 'Heigh-ho, heigh-ho, it's off to work we go.' Chubby whistles the tune from the Disney movie, skipping along. It makes you laugh, and so of course I laugh too.

'Hey, gang. Ready for something nice and cool?' Your mother smiles, offering us ice lollies, ruffling your hair. I very nearly reach out and straighten it back down. Chubby takes two, greedily.

The phone rings, and your mother runs into the lounge. 'Hello? Hi, Gail! How are you? I know, it's stifling. I made the boys some ice lollies. Yeah. Of course. What have you called to say? You can't remember. Oh, good. She said what? Well, I hope you told her. Good for you. OK. Yes, I'll pop over later. Bye.'

She is frowning when she returns, mouth pursed, brows furrowed. 'Honestly, boys. People these days. Do you know what Gail just told me?' She looks at us, flopping in our seats, then shakes her head and laughs. 'Oh, never mind! You three look like you're about to melt. Come on.' She herds us into the lounge and sits us in front of the fan, where we take turns making Bessie laugh. Chubby tells the best jokes, pulling faces and making silly noises, and for a moment I am angry enough to swing the fan into his face because you are looking at him like you looked at me that night. Lovingly.

It has been two years since I moved into your town, and in that time you have grown close to me; you have begun to want my opinion, respect it, to look at me the same way you look at Chubby. It has taken time but finally I have fully integrated myself into your life and your future. But recently, I'm beginning to feel it isn't enough. I'm beginning to wonder what it would be like if it was just us. If Chubby and Bessie and your parents were no longer here and I was the centre of your world. If it was just the two of us. Alone.

*

You saw a woman walking along the street the other day, holding her young daughter's hand. And you didn't need me to tell you the girl was afraid, that the bruises on her arms were fingermarks.

You didn't know I was standing close by but you realised for the first time the world isn't entirely as you expected it to be. That the little town we live in isn't so different from the rest, which is full of cruel, manipulative people. It is full of a rage you never believed possible.

I saw the cogs working inside of your beautiful mind, saw the flashes of shock, horror and sadness seep into your face, and I had to keep myself from running over and covering your eyes.

People are not like you, John, I wanted to say. People are greedy and malicious and they lie and steal. You are special. You are a good one. One of very few. And the world is going to want to hurt you. Want to strip you of your honesty and kindness. It is going to want to change you. But I want you to know that I will never hurt you. You don't break the things you love, and I will never break you, John. I'll keep you safe from the world you are growing up and seeing for the first time. Don't worry, Blue-Eyes.

Thursday 5 March, 1992

I swipe a crumb from the corner of your mouth. You glance at me uncertainly and I wish I hadn't. When you are finished you leave the plate in the sink and we rush to the door, thoughts of the cool river luring us outside. Your mother calls you back. Grinning, she taps her cheek. 'Affection.'

You drop a kiss on her skin and run to join Chubby and I, laughing. I can't help it: I glare at your mother, fingers swiping the yellow vase over the edge of the cabinet. It cracks against the floor, shattered pieces flitting through the air. She gathers the shards up in her hands, muttering under her breath.

I kneel down and help her. 'I'm so sorry, Mrs Graham. It was an accident. I'm really sorry.'

'Oh, it's OK, sweetheart. No harm done. Go on. You three go and play. It's fine.'

I make a performance out of looking over my shoulder so you can see how upset I am. Chubby giggles nervously, skipping ahead of us, fat juggling in time with his feet hitting the ground. You wrap an arm round my neck. 'It's OK, mate. Come on, let's go and cool down.'

I smile, just enough for you to see those words of comfort helped, just enough for you to see I need more. 'It's really OK. It was an accident. You didn't mean to do it. Mum's OK.' A pat on the back. I nod, sigh. Yes, you're right.

You and Chubby run ahead laughing wildly, arms out, feet tripping over the tips of your shoes. I follow slowly behind, hands tucked into my shorts, smiling. Not at you. At your mother.

*

Your arm is wrapped around Bessie, lips whispering a story into the halo of her hair, chin resting on her head. Laughter pours from the open window into the warm night. I climb the branches of the tree outside your house, my clothes tugging on the wood, fingers grazing the yellowy sap. I position myself between two branches and wipe it from my fingers. If I listen carefully, I can just hear your soft, melodic voice lifting over the sound of birds chirping above me. Bessie says something and your head falls back, laughter pouring from your lips. She wiggles under the duvet. You close the book and kiss her head. As you leave, you wave and she waves back.

I watch you appear in the room adjacent to Bessie's. You change into your pyjamas and I run my eyes over your body, drinking you in. The clothes you wore are left in a pile at the bottom of your bed. You pull the duvet up over your head and knock on the wall twice. I glance over to Bessie and am surprised to see her reply with two knocks of her own. You both smile and burrow deeper into the beds. A last goodnight call.

When I rest my head on my own pillow, I hold the hair I cut from your head close to my cheek, running it over my skin. It is soft like your fingers would be on my lips. After I turn the light off, I rest my hand on the wall.

Then I knock twice.

Chapter 38

John

Thursday 17 December, 2015

When you were a boy, you snuck into the kitchen at night and stole acid drops from your mother's hiding place. I can still hear the crackling of the wrappers.

'How do they know that?!' John throws his hands up. 'Even my mother doesn't know that!' He runs fingers through his hair and is surprised to see handfuls come away. He looks at Don desperately. 'How do they know that?'

He shrugs, eyes stuck to the photograph of Bonnie's arm, dotted with rosebuds of blood. A dot to dot, and connecting them is a stripe of blood that makes up the outline of a sweet wrapper. 'I don't know. They're fucked up.'

Jules snatches the photograph up and waves it in front of Alice. 'There isn't going to be any of her left by the time you find her!'

Don puts a hand on her shoulder and she shrugs him off. 'Get off me, Don!' She turns back to Alice. 'It's all right for you. You sent your daughter to France to keep her safe. What are you doing for mine?! This sick bastard has had her for weeks. Tell me WHAT YOU ARE DOING ABOUT IT!'

John takes her hand, a show of support, and looks at Alice for an answer. She has been like a friend to them but now he is beginning to want to shake her.

She looks at him beseechingly. 'You know we're doing our best. I've gone out on a limb with you two, telling you things I shouldn't, keeping you in the loop. I know how you must feel—'

'No! You don't. You can't know how we feel. Your daughter is safe and sound. She's not being hacked to pieces by a sick fuck who's got it in for your husband.'

Don bites his lip, drawing blood. 'Jules, don't say that.'

'Why not? They'll probably start sending us fingers soon. Or toes. Or maybe one day, when we're sipping soup through a straw and the police are about to start on yet another box of doughnuts, they'll send us her head.' Tears drip off her chin and her unruly hair tangles against her wet cheeks. Her eyes are bloodshot and underlined with black, a combination that is a shocking contrast to the paleness of her skin. John looks at his wife and feels the last of his resolve crumble. He wonders how long it will be before they both lose their minds. Perhaps he already has. He hears Bonnie's voice in a silent room, feels her curl up next to him on the sofa. He sees her everywhere he looks. And sometimes he even smiles and opens his arms for her to jump into.

'Jules, that won't happen!' Alice spreads her hands, placating.

'You don't know that!' Spittle flies from the corner of her mouth. John squeezes her hand, feeling her emotion like an electric shock to his skin.

Blood blooms on Don's lip, and for a moment it looks as if he's bitten through a vein. His frightened, round eyes peer at them, like they did when he was a child and cut his leg on barbed wire. 'Hey… hey, I'm just going to check on Kimmy.' He shuffles from the room, wiping the blood from his lip, surprised, as if he hadn't even noticed it was there.

John watches him go, eyes glued to the signs of weight loss. For the first time in his life he can see his best friend is getting thin. The thought of it unsettles him.

Jules glares at Alice, then curls herself into John, sobbing. 'You need to find her, Alice. If things keep going like this, she might not have long.'

'I know. I know. We're doing our best. They'll trip up. They always do. They get arrogant and lose their edge. I've told you this before. Whoever's doing this is leaving no traces for us to find but they will. They will.'

'How did they know about the acid drops? Nobody knew that.'

'You must remember someone, you must! You can't have someone so close your whole life and not know about it! The guys at the station are beginning to think you're in on it!'

'What?! Of course I'm bloody not! Is that why you can't find them, because you're not looking? Because you think you've already found who's responsible?'

'No. Absolutely not. We're doing everything we can.'

'Do more! Do more, Alice!' He rests his chin on Jules's head, closing his eyes. 'You need to find her. Please, *please*, just find her.'

Chapter 39

Maisie

Tuesday 26 January, 2016

'He used to say all mistakes are accidental good choices. Because we learn from the mistakes we make, then move forward. I think that perfectly defines who he is as a person. Positive. Upbeat, kind. Optimistic.'

'I like that. "Mistakes are accidental good choices."'

Heidi presses a photograph into Maisie's hand. 'This is another scan photo – can you put it with the other one, please?'

'Of course. Sweet little one.' She smiles down at the baby. Button nose, fingers spread, chin propped on a small chest. She runs her finger over the picture and sucks in a breath. She's told Ben; she can tell Heidi. 'I was pregnant a year ago, you know. I had those pictures, treasured them like they were made of gold. Hung them up on the wall and looked at them every night before I went to bed. I used to whisper goodnight to my baby, good morning too. A few weeks before my due date, it was Ben's birthday so I was rushing at the last minute to get his gift.' She purses her lips, taking a deep breath. 'I fell down the stairs and had a stillbirth.'

Heidi leans over the bed and rests her hand on Maisie's. 'I'm so sorry. I did wonder. The way you look at the scan photos… it made me think perhaps there was something.'

Maisie squeezes her hand. 'I didn't tell Ben until recently. He didn't know I fell. I let him believe it was just this random thing that happened. For a long time I thought it was my fault, that I killed my own baby. After the stillbirth, we packed everything away in the nursery and left it there. Last Friday, I went in and brought it all into the lounge – photos, toys, things we hid away for so long. It felt good. When Ben got back, we went through his things and remembered him as he should be remembered.'

'Did he have a name?'

'Billy.'

'Will you try for more in the future?'

She looks at Tim, wondering if he is listening. 'No. I can't have children. Billy was just luck, a miracle. We've always wanted kids so it's quite a punch to the gut but we'll get through it.'

'How's Ben? It must have come as a shock.'

She rubs her eyes. 'It did. But I think he's forgiven me. We're going to be OK. I thought he'd hate me. I did kill his son, after all. You know I used to wish I'd died falling down those stairs. Broken my neck or something. Then it wouldn't have just been him.'

'Maisie, sweetheart, you didn't kill him.' She pats her hand, holding her gaze. 'What happened was a tragic accident.'

Maisie nods. It was. It *was* an accident. She couldn't have killed Billy. She wasn't like the mothers on the news who all of a sudden took a hammer to their babies. She would never hurt a child. Even if someone held a gun to her head, she wouldn't.

Heidi moves her hand, shuffling closer in her chair. 'We lost a baby once. Long before our daughter came along. It was a really tough time for us – we were struggling to pay the bills for our flat. Then, suddenly, I was pregnant. I was still only young, a child really, but we knew without a doubt that we wanted a baby. We wanted a family, a little bit like you and Ben. We found out it was a girl and named her Summer. I was terrified, of course – but she gave us hope. She was our little angel.'

'What happened?'

'I miscarried very early on. We were mortified. I could barely leave the house. Tim was working three jobs to make ends meet.' She tucks a strand of hair behind her ear and holds Tim's hand. 'I started to walk to the local park for some time to clear my head. It was so peaceful. It made me feel close to Summer in a way.

'A little while later, Tim took me there and showed me a bench he'd got commissioned in her memory. The inscription read: "For our angel. Heaven is closer than we think." We still sit on that bench even now with our other daughter.'

'That's sweet. Didn't you know Tim was planning it?'

She shakes her head. 'No. He wanted it to be a surprise. We take our daughter there because it feels like our two babies are together. We'll tell her the angel is her sister when she's old enough to understand.'

'So this little one is your third.' She smiles at Heidi's bump.

'I'd love you to meet the baby.'

'Really?' Maisie's chest swells with a burst of happiness. 'I'd love to.'

Heidi kisses her husband's head, a fug of sadness enveloping them. 'Whatever happens, whether he recovers… or he doesn't, I want you to keep in touch.'

'I will.'

'I don't know what's going to happen, Maisie.' She glances at her, and the pain in her eyes makes Maisie feel sick. 'I can't see that this is good, this long with no good signs, but every day when I get up in the morning, I say today will be the day you'll call and tell me he's recovering. He's getting better.'

'Most of my patients' families do. Then, when they come in, I feel like I've let them down. I know that sounds silly but I do.

190

I know what they're going through. My brother, Danny, fell and suffered terrible bleeding on his brain. He was in a persistent vegetative state before he had a seizure and died. I understand how much it hurts. How, at night, you lie awake, praying, hoping, even talking to yourself.'

'That's why you became a nurse?'

'Yes. And I'm glad I did.'

She nods. 'And Tim? What's your professional opinion now? Do you think he'll recover?'

'I hope he will.'

Heidi nods and winds her fingers through the scarf on her lap, a haunted look passing over her face. Maisie bites her lip to stopper the words, then eases herself from the chair and walks down the corridor to hunt for some tea. When she returns she notices a subtle change in the room. Heidi is bowed over her bump, turning her wedding band round and round on her finger. Maisie passes her a hot cup of tea. Heidi lowers it to her knee, the pads of her fingers turning red against the sides. The sharp tang of fresh tea fills the air and drops an intense craving into the pit of Maisie's stomach. 'People always think tea is the solution to everything.'

Heidi smiles, but Maisie can see it is purely for her benefit. Maisie has heard grief described countless times and in countless different ways. For some it is a pit in their stomach, a hole, an emptiness that steals away the significance of the days. For others, it is a pressure building up in their minds, making life impossible to live as they would have done before. For Maisie, grief is a burden strapped to her chest, the straps cinching tighter and tighter, robbing her of breath and of the hope of ever getting it back. She wonders if it is the same for Heidi.

'How is your daughter today?'

'She's… she's OK. She's getting better. It's a long process, though. The doctor said she'll need to keep the cast on for a few more months.'

Heidi curls into herself, arms wrapping around her bump, expression unfurling like a ball of wool. Maisie takes the cup and glances at her fingertips. Did she even feel the tea burning through the cup?

'Heidi?'

Her expression creases into a thousand folds. Her lips part and stretch back over her teeth as tears slither down her cheeks. Maisie wraps her arms around her shoulders, wishing she could do more. She holds her as she shakes in her arms. How would she feel if Ben were attacked in the street? She almost finds it impossible to imagine. A fug of fear and dread radiates from Heidi, wrapping a fist round Maisie's heart. She has seen varying shades of grief but none like this. There is something else woven through – she can see it in the way Heidi fiddles with her scarf or bag, the way her hands begin to shake and she stuffs them under her legs. There is more to it.

Heidi sits up and mops her tears away with the cuff of her T-shirt. 'I'm sorry, sweetheart.'

'Hey, don't be sorry. It's OK.'

Heidi smiles and pulls herself from the chair, dropping her bag and picking it up with shaking hands. 'I'd… I'd better go. See you tomorrow, Maisie.'

Heidi opens the door and lets in a peal of noise that washes over Maisie in waves: snippets of conversations as nurses deliver sad words to sadder families. The tap and rub of shoes across the floor. The sway and brush of uniforms across exhausted limbs. The crackling of gum circulating round a mouth. Then, all of a sudden, it is gone. And all Maisie can hear is Tim's slow draw of breath and the sharp, broken sound of her own.

Chapter 40

Miller

Sunday 8 March, 1992

I couldn't help myself. I wanted to see her cry. I wanted to see you comfort her, rub her back and whisper consoling words. If you knew, you would block me from your life, tell me to stay away from you and your family, protective of those you love, fearless of those who might cause them harm. But you don't.

It didn't take much effort. I wet my fingers and closed them over the flame, snuffing it out. Then I brought my hand back in a fantastical wave. A magician's wave. She thought I had super-powers; she wanted to be like her big brother's best friend. When your mother called you out of the room, I waved her over and whispered into her ear, 'You can have magical powers too, but first you've got to touch the flame to prove you're brave like your brother, Johnny. Can you do that? Can you be brave?'

She nodded, face shining with excitement. 'I can do it.'

'Good. But you have to promise you won't tell anyone. Not your mummy or your daddy. And definitely not Johnny because he will be cross. Promise, Bessie?'

She nodded again. 'Promise.'

'OK. When you're ready, reach out and touch it. I'll be right here.' I stepped back as she stepped forward. She finally reached out, but I was already in the kitchen with you and your mother. No blame would find me if I was by your side.

You moved with such speed, such purpose. Face black with fear. I could almost taste it in the air, streaming off you in thick rivulets, choking the room. Her wails rung out, your voice called her name. Your mother and I followed at your heels. Bessie was on her back, rolling around, red face bunched up, thick tears smeared across her cheeks. Your mother sank to the floor and gathered her up in her arms, rocking and soothing her. You knelt next to Bessie and stroked the hair out of her face.

'Bessie, what did you do?'

She sobbed into her mother's arm, slowly offering her burnt fingers up for you to see. 'Oh, no!'

Your mother carried her into the kitchen and told her to put her fingers into a cup of water. 'You must, Bess,' you said when she shook her head. 'It's nice and cold. It will make you feel better.' She shook her head. 'Shall we do it together?'

A nod.

'OK. On three. One. Two. Three.' She cried out, biting her lip. You smiled at her. 'Well done, Bess.'

'John, take her. I need to find the lavender. She'll get blisters.' Your mother passed her to you and dashed out of the kitchen. Her feet thumped up the stairs. You rocked Bessie in your arms like you saw your mother do, shushing and cuddling, telling her she mustn't touch flames. It was dangerous. That she was brave for putting her fingers in the water. She nestled into your shirt, the noise dying in her throat.

I stood by the door, a look of perfected concern on my face, a feeling of excitement and love blooming in my chest. How beautiful you were, John. Sitting with her in your arms, rubbing her back, kissing her head. I was so happy, seeing you like that.

But then it changed.

'I love you,' you said, and then I wanted to rip the brat from your arms and drown her in the river. *I* wanted to sit on your lap and fall asleep against your chest. *I* wanted you to whisper and cuddle me and kiss me. *I* wanted you to tell me how much you loved *me*.

Death.

That is what you are thinking of now, I can see it on your face. You are thanking those 'lucky stars' that her shirt didn't catch the flame, that hers was a case of burnt fingers instead of burnt body. Your hand tenses around the bandaged mass of hers. Despite the questions thrown at her through the panicked lips of your father when he returned home, she only said, 'I wanted to be a magician.' That made me smile.

Good girl.

She skips along by your side, young mind already beginning to forget the blinding pain that brought tears to her eyes. But you can't forget. 'What shall we have today?' you ask, smiling down at her.

'Acid drops!' She swings her arm around, giggling.

'OK. A bag of acid drops. Shall we stop on the way home and eat them by the river? What do you think? I already asked Mum, she says it's OK.'

'Yeah! Want to, want to!'

I see you nod from behind a tree. I asked once if I could come with you and Bessie to get some sweets on Sunday. You politely said that Bess preferred it to be just the two of you. A kind, thoughtful reply. But I know it wasn't Bessie. You want Sundays for yourself. Quiet time with your sister. They mean something to you, something so much more than the times you spend with me. I can't describe the anger I felt when you turned me down. But no matter. Nothing lasts for ever. Those special Sundays certainly won't.

As you take off down the street, bag of sweets passing back and forth between you, I rush into the shop, buy a bag of acid drops and follow close behind. The sun is shining down hot on our backs, and if I strain my eyes, I can see beads of sweat forming on your neck. When you and Bessie flop down on the riverbank, tipping your heads back and dropping in sweets, laughing, sharing jokes, I sit further down and tip *my* head back and drop one in *my* mouth. I don't like sweets, but when you suck on yours I want to know what it feels like. Bessie throws a pebble into the river, giggling as it sinks with a soft plop!

'Whoever can throw one furthest away wins the last acid drop,' you say.

Of course, you let her win. You swing your arm back and watch the pebble fly through the air. I throw one in the opposite direction. When you sit back down and fiddle with a twig, I pick one up and fiddle with it too. When you wrap an arm round Bessie's shoulder, I wrap my arm round my own, pretending it is yours. And when you laugh at something she says, I laugh too.

*

I climb the tree outside your house and watch through Bessie's window every night. I am beginning to think I am making an impression in the bark. It is warm now but even when the nights grow shorter and the temperature drops, I'll climb this tree and fold my hands into the pockets of a woollen jumper just so I can watch you. Just so I can be with you.

Tonight, you are sitting at the bottom of the bed, legs bobbing up and down, hands fidgeting. Even without these signs, I can tell by the way you are biting your lip that you are excited. Bessie is tucked up in bed, puzzled by your behaviour. Another thing I have grown a skill for since finding my spot in this tree: lip-reading.

196

Can I have a story?

You can, but first I've got a surprise for you. Do you want to know what it is?

Yes, please.

Close your eyes.

OK.

Are they closed tight?

Yes.

Good.

I do exactly as you say, imagining the surprise is for me. When I open my eyes, you are holding a stuffed teddy bear, smiling like you have never smiled before.

Ta dah! you say, offering the bear into Bessie's waiting hands.

I love it! she squeals.

So do I.

My fingers itch with desire. If it wasn't for a twig sticking painfully into my ribcage, I think I would dive into the room and snatch it out of her hands. I can only imagine how much it cost you, how much it took out of your piggy bank. That is not a cuddly toy. It is a symbol of you. Of love and friendship. Of everything I want.

When you and Bessie go out the next day, I take the bear from its place on the bed and hold it in my arms. I can smell Bessie but I can also smell you. I can feel you in the fibres of the fabric. I can feel your love surrounding me, filling me up, making me whole.

Tuesday 10 March, 1992

I see a couple walk hand in hand across the street. They look at each other the way your parents look at each other, the way Mother used to look at Father when Mary was alive. It isn't love. What *I* feel for *you* is love, and that is something they will never feel. No one ever will.

The girl leans over and kisses him. When she pulls back, the boy smiles and squeezes her hand. I want this and I want it with you. I want to walk along the street, holding your hand, and oh so casually lean in for a kiss. Just the thought of it makes me feel light-headed. Can you even imagine?

*

You and Chubby are riding your bikes, cycling up to each other, whipping out your arms and high-fiving as you pass. Twelve years old, hanging on to the precipice of childhood, ready to fall into the abyss of adulthood. The last vestiges of it shine in both your eyes. Chubby is laughing and screaming at the top of his lungs, cracking jokes about his weight. I sit on the pavement, warming my fingers on the tarmac, enjoying the sound of your voice, singing the latest song Chubby and you adore. And which makes me squirm. Father once said that people who don't like music are psychos. I told him I was one of them. He didn't know what to say then.

Chubby giggles and you tease him, saying he sounds like his mum. He laughs, wagging his finger at you.

'Yeah, but you sound like your dad when you snore,' he shouts.

A woman walking past looks at you as if you are a monster. You and Chubby turn red-faced. You are drunk on the sun and sugar and the promise of another day tomorrow.

'Again, John!'

You turn your bike around and pedal as fast as you can towards Chubby, reaching out for a high five. The next time, you both go faster, then faster and faster, going further and further from my spot on the pavement.

You don't see the rock in the middle of the road. And as you go speeding towards it, I am on my feet, waving my arms, screaming a warning. But it is too late. In an instant your body slams against the ground, skin scraped across the tarmac. I think I can smell the blood on your leg even as you pull yourself up to inspect the wound. I run as fast as my legs will carry me, my chest aching with fear. Chubby gets there first and kneels down next to you, laughing at something you say.

'JOHN!' I bellow.

It makes you jump, I think. You shake your head. 'Don't worry. It's fine. Just a bit of a graze. It's stopped bleeding already.'

'I'll go and see if your mum has a plaster.' Chubby rushes off into the house.

I bend down beside you and put my fingers close to the wound, searching your eyes for signs of pain. I am panting, gasping, my heart hammering away like ten drummers have started banging away on the same instrument.

'John, are you all right? Are you OK?!' I wrap my hands around your leg, catching myself before I cup your cheek and brush the hair off your face. My hands begin to shake and so I hide them in my pockets. I am panicking but I try and keep a calm façade. It must work because you are perfectly fine, prodding the wound like it is something magical.

'I'm good. That was fun. I think I flipped! Did you see? I kinda want to do it again. Yeah, no, I *definitely* want to do it again. *So* fun! I'm *sure* I flipped. Wish someone had recorded that. I could have shown everyone at school!' You clap your hands, delighted.

I am lost for words, horrified by the blood on your skin, by the look of amazement scrawled across your face. You are injured. Wounded. The graze will leave a scar on your perfect skin. You will be this way for the rest of your life. My mouth pops open and I quickly close it, feeling my eyes bulge in their sockets.

You mother walks up to us, first-aid kit in hand, Chubby trotting along at her heels, saying how 'awesome' you were when you flipped. I deny the urge to snatch the kit from her hand and fix you up myself. Her slowness makes me dizzy with anger. How can she be so blasé? You are hurt, bleeding. Is she blind? HURRY UP, I want to scream.

'OK, sweetheart?'

'I'm fine, Mum. It was actually really fun! I flipped. Chubs told you, right?'

She laughs.

She laughs!

'He did. It's fine now but make sure to be a bit more careful, OK?'

'OK, Mum. Thanks.'

She wipes the graze and sticks a plaster over it, smiling. 'There we go. All better.' With that, she kisses your head and goes back into the house.

All better?

I feel my face flush, my legs begin to tremble. How dare she leave you! How dare she say, 'all better'! How could she be so calm?! How could she walk away? How could she not *care*?!

You and Chubby resume pedalling on your bikes and I return to my spot on the pavement. I have never been so angry in my life. I have never hated anyone as much as I hate your mother. I have never wanted to hurt anyone as much as I want to hurt her. She'll regret not giving you the care you need. I would have. I would have held you and spoke comforting words. I would have kissed away your pain. Carried you to the hospital and waited with bated breath while all the nurses cleaned and bandaged your leg properly. I would have been a better mother than her.

Chapter 41

John

Friday 18 December, 2015

When he was five years old his mother dug holes in the back garden and filled them with water so he could splash in his new pair of wellingtons. He did the same for Bonnie when she turned three, laughing as droplets of muddy water flew through the air. He looks at the picture now, wondering with a peculiar calmness how life has taken such an unexpected turn.

And there is nothing he can do to prevent it getting any worse. He's ripped his hair out searching his mind for memories – any memories – of someone hanging around when he was young. Someone who watched him and followed him. But there was no one. He wishes he could remember someone so Alice would have more to go on. But he can't give them what he doesn't have.

Jules is growing more and more frustrated with him as they feel the clock tick down the seconds to Bonnie's demise. But what can he do? He can't rewind the past, can't hop in a time machine and revisit his childhood. He's gone through every message that has been left for them to find.

So far there have been five. When will the sixth arrive? He has no doubt it will. Why stop terrorising someone if you are enjoying it? No, this person will have to get bored before they kill Bonnie. Until then, they'll just pick off bits of her like a bird picking at a worm. He doesn't dare imagine how frightened she is. He just hopes she knows how much they love her and that they are trying their hardest to find her.

'John?'

He smiles at Jules and invites her into his arms. 'I wish you'd met someone else. I wish you hadn't married me and you'd had Bonnie with another man.'

She looks up at him. 'You shouldn't wish that.'

'It's my fault this creep's got Bonnie. If it wasn't for me, you'd both be having breakfast now, laughing at something on the radio. Bonnie would be nibbling some fake bacon and you'd be reminding her to use her knife and fork.'

She shakes her head. 'Not your fault, John. None of this is.'

'How can it not be?'

She takes a step away. 'Because you aren't the bastard who has Bonnie. You didn't kidnap someone else's child. You aren't sending sadistic photos to the family. You haven't done anything!'

He nods. She rests her head on his chest. 'How long do you think we have?'

'A few weeks. How long would it take for you to get bored? We've had five messages now – that would be enough for some.'

'It's like they're taunting us.'

He shakes his head. 'All of my memories feel tainted now. Was this person there when I was born? When I lost my first tooth? When I learnt to swim? When we met? Were they there when Bonnie was born? When she lost *her* first tooth or when *she* learnt to swim? They could have been there for everything and we were too stupid to notice.'

'We weren't stupid, John. This person's clever. They're making *Bonnie* sign their sick messages, for God's sake.'

John nods, looking at the collage of photographs sticking to the wall, all of Bonnie and in all of which he can see the shadow of someone who doesn't belong there. He can see a foot in one, a hand in another, lurking at the edge of the shot, on the periphery of their lives.

He wonders for the hundredth time how long Bonnie has. He looks at the pictures, at her sweet eyes and wavy brown hair, at the smattering of freckles and gap-toothed smile, thinking they should have done better. They should have done so much better.

*

He'd read about the kidnapping of a young boy in the *Daily Mail* over a year ago now. Lucas Styles. Six years old with blond hair, blue eyes and a lisp. The police searched high and low for him, until after three months they found his remains beneath a wind turbine on the outskirts of Manchester. His parents were crippled by the loss of their son. The father, Gerald, hung himself in his garage and the mother, Carrie, suffered a mental breakdown soon after. John followed their story with a crippling pain in his chest. Like a needle burrowing deeper and deeper into his skin. Whenever he glimpsed a picture of Lucas or his parents, he felt as if someone was throwing punch after perfectly aimed punch at his heart. He'd thought he understood their pain then. But now he realises he wasn't even close. The true agony of losing a child exists in another orbit entirely to the mere thought of it. It shreds your perception of life, of people, of every facet of who you are, tearing away the armour you wear to protect yourself until every scratch and every scrape is a scratch and scrape to your soul.

John wishes he could ask Gerald if he saw Lucas everywhere just as he sees Bonnie. He wishes he could ask Carrie if she heard Lucas call for her just as she woke, and if she leapt from the bed and searched for him. In the bathroom, in the kitchen, in the garden. He wishes he could ask how they lived through the days of guilt, shame and utter fear. Because his grasp on these long days is slowly weakening.

He now knows that, when he sees Bonnie, his imagination is tricking him, hope shaping the outline of a girl and desperation colouring life into her body right in front of his eyes, like a child with paper and a set of crayons. But like a dream, like a fantasy, he knows it is a product of grief.

John rubs his sore neck and watches people go about their lives from the safety of the café chair. In front of him is an untouched slice of cake. He won't eat it. He can't. He only bought it because he felt he should, like a muscle memory from a time before this. He is surprised at how the weight has dropped off him. Any more and his body could be deemed skeletal. But he can't muster the energy to remedy it. Instead he pulls a photo of Bonnie from his pocket and weaves his way into the tide of bodies that surge along the street. He holds the photo out and preys. 'Hello, have you seen this girl? Excuse me, do you recognise my daughter? Please, have you see her? Have you seen this girl? Please look at the picture, you might recognise her. Are you sure you haven't?'

Words tumble from his lips. They look at him, smile and shake their heads, before moving on, happy in the glow of Christmas. There isn't much point to this, he knows. He probably shouldn't even be doing it. Alice would be furious. She is the one who will find her, *if* she can find her. He is not a police officer, he is not a detective. And the likelihood of someone having caught a glimpse of *him* moving her somewhere is small. But by doing this, he feels as if he is trying. He is going to do everything he can to find her.

John can see Bonnie in the way a woman's hair flutters across her shoulders. He can see her in the smile of a girl who cycles past, red-faced and sweating; in the frown of a distressed waitress who huffs and puffs when no one is looking; in the chipped fingernails of a boy who nods his head in time to a scrap of music. He can hear Bonnie's soft voice in the voices of a group of children touring the town; he can see flashes of her in all of them. The eyes, the nose, the hair, the smile. She is there, or facets that resemble her. And each one is a crippling stab to his heart.

John thrusts the photo into hands and in front of eyes. No response, no recognition.

As he turns to make his way home, he glimpses a girl walking in the opposite direction. Her hair is tied up, freckles spotting her skin, a blush creeping up her neck. John hurries towards her, hoping and hoping and hoping. He stops a few steps away and watches.

It's her.

But it isn't.

John turns and continues home, under the weight of yet another trick his mind has played on him. It isn't her.

She is none of those strangers.

Chapter 42

Maisie

Wednesday 27 January, 2016

His fingers stretch across the skin of her neck, slowly, as if memorising every inch of it, as if he is savouring it somehow. She watches the path his hand makes, her stomach churning. Heidi does not seem to notice; her eyes are trained on Tim. Or perhaps she is just used to it? Maisie doesn't know, but what she does know is she doesn't like the way he is touching her. There is something… *odd* about it.

Her eyes travel from his feet to his head, studying him more closely. He is tall, well-dressed, beard trimmed, eyes red-rimmed. When he smiles, it is a warm one, one she guesses has disarmed many women in the past. When he jokes, she thinks they have been designed for maximum effect, ones to break the ice, ones to comfort, ones to silence. He is trying to lift the atmosphere and, in another situation, perhaps it would work. But not here. Not now.

She smiles at something he says. If it wasn't for the feeling in the pit of her stomach, she would chat with him. But now she can't. She wants him to leave. Her feelings have nearly always been right and now she can't marry this feeling with the man she thought he was.

It is the way he touches her: a loving way, a tender way. As if he is her husband, her lover. Maisie hasn't seen it before now and it bothers her that she might have missed it. Watching his fingers graze Heidi's skin, Maisie has to stop herself from swatting him away.

'I keep telling myself, "He's going to recover, he's going to recover." Like a mantra.' Heidi runs her fingers across Tim's hand, the haunted look in her eyes expanding across her face. Maisie hasn't mentioned what happened between them before, the way she sobbed in Maisie's arms and then abruptly left. She's unsure whether to bring it up.

'Are you doing that too?' Heidi asks.

He kisses her head. It lingers too long. 'All day, every day.'

Maisie knows no positive signs at this stage are in fact a bad sign, so she steers the conversation onto a lighter track. 'What will you do if he recovers? What were your life plans before he was attacked?'

Heidi glances at her. 'We were planning to move to Spain. Start a new life in the sun. The move had been on the back burner for a while, then a few months ago we just thought, why not? We only live once. If he recovers, once he's better, we'll probably carry on with those plans.'

Maisie nods. 'That's good.'

He shifts from foot to foot. 'Yeah... yeah, but... but not straight away, of course?'

'No, he'd need time and lots of it, but we'd go eventually. He was so excited about the move before...'

He drops his hand from her neck, fiddling with the seam of his jacket behind his back; Maisie can see in the reflection of the window.

She ventures a question. 'That would be hard for you, wouldn't it? You'd miss them?'

'Oh, God, yeah! I'd miss them every day!'

Heidi pats his arms. 'You'd be over all the time.'

He smiles at her warmly. Maisie studies him, thoughtfully. Is he sad? Is he distraught at the prospect of his friends leaving him behind? She knows she'd hate it. Does he feel bad because he wants to go with them but can't? Or is he jealous? Does *he* want a fresh start? A new life in the sun?

Watson casts his gaze to the floor, biting his lip. When he looks up, she sees fear streaked across his face like red paint across a white wall.

Chapter 43

Miller

Thursday 12 March, 1992

Music blasts from your bedroom. The crash of drums and peel of guitar strings. This particular flavour of music is a phase I know you will abandon eventually. And your parents will be thankful when you do. As will I. Although I think I will miss the way you bop your head in time with the rhythm and the way you close your eyes and pretend you are playing the guitar.

Today you are cross about your homework, frustrated at the maths equations that block your path to good grades. I offer to help you but you turn me down with a mumbled 'no thanks', jutting out your bottom lip.

'I don't mind. Really. We could go through it now?'

'No. I don't want to.'

I know I am pushing you but I can't help it. I want you to have a good education. I don't want to see you struggle later when there are no excuses and being ridiculed is just another part of the day. I don't want that, John. I want you to be respected, admired, loved for what makes you special. The world is going to swipe at someone as good as you; please don't give them a reason to.

'Oh, come on.'

'No!' You put a hand to your face, tears threatening. I take a step back. Just one because I know you like to feel space around, otherwise you feel trapped.

'OK.' I turn and leave, knowing later you will come to apologise, to ask if we're still friends. Of course we are, I'll tell you. Do you think anything you do or say will ever scare me away?

Friday 13 March, 1992

I take the teddy bear with me on my jaunts to the tree now. And I hold it so tight, I worry the stitching will come apart. Bessie was mortified when she realised she'd lost it; you were heartbroken, wondering how you could ever replace it with the pocket money left over. I want to tell you it is not being wasted. It is being loved and stroked and played with. In a way, when I stick it under my arm at night, I feel as if you are there. It's a comfort, John.

You kiss Bessie goodnight, then, when she points beneath her bed, a look of fear on her face, you fetch a ball of wool and wind it round the bed's legs, saying the pesky monster will trip and fall flat on his face if he visits tonight. She laughs, nods, comforted. And with one simple action, you have rubbed away the childish fears that haunt your sister. This is why I love you, John. I love the kindness of your beautiful mind.

When you turn the lights off and climb into bed, I lean my head back and smile to myself, thinking how sweet you were earlier munching on your apple.

We were sitting on the pavement, you, Chubby and I, talking about the latest adventures of Elaine and Rupert at school. 'They kissed,' you said, eyes widening at the prospect of being so close to a girl. I found it hard not to laugh.

'I kissed a girl ages ago,' Chubby said, smirking.

Your head swivelled round. 'What?! You kissed a girl?'

'Yes.'

'Really?'

'No!'

You both burst out laughing and I followed suit, wondering what the joke was. Although maybe a joke isn't even needed. You are only young after all.

You took another bite out of your apple, and I watched a drop of juice slide down to your chin. I swiped my finger across it and hid my hand behind my back. When you and Chubby turned to watch a cat across the road, I stuck my finger into my mouth and sucked. Sucked and sucked until my finger went numb.

And I can still taste it now.

Sunday 15 March, 1992

Last night I dreamt Bessie and I stood either side of you, hands outstretched, a plea in our eyes: save me. The world was burning and bodies – your mother and father and Chubby included – were in piles, expressions vacant, staring up at the smoky sky. You had a choice. Save the one person you loved the most.

And you picked her.

You and she walk hand in hand down the street, as you have done so many times before. And yet this time feels different. The chorus of tyres rolling along the road and the chatter of neighbours discussing the latest episode of *Emmerdale* all ring with a note I can't put my finger on. But I know I haven't heard it before.

The world we live in, John, is different today. Subtle things. Only subtle things. Well, perhaps not to you and Bessie. Perhaps not even to the people who talk and smoke and laugh, idling in doorways, on benches.

It is now I realise. It's not the world. It's in my mind. The domain has shifted and suddenly the path I have been on these past few years is different. A new one lies before me. One with her out of the picture.

I think it is because of the dream, the way you took Bessie's hand with barely a thought for me. I know you love me, John – as a friend. But not as much as you love her. You love her in a way I can never hope to compete with. Certainly not while she laughs at your jokes and nestles her head into your chest. Not while she is walking and smiling and breathing.

Chapter 44

John

Sunday 20 December, 2015

The sixth message is short. It reads simply:

> She has your nose, John.

It isn't the message that troubles him, it is the photograph. Bonnie is sitting with her back to a stone wall, her eyes vacant, empty. This is the second close-up photograph of her face and the contrast to the first is stark. Now she looks as if she is just a shell, empty. She looks as if she has already been broken.

His beautiful little girl is gone. She doesn't even look like herself anymore. The six years of life he and Jules tried to make special are just a single brushstroke in a whole portrait of grief and pain. Nothing against the backdrop of her life now. She's been gone for three weeks. He wishes it could have been him. Why couldn't it have been? Because taking Bonnie has hurt him a thousand times more than any torture ever could.

In the mornings John opens his eyes, then immediately closes them again, thinking if he goes back to sleep, he'll forget. Everything. A slate wiped clean. And then he wonders, what if he never woke up? What if he slept for the rest of his life?

Thoughts of Bonnie, Bertie, Jules and Don are what pull him from that worrying stupor. And they will keep doing so, anchoring him to his life.

The sixth photograph was found in Alison's handbag at the gallery. He'd suspected she would be next. Alice had watched the gallery's CCTV but so far turned up nothing, which led them to believe it had been slipped into her bag when she left for lunch. She was questioned and questioned over and over again, teary-eyed and distraught, but her answers were the same each time. She noticed no one. No, no one followed her. Yes, she was sure. She only put her bag down for a moment as she was ordering her food.

John has known Alison for years. She is one of Jules's closest friends and yet he can't help but feel suspicious. What if it is her? What if this is all a ploy to make them think she is a victim? No, it can't be. She doesn't have a grudge against him, doesn't want revenge. She doesn't have a bad bone in her body.

But who does that leave? Maybe it is Alice. It can't be her either. He is getting paranoid.

John rubs his neck as his head spins. Jules is sitting beside him, picking at a scab on her wrist as if it is the reason behind all their worries. Don paces with his hands tucked into his pockets, wild eyes roaming the room and feet beating out a rhythm which matches the sharp tones of their heartbeats.

And it is then he realises the problem. They aren't behaving like something bad has just happened, they are behaving like something bad is about to.

Chapter 45

Maisie

Thursday 28 January, 2016

He holds her in his arms like she is his daughter. Lovingly, tenderly. The way she looks at him and the way he looks at her. Maisie wonders for a moment if he is her real father. If Tim is no relation. She feels guilty for thinking Heidi would cheat on Tim but there is something in the way Watson looks at her. Something that shouldn't be there.

Watson kisses Heidi's daughter on the cheek and cups his mouth, speaking into his hand. The girl giggles. He winks. A joke, then. But what?

Heidi smiles. His influence, Maisie supposes. They walk down the hall to Tim's room, and they look as if they are a family. Watson throws his head back and laughs. She learnt a long time ago to trust her instincts but she can't help but wonder if she is wrong about him. Heidi loves him, the little girl loves him, Tim loves him. Even she herself believed him a kind, compassionate friend. Or more, even. Perhaps that is the reason for Heidi's behaviour. Are they having an affair? Were they together when

Tim was attacked? Does she feel guilty? Is that what she's hiding? Maisie feels her heart thump faster in her chest. A flush of concern sinks down her spine. Is that it?

'Lailah, what was your first impression of Watson?' She gestures to him.

She follows her gaze and grins. 'Oh, him. I think he seems sweet. Cute too. He's pretty torn up about Tim. Nice, though, that he's looking after Heidi and her daughter. Why?'

Maisie shrugs. 'No reason. Just wondering.'

He collects admirers like her mother collects dirty looks for her wacky dress sense. The only person who hasn't been susceptible to his charm is the man in the Armani suit. Now Maisie is beginning to wonder if it had been more than a tiff. More than a few mean words thrown in an argument. Does the man in the Armani suit know about them? Did he catch them together? Are they really having an affair?

How could he want to be with Heidi when Tim is in such a terrible state? It is a betrayal. One that is almost too much to comprehend. And what about Heidi? Would she really cheat on Tim?

'Do you think Watson likes Heidi?'

'Well, of course. They're friends.'

'Never mind.'

'Oh, you mean *like* likes?' Lailah shakes her head. 'No, I think he loves her as a friend. Only a friend.'

Just her then.

'Why all the weird questions? I thought you liked him.'

'No reason.'

'Mae, I can see something's bugging you. What is it?'

'I think there's something going on between them.'

Lailah puts down the box of surgical gloves and looks at her. 'Is that a hunch?'

'No,' Maisie says, meeting her gaze. 'A concern.'

216

Chapter 46

Miller

Wednesday 18 March, 1992

It was me.

Why, you ask.

Are you sure you really want to know?

OK.

You. Everything is for you. Even the death of her.

You and Chubby are out with your mother, fetching the shopping, sneaking sweets and crisps into the trolley. We plan to walk to the park and play catch when you get back. But by then, I will have changed your life drastically. I almost wanted to tell you to savour that trip to the shop, the ease, the happiness, because soon all you will feel is pain beyond belief. I'm doing this for you and I. If we are ever going to be one, we must take away the person separating us. It's going to hurt for a while but in the end you will be better for it. I can make you happy, John. I can give you a life that will make you smile the moment before death slips you away, times that will make you laugh and jump for joy. I can give you so much more than she can.

I hear her giggling now, you know. That soft, light voice drifting down the stairs. Your father is talking to her, telling her not to splash, laughing with her when she does it anyway. You'd be smiling right now. If you heard her voice, you wouldn't be able to help it.

Mother rings the landline at the appointed time, and your father leaves Bessie in the bathtub to get it, muttering 'I'll be back in a minute, sweetie'. Mother doesn't know my plan; she simply thinks I'm trying to get you to myself, away from your father. If she knew the truth, she would have never made that call.

I take the steps two at a time, springing up to the top floor as lightly as I can. I used to make Mother jump, used to tiptoe up behind her and blow on her neck. I remember it well, the flush of adrenalin as I watched the hairs on her skin rise up, the thrill of making her quiver.

She calls out when she sees me, arms opening for a cuddle. I put my finger to my lips. You'd think my heart would be hammering in my chest by now. But it isn't – it's calm. I'm calm. The calmest I've ever been.

She looks as me with eyes as big as saucers and for a moment I wonder if she knows. I wonder if that little heart just stopped in that little chest. I wonder if those little eyes are looking at me with a plea, a fear, a little inkling of what comes next.

She mutters my name again, hushed, hesitant. I walk to the side of the bath and smile… at you. At the thought of you, John.

Your father is arguing with Mother in the other room, distracted, cross, confused.

I run my hands along her bare shoulders, and she shivers, pushing my hands away. Her nail digs into my left forearm, peeling back the skin. Blood buds along the cut, dripping down my arm. Shaking her head, she shifts onto her knees and pulls herself up

218

with the handrail. I push her back down and tears brim over in her eyes. I lean in close and whisper, 'Would you like to meet some angels?'

She nods.

Do you want to know what I do next, John? Are you sure?

OK, then.

One, two, three… finger by finger, I squeeze down into the soft, pale skin of her neck.

Four, five six…

She reaches out and grasps and grasps at thin air, small fingers searching for some salvation, even as her young face submerges and her lungs fill with water.

Seven, eight, nine…

It doesn't take long. I stroke her hair and smile into her frightened brown eyes.

Ten, eleven, twelve… I squeeze down until her arms grow limp and the last moments of life bleed into nothing.

When your father finds his daughter floating in the bath, you, Chubby and I are already making our way to the park. You both look at the blood on my arm, fascinated by the way it dribbles down.

'That's going to leave a scar. You know it looks a bit like a question mark. How did you do it?' you ask.

I smile. 'Slipped in the bath.'

Thursday 19 March, 1992

They come to you in waves, the wives clutching their hands to their chests, the husbands folding their arms in front of their stomachs, heads bowed, all wearing expressions they deem suitable for the occasion. Unbidden, they are trespassers on your grief and it's as if they've pulled their expressions from their wardrobes, along with the black clothing they donned this morning. But their otherwise perfect appearance is bereft of the most crucial component: sincerity.

You and your parents barely notice. You accept their condolences and pats on the back with good grace, but I can see behind the well-mannered veneer to the part of you wanting to be left to the solitude of her absence. I've lost count of the times I've witnessed them smile, stroke your cheek and mutter to your parents, 'Brave little soldier.' You only nod and force a smile onto your lips, awaiting the next chorus of 'Ohhs' and 'Ahhs,' closely followed by the ensuing pulse of 'Such a shame, such a terrible shame'.

As they leave, the expressions they wear already slipping, I walk up to your house and ram my nail into the puckered scratch that runs across my forearm, tears of pain slipping down my skin. Smudging them across my face, I knock on the door and wait. When you appear, you take in my appearance and I yours. Despite watching from afar all morning, I hadn't realised how your posture has slumped, nor how your eyes are rimmed red.

'I'm sorry, mate,' I say, and like those before me I pat you on the back and smile; a mechanical act but an acceptable one.

You nod and step aside: an invitation into your home, to share in your grief, but most of all an invitation to comfort you. If only I could, properly. If only I could gather you up in my arms and stroke your short brown hair, kiss each of your fingers and banish the pain. The desire to do all of this, my beautiful boy, is nearly impossible to ignore. But I must. You need your friend. You need the person I've given you. You need the illusion. The good-little-boy pretence. The neighbour. Not me. Not the oddity. I realised a long time ago who I needed to be and what I needed to do to achieve in life. You don't have to look hard to see that 'good boys' go further. They get what they want when they are as sweet as me.

It doesn't matter that this is a pretence, though. Even being with you as someone else is good enough for me.

My hand lingers a second too long and you pull away, but you do not close the door. I follow you into her bedroom, where I can see you and your parents spent last night. Wads of used tissues are balled up like confetti across the bed. The pink duvet is rumpled and creased. And already, her posters are beginning to peel away. Strewn across the floor are her things: bears, dolls, storybooks, the shrapnel of four years of her life already slipping into the past. You perch on the bed and look at it all, hands tucked beneath your legs so I can't see them shake. I sit close – this way you can feel me beside you. The smell of cheese and cucumber sandwiches wafts from your mouth. I imagine you ate them to assuage your mother's concern, each bite tasting of ash on your lips.

You look at her toys and books, your lips parted in an 'O' shape as if you can't quite believe the ferocity with which life has taken a swipe at your family. Tears trickle down your cheeks. My hand itches to wipe them away but I keep myself in check and instead pat you on the back again. That is the limit, the boundary. You slump into me as if I have stolen your remaining strength and begin to weep. And even as you do this, you are silent. We sit like this for what seems like hours. But it can't be because when I leave you in her room, the sun is nudging its way into the middle of the sky. I take off down the street, words that have been bandied about by the neighbours repeating themselves over and over again in my mind:

'Sweet girl. Funny girl. Happy girl.'

I stop and look back at your house. Through the crack in the curtains, I can see you, curled up in your mother's arms, bright-red cheeks scarred by the pale tracks tears have made down your skin. Your mother rocks you to and fro. The last vestiges of strength that have kept you on your feet all morning burn up and slide away. And I turn away and smile.

Sweet girl. Funny girl. Dead girl.

We walk side by side, companions, friends, lovers. Your hands are hanging by your legs and your face is drawn, haggard, corrupted with a grief that makes you look as if you are about to fall to the ground, curl up and cry. Since her death, you've been clutching your stomach as if there is a slice straight through the middle and, any moment, you will fall to pieces. I like the look of it because I like to imagine myself crawling after you, picking up those pieces and putting you back together again. Like Humpty Dumpty. But with so much more love.

Your mother worries this walk we are taking is unhealthy but I understand why you need to do it: to be close to her, or her memory at least. To the last few times you held hands and giggled, sharing secrets and promises.

Your mother blames your father and he blames himself. You, on the other hand, blame no one. You don't care for accusations thrown like grenades across the room; you don't care for appointed blame and crocodile tears. These things barely even graze the wall you hide your heart behind, the place you are lying in a state of agony, mourning the loss of Bessie. I can see it in your eyes, the shut-down look of you. I want to tell you that I'm going to make it my mission to knock down that wall and offer you a life free of pain and free of loss. A life with me in the middle.

Chubby, for once in all the years we have known each other, is lost for words, humour eluding him. He cries for you and he cries for her. Patting your back and saying he's sorry. That is all he can offer. I can offer more.

When I asked if I could come with you this morning, you said no. When I asked again, you gave in, and now we walk together like you did with Bessie, the sweetshop and those acid drops luring us forward.

It is a risk, I know. But this is the only time I can take this chance and not be deemed strange. You might pull away, you might even look at me in disgust. But I don't care. I want to touch you. I want to hold your hand like Bessie did. I want to know what it feels like. What she felt like, walking beside you. I reach out and entwine my fingers through yours. I hold my breath, then let it out when you squeeze my hand. You think I am trying to comfort you, trying to help you. I'm not, I want to say, not right now; now I just want this for myself.

We walk on in silence, and I work hard to conceal my happiness. Because now, here we are, doing the exact same thing you did last Sunday with her. Because the moment you backed down was the moment you agreed to let me be Bessie. The new Bessie. Now the special moments you had with her will be the ones you have with me.

Chapter 47

John

Tuesday 22 December, 2015

'Hey, guys! I didn't think you were going to make it!'

John forces a smile onto his lips and gently puts Bonnie on the ground. She waddles up to Don, hands grabbing at thin air, calling out his name.

'Bon-Bon!' He sweeps her up into his arms and bounces her up and down, before patting John on the shoulder and kissing Jules's cheek. 'Mwah, mwah. So, how are we today then?' He looks at them, happy expression slipping. 'Oh, what's happened? You both look terrible. What is it?'

John wraps an arm round Jules and shakes his head. 'Nothing. Really.'

'Johnny, mate, what is it? We've known each other for ever, I can see something's wrong.' He touches his arm, eyes growing round with concern.

'Don, don't worry about it. Nothing's wrong. Come on, we came here to have some fun.' He pats his hand away, gesturing to the barbecue.

'Mmm, well, all right.' He smiles. 'Fun's on the menu for this evening and a lot of it.'

'Hey, John, hey, Jules.' Kim flags them over and John is relieved, waving, pretending everything is OK. 'How's things? Good? Great! Oh, congrats on getting shortlisted for that award, love. How exciting.' She kisses him on the cheek, warm and sweet as ever.

'Thanks, Kim.'

'You know, Don forgot to tell me. What a plonker. Too busy eyeing up a Porsche driving past.'

Don laughs, passing Bonnie to Jules and wrapping his arms round her waist. 'Well, actually, I was looking at the woman inside the car. You do realise I'm trading you in as soon as you hit forty.'

She chuckles, swatting his hands away. 'Oh, really?'

'Yep! Enjoy life while it lasts.' He kisses her.

'What if I trade you in, huh? Get myself a younger, thinner model?'

He gasps, clutching at his chest. 'You wouldn't!'

She giggles. 'I would.'

He gestures to his heart. 'You're breaking this right now, you know. Breaking it. It's shattered.'

'Awww.'

He takes her hand and squeezes it. 'You love my fat – it makes me cute.'

She sighs. 'Yeah, you're right, I do. I suppose I'm stuck with you then.'

'Yep.' He grins.

John watches them both, inexplicably removed from the moment. Normally their banter would have him in fits but he feels cold, empty. He looks at Jules and knows she feels the same. They didn't want to come to the barbecue but Bonnie had been looking forward to it.

He makes himself laugh but even to his ears it comes out harsh and forced. Don sends him a questioning glance, then reacquaints *himself with the barbecue, wielding the tongs like a set of drumsticks. Kim tucks herself under his arm, nursing a champagne flute.*

As they talk, John smiles, leaving his reactions to instinct. He nods when they nod and smiles when they smile, laughing on occasion, hand firmly wrapped around Jules's waist. They are propping each other up the same way Bonnie props her dolls up against a wall.

John feels the force of their happiness crash into him, wave after wave, and it makes him want to sit down and rest his head in his hands. But he won't. He knows Don hasn't realised and he doesn't blame him. He wishes he could forget about it but he can't.

Jules squeezes his hand when they finally close the car doors and make their way home. John nods at her, then covers his eyes so Bonnie can't see him cry.

*

He looks at the words and feels as if the floor has given way beneath his feet. Jules buries her face into his shoulder, arms wrapped round his waist, supporting him like she did at the barbecue on the anniversary of *her* death in 1992. Alice is looking at him, expecting tears, fury, but he has nothing. He feels empty, drained of all emotion.

'John?' She takes a hesitant step forward, as if she is worried he might crumble and she will be trapped beneath the debris. 'John?' she says again, sympathetic eyes searching his face.

He looks at her and hands back the sealed bag, inside of which is the seventh photograph. She takes it, then reaches for his hand. 'John, I'm so s—'

He turns and walks away with Jules, the image of Bonnie's crippled body the backdrop to the message that will for ever be burnt into his mind.

I think she would have loved Bessie.

John holds Jules close and, when he closes his eyes, he can see them together: his sister and his daughter smiling, entwined in each other's arms. He can see a future, a different one. One in which she lived, grew up, married, had children of her own. One in which they laughed at each other's wrinkles and soft edges, at the grey hairs and rickety bones. At the times gone and the times coming and everything in-between.

If he could answer the message, he would reply, 'You're right, she would have.'

Chapter 48

Maisie

Friday 29 January, 2016

'How long have you known Watson?'

'Years. We met when we were very young. Why?'

'I was just wondering.'

'He's been wonderful since Tim was attacked. He's practically living with us, cooking, cleaning, driving us around. I couldn't have done any of this without him. He's been my rock. I'm really grateful.'

'That's good of him.'

'Yes. He's a great guy – just gone through a bad breakup, though.'

Maisie injects the needle into Tim's vein and withdraws a sample of blood for testing. 'Really? I wonder why they broke up.'

'His partner claimed he didn't spend enough time with her – said he spent too much time with us. He was distraught, told her she was selfish and that his friends needed him. But she said it had been going on a lot longer than the past month. I think maybe she's probably just stressed.'

'Do you think they'll get back together?'

'No. No, Watson was upset but he said it was probably for the best. He slept on our sofa that night, couldn't bear to go home to an empty house.'

'Poor guy.' Maisie forces the words out of her mouth.

'He'll be OK.'

'Do you think she was right, his partner? About him spending too much time with you?'

Heidi shifts in her seat, frowning. 'No, I don't think so. We've always been very close. Watson and Tim are two peas in a pod. Most of his family have passed away. His mum doesn't talk to him. He's only really got us.'

'It's nice you all have each other.'

'You know, last night, I was sitting at the table fretting, and he came in, stuck on some music and we danced around the kitchen. It was really sweet because that was what Tim and I used to do. It was like he was trying to remind me of happy times, give me hope.'

So they haven't been having an affair. But Watson obviously wants Heidi for himself. Maisie nods, surprised Heidi doesn't see what is right in front of her. Should she tell her? She has known her for nearly a month, he for years. Why would she believe Maisie over him?

'That's sweet,' she says, biting her lip. How can she tell her? 'Your friend is trying to take your husband's place?' That would sound terrible.

'How's he coping? I mean with the breakup on top of what's happened to Tim.' She gestures to him, wondering if he can hear them in some far-off part of his mind, and if he can see the wood for the trees.

'Well, he's broken up but he's covering it up, trying to be strong for me and my daughter. He doesn't think I know but I hear him talking to Tim sometimes. Asking for his opinion, wanting to know what he thinks he should do about work and the breakup.

It's heartbreaking.' Heidi rubs her bump, gazing at Tim with a finality that makes Maisie's stomach clench. 'I'm trying to get our daughter ready, talk her through things, make sure she understands what's happening. She's too young to deal with all of this.' She runs a hand across her face. 'If Tim doesn't recover, she needs to know he loves her. I tell her every morning and every night, "Daddy and Mummy love you." I tell her so much. You want to know what I'm most afraid of?' She gathers Tim's hands up in her own and kisses his knuckles, voice catching in her throat. 'It's that she'll forget him. That the memories they built up together will fade and one day, when she's older, Tim will just be a man she *used* to know. That's all.'

'You and Watson will remind her.'

'We will. But what about this little one?' She touches her bump, tears brimming in her eyes. 'My baby will never know Tim. Never know how special he is. There is only so much I can do.'

Maisie leans forward and pats her hand. 'Don't give up yet.'

'I'll never give up, Maisie. Tim isn't someone anyone would ever give up on. But I'm afraid and I need to get my daughter ready. And I need to be ready myself, for when this little one comes along. The longer he's this way, the less likely it is he'll recover. That's what I've read. Well, I need to be prepared for both scenarios. Tim would want me to be ready.'

Maisie understands, but to her ears it sounds as if a small part of Heidi is losing hope.

Chapter 49

Miller

Tuesday 14 May, 1996

What separates you from me is the ability to see good in others, to seek it out and appreciate it. The worst thing I have ever heard you say about anybody is, 'They need to dust down their jacket of morals.' That made me smile because you sounded wise beyond your years. My John, an old soul.

When Ginger Addams moves into our small town, she steals your heart within an instant. You look at her as if she is the epitome of all the goodness in all the world, but I know, deep down, hidden under the debris of your infatuation, your first love, you see she harbours a bad side.

She rests a hand on her hip, thrusts out her chest and parts her lips, smiling, obviously taken with your good looks. She flicks her red hair over her shoulder, and I think how well her name suits her. Ginger.

'So, what's your name?'

'Johnny Graham.' You are nervous, self-conscious, palms sweaty, fingers fiddling with the bracelet around your wrist.

'Nice to meet you.' She glances at Chubby who is standing by your side, comrades-in-arms, just as always. 'What are you?'

He laughs, thinking she has made a joke. You frown, surprised, and she sees it, makes a quick examination of the situation and changes her approach accordingly. 'What's your name?'

'My friends call me Chubs.'

She nods, eyes flickering to you, as if to say, Aren't I doing well, talking to your fat friend? Aren't I lovely? You smile, fooled by her act.

I watch through my open window, the sound of your voice blowing in on the breeze, and I want to scream at you to turn your back and walk away. But you are smitten, and she won't do anything to put you off because she wants you, John; she wants you more than she has ever wanted a boy before. I can see it in her eyes: lust, desire, a need to have you and to conquer you. Another notch on the bedpost. But you, my beautiful boy, you won't be one of them.

Wednesday 15 May, 1996

Your parents found a way to work through their grief and the blame they'd assigned for the death of their daughter. They took a moment at the end of the day and told each other how they were feeling, and slowly they found their way. You were the one who suggested they do this, another facet of that wise old brain, and it was because of this they soldiered on. You know, I used to call you my wise old owl because you seemed to know what would help people. You knew how to cheer Chubs up when his parents told him he was a disappointment, how to mollify your father when he worried he wouldn't be able to pay the bills on time, how to calm your mother when memories of Bessie made her sick with grief. You knew as if on instinct what to do and say and when to do and say it. My wise, wise boy.

You are sixteen years old and even now I can see vestiges of the boy you used to be shimmering beneath your face. It is there when you lift the cigarette to your lips and inhale, the wonder and excitement dancing across your features making me want to laugh. You pass the cigarette you snuck from your father to Chubby. He giggles like the child he still is and always will be, hopping up and down on one leg, fat juggling round his middle

'Aw, this is awesome. Your dad doesn't know you took it, does he?'

You shake your head, grinning. 'No. I don't think he'd mind us trying it this once anyway.'

Chubby's eyes widen. 'Cool!'

I smile, taking a turn with the cigarette. You watch me draw with big eyes, lips parted in awe, and I want to cup your face in my hands and kiss your nose. How beautiful you are.

'So did you ask Ginger out this morning or did you chicken out?' Chubby flaps pretend wings, clucking into your face.

You blush, suddenly finding an intense interest in the floor. 'Oh, I did. She... she said yes. We're going to catch a movie tomorrow.'

Chubby bounces on his toes. 'So, do you think you'll kiss her?'

'I don't know. If she'd like me to.' I smile at this answer; so many boys would do it regardless of her wishes, but not you.

'You've got to come round and tell us as soon as you do. I wonder what it's like, like if it's really wet and disgusting.'

You shrug. 'Same as when your mum kisses you, I suppose.'

'Eww, don't say that. And especially don't say it tomorrow, you'll ruin the mood.'

You laugh. 'Of course I won't.'

'You don't think she'll want more, do you?' He raises his eyebrows, nudging you in the ribs. I want to hurt him when he does this; I want to thrust my finger into his eye and make him cry out.

The colour drains from your face. 'Er... I don't know. I... I think I'd like to get to know her first.'

Chubby nods. 'I wonder if I'll ever get a girlfriend. Do you think a girl could ever like me? I could lose some weight, comb my hair – Dad's always telling me to.'

You wrap an arm round his shoulder. 'Of course you will. Girls think you're really funny.'

He grins, looking at me. 'What do you think?'

'You won't have any problem, Chubs. They'll be lining up at your door.'

If it wasn't for you, I'd tell him that no one will ever look at him twice. I smile and nod, taking another drag on the cigarette before giving it back to you.

The cigarette makes two more rounds before it burns to the nub. You drop it on the floor and stamp on it the way you've seen your father do. We smile at each other, then we burst out laughing because it tasted awful.

Thursday 16 May, 1996

I brush my fingers across the tree trunk where you have cut both your initials. A splinter sinks into the soft skin under my nail. I wince and suck the blood through my teeth but the splinter digs itself further into my skin. I ignore the pain and follow the path you have made through the park, seeking out your size-six-and-a-half shoes. I can see you further ahead, holding her hand, laughing at something she said. I stop when you slowly lean forward and press your lips to hers. I feel as if you have just taken a pair of scissors and cut straight though my body, and in a minute the pieces of me will blow away like petals in the breeze. You are nervous, frightened even, of doing something wrong, but she does not care. She hasn't noticed the way your hands clench, or how your neck tenses, the muscles bunching together. Her hands slip over your back, down, down, to the waistband of your jeans, her fingers exploring the length of you, as her tongue forces its way into your mouth. You pull away, surprised, give a nervous smile, then kiss her again. She presses her body against yours, running her hand through your hair, and it makes me want to be sick into the grass.

She lowers herself to the ground and pulls you with her. You are stiff, uncomfortable, but you are fascinated by the lure of something new and unexplored and she is the most beautiful girl you have ever seen. As she kisses you, I roll my tongue back and rub, imagining it is yours and you are doing to me what she is doing to you. She brushes her finger along your jaw and I do the same with mine, slow, seductive, for a single solitary moment the anger slipping into a pool of pleasure. But when I open my eyes and see her tug on your hair, I want to drag her off you with the back of her own hair. You deserve more sensitivity and tenderness. You are special and she is not worthy of you.

You walk back hand in hand when you have finished. She is oblivious to the fact that this simple act would have been enough for you. I follow behind, listening to her rant about the latest fashion trend, my body trembling when she calls you 'babe', as if you are her child, her possession, her thing. You are not, you will never be. You are special. You are more than she could even aspire to be. And you are *mine*.

Sunday 19 May, 1996

'You do realise he isn't going to sleep with you, don't you?'

She looks at me in surprise. 'What are you talking about?'

'John. He won't sleep with you. He's saving himself for his future wife. You haven't got a chance. I just thought you should know.'

Her mouth opens and closes, then her face wrinkles in disgust. 'That's so weird. Why would he do that?'

I shrug. 'Who knows? He gets these ideas into his head sometimes and he just won't budge.'

'He told you this?'

'Yeah. He tells everyone. He thinks it's cool. Thinks it's honour-able. I don't know, something like that.' I shrug again, playing the nonchalant character I think she is most likely to listen to.

She pulls a face and walks away, swinging her hips to catch boys, lips pouting, chest pushed out to display her breasts like confectionery at the newsagent's. She is walking, talking tempta-tion and the game she plays is one of luring as many boys to her bed as possible. But not you. Not anymore. If she can't win the game, why would she even want to play?

*

Your eyes are red, cheeks puffy, confidence broken with one fell swoop. You told me she turned up and said she didn't want to see you again; had met up with an old boyfriend and realised she still loved him. You only knew her for a few days but she was the first girl you ever liked and she shattered your confidence like a ball thrown at a window. I hate to see how I have made you feel. I want you to be confident, happy, but not with her. She doesn't deserve you. You are not a pawn to be used in a game. I can rebuild your confidence, brick by brick, just give me time.

'I… I thought she liked me. She said she did. I don't get it, what did I do wrong?' You are staring at the floor, looking as if you are about to cry.

'I don't know. Just forget about her. She was a bit weird anyway.'

'But what did I do wrong?' You peer up at me, begging for an answer. I have none to give.

'Nothing. You didn't do anything wrong. You're better off without her.'

'Yeah. He's right, Johnny.' Chubby fiddles with the yo-yo in his hand, nudging your foot with his own, trying in his little way to imbue a sense of confidence in you.

'She doesn't know what she's missing.'

236

'Yeah!' Chubby punches the air. 'It's her loss!'

You smile, nod, thank us for coming round. We pat your back, taking turns to make you laugh. I can see it is going to take longer, more than a few jokes to build you back up again, though. But that's OK. Unlike her, I know how to handle someone as precious as you. You're going to be just fine, babe.

Chapter 50

John

Sunday 27 December, 2015

He doesn't speak. He doesn't even cry as he hands her the photograph.

Twelve cuts for twelve ribs.

Each one running down the side of her body, weeping blood.

Tears streaking her face like pen marks down a piece of paper.

Bones broken, skin torn, a scream for help.

On the back, a message:

I think she's had enough now.

Chapter 51

Maisie

Saturday 30 January, 2016

'Can you squeeze my hand, Tim?' She rests her forefinger in his palm and waits. Nothing. His eyes rove around the room, flashes of emotion streaking across his face, disappearing just as fast as they came. 'Can you squeeze my hand, please, Tim?' She tries again.

Nothing.

She sighs, scribbling across her clipboard, then picks up a tennis ball and moves it from hand to hand in front of his face. His eyes fix on it for a moment and, for a handful of heartbeats, Maisie is overwhelmed with hope. But then his eyes begin another blank turn round the room.

'Tim, if you can hear me, I need you to blink twice. Can you do that for me, please?'

Nothing. She makes another note on her clipboard, then throws back his covers and runs her pen down the sole of his foot. She is about to turn away when she sees his toes twitch.

She takes a breath to steady herself. Her pulse quickens. 'Can you feel that, Tim? Can you feel it? Wriggle your toes for me, Tim.' She runs her pen across his foot. Another twitch.

'Oh my God.'

She drops the clipboard on the bed and bends over his chest, searching his face, her nerves on edge, as if an electric current has run through her body. She gathers a fold of his skin between her fingers, says a silent prayer, then pinches.

'Lailah! Lailah!'

'What?! What is it?' She runs into the room, eyes wide, arms open. 'Maisie?'

A bubble of joy bursts in her chest. 'Watch, watch!'

She pinches his arm, again and again to be sure. When she looks up at Lailah, she is laughing. 'He... he... did he just...?'

She nods and pulls Lailah into her arms. 'Yes!'

Chapter 52

Miller

Wednesday 8 October, 1997

I see the way they look at you. All those wicked girls with their honeyed skin and bright eyes. They look at you the way Mother looks at the dress she wants in the window of Debenhams; they wonder how you would look by their side, and if they could make the other girls jealous. I'm with Johnny Graham. That's right. He picked me. Me, not you.

You do not notice. There hasn't been another girl in your life since Ginger; I think that still hurts you in a way. But just as I promised, I have built your confidence back up and now you walk down the street with your head held high. Chubby likes to pretend the girls are looking at him, likes to think he could make them swoon with just one glance.

The girls angle their bodies at you, licking their lips and flicking their hair. Times like these, I want to grasp your hand, a clear message in the touch: he's taken.

He just doesn't know it.

There is a new girl at school now. She moved into our village with her affluent parents, nice clothing and expensive jewellery, and although she has aimed a few curious looks at you, I can sense that, to her, you are not an object. Not an accessory to flaunt. I watched her in class the other day, you know, and I thought to myself, if you were ever to be with a girl, she should be the one. No one will ever be good enough for you but I want you to have diversity in your life, I want you to feel alive, I want you to be touched and kissed and treated well. I want you to live to the very extent of life. I want you to run and laugh and scream, but at the end of the day I want you to come home to me so I can mend your raggedy heart and kiss away your troubles.

Don't forget you belong to me.

'What do you think of the new girl?' I ask, wrapping an arm around Chubby, so you can see I am bringing him into the conversation. Chubby thinks I am as kind as you, the best friend in the entire world, but I'm not. Not to him at least.

'She seems nice. Have you talked to her?'

'No.' I snigger. 'You should see the guys in my art class. They're practically drooling. It's disgusting.'

Chubby laughs, skipping along beside us. 'She's pretty. Do you think I have a chance?'

'No, I don't think so, Chubs. I'm not sure she's into the whole dating thing.'

'That's probably a good thing. I'd only break her heart.'

We laugh. 'What movie have you got that from? Chubs, you can't bear to stand on an ant, so you're not going to be able to break anyone's heart.'

'Has she even talked to anyone yet? The girl?' you ask, and I have to look away so you can't see my smile.

'Whyyyy? Do you like her, mate?' Chubs bumps your hip, grinning.

'I don't know. I haven't met her.'

'What about you? You're in her class.'

I shake my head. 'No, she keeps to herself.' I plan to, though.

I plan to smile my best smile and talk to her after class, laugh when she makes a joke, show interest when she talks about art. And then I'll introduce her to you. And the rest will take care of itself. She won't be able to resist you, John. And it's better her – someone I have picked – than a girl like Ginger.

Don't you agree?

*

You'd carry him home if you could. I know you would.

He is shuffling by your side, right arm hooked round your shoulder, left dangling to the floor. His face is bloody, nose slightly crooked. When you found him, you rushed to his side and cupped his head in your lap, patting his chest, asking him to look at you, to answer you. At first he didn't respond and that scared you, didn't it? But when he did, you sighed and looked to the sky as if in thanks to a hidden entity.

You think I have just spotted you when I come bolting down the street. It isn't true, though. I've been watching you all day. And as I shout Chubs' name and don a look of panic, I wrap his free arm around my neck and shuffle along with you both.

'Chubs! Chubs, are you OK? What… what happened, John? What happened to him?' I look at you imploringly.

'Marcus and his band of idiots got him after school. I found him at the back. I think he's OK. His nose is broken, though. Can you run and get his dad, mate? I think my knees are about to buckle.'

'Yeah, yeah.' When I return with Chubs' father, you are sitting with him on the curb, legs shaking from exhaustion, arms flopping over Chubs' sobbing form. 'Hey, hey, mate, come on. It's OK. Everything's going to be OK. You'll see.'

He shakes his head, leaning in to you. 'Everyone at school's going to think I'm weak!'

'They won't. I promise. Why did they come after you?'

Chubs hiccups, snot running in rivulets down his lips. 'They said I was fat. Said I couldn't fit through doors properly. I can, though, I really can, Johnny. It's not true!'

You pat his back and hold him close. 'I know it's not, Chubs. They're just bullies. Don't go anywhere on your own. Let's stick together. It's got to be harder if we're together.' You rest your head on his. 'Does your nose hurt?'

A stupid question. And yet it makes Chubs chuckle just as you knew it would. 'Yeah. A little bit. It was a lot worse a minute ago. Do you think I'll look like that guy on telly now? You know, the tough guy with the bent nose?' His expression brightens.

'I think the doctor will put it back, Chubs.'

'Oh, oh, yeah.' He casts his eyes to the ground. 'Maybe you shouldn't call me Chubs anymore…'

You nod sadly. 'OK. Good thinking, mate.'

He smiles, bumps you in the ribs with his fist. 'Thanks for helping me home.'

You smile back. 'No problem. We'll always be there for each other.'

You stay with him that night, curled up on the floor of his bedroom, so when nightmares of Marcus come and scare our little friend, you can reach up and pat him on the back, reminding him he is safe. It makes me smile, you know, how thoughtful and considerate you are. When I go to bed, I smile because you are my special boy.

Special. Special special special.

Chapter 53

John

Tuesday 29 December, 2015

He'd always hated that red jumper; the only reason he'd worn it was because his mother bought it especially for him and he didn't want to hurt her feelings. He can still remember the way it made his skin itch.

In the picture he's standing with his two friends, Miller and Don, smiling, wishing he could rip the jumper off and throw it into his neighbour's garden. His eyes flicker back to Miller and, with the weight of an anchor, his heart falls dormant to his feet.

Miller.

The photo album slips from his fingers and lands on the floor. He doesn't pick it up but stares ahead, as if someone is dangling something in front of him, hundreds of memories swarming through his mind.

He and his father going to the river to play, swapping stories and pieces of information like cards in a game; helping his mother dig a vegetable patch in their garden, the sun hot on their backs, soil soft under their fingers; walking to the sweetshop every Sunday with Bess, holding hands like nothing could ever part them.

Idling away year after year in the company of his two friends, playing games, sitting by the river, sneaking a fag from his father's stash, partying, arguing, laughing. There was so much laughter. He struggles to reconcile those glorious, sparkling days with the darkness that swamps him now. He draws a breath and picks up the album, rubbing his hand over his face.

Miller.

He hardly even notices when his hand begins to shake. He turns the page, then turns another, and again and again, the face of his old friend tumbling through his mind. Miller, Miller, Miller. He is in all of the pictures. Him. Don. Miller. Together, friends. They thought for ever.

Can it be him?

He shakes his head. It can't be, can it? He didn't have a bad bone in his body. He was kind and funny. He was a sweet boy. He can't have a grudge against him. He wouldn't want to hurt his family.

But…

He flicks through the album Don found in his wardrobe, pausing when he sees a photograph of him, Jules and Don, slumped across each other, laughing at something beyond the camera. To the side, Miller sits with his arms crossed, swiping a glance at Jules from the corner of his eye, the look of a haunted man, something morphing his features into a permanent grimace.

And then John remembers. He remembers the summer Miller changed: the way he kept his distance, kept his eyes cast to the ground, kept the bond they had built as children locked away to crumble and to rot. He'd tried to mend the rift, bring him back into their lives, but he couldn't.

One came and one went. One to happiness and one to loneliness. The bond of their youth left to wither under the arrival of someone new.

He stands with his back to the album: out of sight, out of mind. Or so he wishes. Thoughts of the past turn around in his head.

Don paces the room, running fidgety hands through greasy hair. Jules sits at the dining table, lost, just as he is, in the years before. 'I… I always thought he was lovely. He made us laugh. Took care of us all.'

Don comes to a halt and shakes his head. 'No, there was another side to him neither of you saw.'

John frowns. 'What do you mean?'

'I was riding my bike by the river one day when I fell in. I screamed and screamed for help. Miller came, and I thought he was going to pull me out. I thought he'd come to help me. But when he knelt down, he… he pushed me under, John.'

'No, he couldn't have. He wouldn't! This is Miller, Don. Miller.'

Don sighs, lowering himself into a chair like an elderly man. 'I thought he was joking, you know. That's what we did. Joke. I thought he'd pull me up, pat me on the back and say something to cheer me up. I was so relieved when I saw him. But he didn't. He kept me under the water until I thought I was going to die.' Don covers his eyes, massaging his temples. 'At the last minute, he pulled me out, but you should have seen the look on his face. He wasn't joking. He was angry, John.'

John eases himself to the floor, legs buckling at the last minute, tears prickling his eyes. 'Why didn't you tell me? Tell anyone for that matter?'

Don looks at him with an expression that breaks his heart. 'Who would have believed me? Everyone loved him, everyone thought he was an angel.'

'Why not after? Why didn't you say anything?!'

'I just told you: because no one would have believed me, John! You wouldn't have!'

247

'I would. You were my best friend.'

'So was he! So was he, John.'

'That doesn't matter anymore,' Jules shouts, throwing her hands in the air. 'What matters now is getting Bonnie back.'

John nods, slumps back against the wall. 'Why didn't we think of him?'

'Because we made ourselves forget, blocked it from our thoughts. Because when he moved away it was the easiest thing to do for a bunch of teenagers,' Don says, meeting his gaze, a shadow passing over his face. 'Because when the two of you got together, he felt you had betrayed him.' He sighs, lowering his face into his hands. 'Because he loved Jules more than anything else in the world.'

Chapter 54

Maisie

Sunday 31 January, 2016

Maisie counts the seconds, tapping her finger in time with the pulse of the room, which throbs with an intensity she hasn't felt for a long time.

She watches the doctors perform their actions with her heart in her mouth, prepped to jump in at the slightest notice. Lailah stands sentinel by her side, flashing her looks of fear and looks of hope.

The room is heavy with whispered words and the rustle of their uniforms. Maisie holds her hands in front of her stomach, hoping with everything she has that this is what she thinks it is. Please, please, please. Please, let this be it.

She closes her eyes and sends a silent prayer into the universe. When she opens them and looks over the doctor's shoulder, a shiver runs down her body.

'Call Heidi!'

Chapter 55

Miller

Thursday 23 October, 1997

I sense with a feeling in my bones that this is it now. There will be no parting over loose morals, or words thrown over the course of an argument. There will be no playing away or punches given and taken. There will be nothing of what other couples take on the chin. Because you both transcend those around you and your relationship will endure. Within an instant, I've set the course for your joint future.

You smile and offer to carry her bag, and I want to clap you on the back and tell you, 'Well done.' Chivalry is losing in the race against arrogance and you, I feel, could pull it round again.

'Thanks,' she says, smiling.

'No problem.'

You've been walking her to school every day now for the past few weeks, asking her how she is, being the gentleman, something that puts you in stark contrast to the bad boys and cool dudes. She sees it. So do other girls. I told you this would happen. I told you people would swarm to you, some vying for attention, others wanting to hurt you. You didn't realise, but just the other day, I stopped Nick Kingsley from taking you round the back of the school and beating you within an inch of your life. I won't tell you how because I know it will make you screw up your face and clutch your stomach.

'Some friends and I are going for a picnic later at the park. Would you like to come? I think you'll like them – they're really funny.'

She nods. 'OK. Thanks.'

She doesn't speak much. Instead she likes to listen to you talk about your parents, Chubby and I, writing, music, school, even the weather. You worry you're talking too much, but don't. She thinks you are perfect.

She always will.

Thursday 30 October, 1997

I know you think I like her. Fancy her. I saw the way you kept glancing at me yesterday, sadness and concern in your eyes. Don't worry, I wanted to say, I'm not going to try and claim her for my own like all the other boys do. I'm not interested. When I look at her I'm thinking of you, how I have made a good choice allowing her into your life. You'll learn from her and she you, you'll support one another through the hard times that await in the years to come, you'll comfort and love and make each other happy. I want this for you, John; you're my little angel, my beautiful baby boy. I watched you grow up, I built your confidence when it tumbled, I fed you when I worried you were thin, I put a cold cloth on your forehead when you were ill. You and she will never have what we have. But I want you to live life to the full. These times with her aren't our end, they are our beginning.

Chapter 56

John

Wednesday 30 December, 2015

The man stands with his back to John, left hand digging deep into his trouser pocket, right hand spooning sugar into a milky cup of tea. A swift ping alerts them to a message on his phone. The man turns and pokes at the screen and John takes the time to study his old friend. Wrinkles edge down his forehead and across his cheeks like lines in a piece of paper. His shirt, so crisp and neat, bulges up at the back where he has forgotten to tuck it into the waistband of his trousers. A silver wedding band glistens on his finger and catches John's eye, then disappears from view as he stirs milk into their tea. His still-thick hair is slicked back across his head, and in another life John might have poked at his luck in keeping a full head of hair. But how can he? The bond that bridged their lives together as children is so deeply settled in the past, he can't find a way to bring it back. How does he behave? What does he say? His question can wait for later; first he wants to get to know the man his old friend has become.

Before knocking on Miller's door, he'd sat in his car, staring up at the grand house, wondering how their friendship had come to this: John Googling him on the internet and arranging to meet after so many years apart and now sitting outside his house. It hadn't taken much effort to find his work details online and, after eventually getting past his secretary, their conversation went from a few stilted words to a blast of conversation booming down the phone.

'You look different, Mill. You look good.'

He smiles and turns, raising an eyebrow at John. 'I suppose I do. You look the same.'

'How have you been all these years?' John takes the steaming cup from his hand and follows him into the sitting room, running his eyes across the photo frames that paint a happy life. Three cream sofas sit at right angles round an old oak coffee table. Knick-knacks, balled-up notes, jewellery, crumbs, and the latest state-of-the-art tablets are sprinkled across the sideboard to his right. A sixty-inch flatscreen TV sticks to the wall like one big eye reflecting their own small silhouettes back at them. John's surprise at his friend's obvious wealth makes the words stick in his throat.

Miller catches him looking and shakes his head, gesturing across the room. 'It wasn't always like this, John.'

'What do you mean?' John takes a seat and feels himself sink down into the sofa cushion.

Miller runs a hand across his face, the wrinkles burrowing deeper into his skin as he frowns. 'You don't really want to know, Johnny. You have a perfect life. Why would you care about anyone else's?'

The words come as a blow to John despite the years. 'Mill, you were my best friend. Of course I care.'

Miller taps the floor with his foot. Quick, sharp movements that set John's teeth on edge. 'You were mine.' It comes out as a whisper.

'Why did you leave? Why did you shut yourself down? It's because of Jules, isn't it? You loved her.'

His foot stops tapping. 'What? No, I didn't. I didn't leave because of that.'

'Then why did you?'

'Because something… something happened that changed things. I had to leave. I was scared. I was only young, John. I didn't know what to do. It was easier just to run. I lied to my parents, told them I was being bullied, and they moved us away. I didn't want to leave you, though. You were my best pal.'

John nods. 'What happened?'

'It doesn't matter now.' His foot resumes tapping out a rhythm in the floor and his finger digs and digs deeper into a cut on his hand. Tap. Dig. Tap. Dig. John looks away when his hand starts to bleed. Even then he keeps digging, as if the answers to life are buried beneath his skin.

'Of course it matters. What happened, Mill?'

'Our lives went separate ways, Johnny. I read about you in the papers. Famous writer. You always wanted to be. Well done. You got everything you wanted. You have Jules, you have a daughter, a career, a home, a life. For a long time, mine wasn't like that.'

John takes a sip of his tea, if only to calm himself. 'Tell me.'

Miller stares at the floor and sighs. 'When I moved away, things went from bad to worse. My parents died, I lost the money I had saved. I was forced into a job I hated, into a flat where I had to push the bed against the door every night. Told myself it would get better, that I'd get myself out of this hole. That maybe, if I was brave, I'd find you. The only reason I didn't was because I got ill. Leukaemia. Those were some of the worst days of my life.' He rubs his eyes. 'At one point, I hoped I would die. I know that's selfish but I did. I couldn't help it. I'd had enough of the neighbour's boys coming every night and trying to get in, I was sick of not having enough money to eat, I was sick of being alone, staring at the wall, wishing I was a boy again, running about with

254

you and Don.' He smiles, wiping away a tear like it is burning his skin, like a child would, palm flat against his cheek. 'Bad times hurt, John. They cut you so deep it's only when you're on your knees you realise this type of cut can't be healed. You don't know what this is like, I can tell by the look of you. You've had a good life.'

John swallows the lump in his throat. 'I'm sorry, mate. I'm so sorry.' And he means it. He means it more than he has meant anything in his life.

Miller nods. 'It's OK.'

'Then what happened? After?'

'I survived, kept this picture of us, looked at it, sort of told myself I could have that again.' He pulls a crumpled photograph from his pocket and passes it to him with a shaking hand. 'That picture got me through.'

John holds it in his hand and smiles. It is the same picture Don has in the album. 'I hated that red jumper.'

'I know. Didn't want to hurt your mum's feelings, though, did you?'

He chuckles. 'No. I used to lie awake at night imagining sticking it on the fire.'

'Do you remember those times by the river, throwing rocks and talking about rubbish?'

'Yeah.'

'I missed them.'

'I've missed them too.'

A nod.

'Later the leukaemia came back to bite me on the bum. Worse than before. Lot worse. I was sitting on my bed one night, listening to the neighbour's boys shout at me, and I thought, "Why don't I just stop this?" I kept ten packets of painkillers and a bottle of vodka in my drawer. The leukaemia was getting the better of me so I thought I'd get it over with. I sat on the bed and held that picture in my hand, thought I could go thinking of you and Don. With every pill I swallowed, I felt a little bit more relieved. It would be over soon. I wouldn't have to live that life anymore. I'd find those days with you and Don and I'd stay there for ever.'

John rubs his finger across the picture, not daring to look up because, if he does, he knows he won't be able to stop himself from crying.

'You didn't come and look for me, John. You forgot about me, didn't you?'

He shakes his head. 'I didn't forget. I blocked you from my mind, threw away my photos of you, stopped myself thinking about you until it became natural. I was hurt, Mill. You just left. If I'd have known what happened to you, I would have come and found you. I would have helped you.'

'I know. I know.' Miller begins tapping the floor with the other foot. 'And I know you mean it. You always were honest. Some things don't change.'

'What happened after you…'

'Tried to top myself?' He smiles. 'It almost worked but those boys broke down the door, got scared when they saw me, ran, left the door open. A woman on her way to see her sister looked in and rang for help. She saved my life. And although I thanked her, I wasn't grateful. I hated her. It should have been someone else she saved, not me.'

'Mill, don't.'

'It's true. Anyway, that was that. Got myself out of that flat, exchanged it for one that was a whole lot worse, but I didn't have anyone trying to get in at night. I got some help from a counsellor, survived the leukaemia. Life slowly improved. Sorted myself out. Studied. Worked hard. Got a job I love. Met my wife. Things are a lot better now than they were then.'

John nods, reaching across and taking Miller's hand. 'I'm sorry I wasn't there for you, mate.'

He smiles and squeezes his hand. 'You didn't know. Anyway,

enough about me. That was all in the past. Tell me about you. I know you're an author, quite a good one if that last book was anything to go by. How is Jules? Are you still with Jules?'

'She's... she's OK.' John braces himself and slowly begins to tell Miller about Bonnie, each word feeling like it's sticking in his mouth. He starts with how they first thought she'd gone for a walk and got lost, and finishes with the last photograph they received. Miller is silent through all of it, his eyes pinned to the floor, his fingers steepled together. John notes his reactions and waits for him to say something. When Miller eventually meets his gaze, John knows with a certainty in his gut that he is not the person they are looking for.

'Jesus. Johnny, I'm sorry. I... I can't even imagine what...' He pauses and leans back, eyebrows rising high into his wrinkled forehead. 'You... you came here because you thought I might have taken her, didn't you?'

'Yes. I had to be sure.'

Miller nods, biting his bottom lip. 'I understand. I wish you had just said it first off, though. So. Tell me. What do you think? Do I have your daughter? Is it me?'

'I'm sorry, mate. I am. But if you were in my position, you'd do the same.'

Miller leans back into the sofa, a deep sigh scraping past his lips. 'Yeah. I know I would. Is there anything I can do to help you find her?'

'I don't think so. Do you remember anyone from back then? Did you see anyone?'

'No,' he says, but John wonders if he is keeping something back.

'OK. Thanks, mate.' John stands and gently pulls him into his arms. 'Don't think I'm falling out of touch with you again, Mill. You're stuck with me this time.'

Miller tucks his head into his shoulder and pats his back. 'It's good to see you again, Johnny.'

257

He looks at Miller and smiles, thankful he's at least found Miller in the search for Bonnie. 'I'll see you soon, mate.'

As John turns to leave, Miller looks at him with something that sends a shiver down his spine.

'I hope you find her, Johnny. I really do.'

*

The letter is addressed to John. He can still recognise Miller's thick scrawl after all these years. It is propped up against his door. Inside is a note with four words that frighten him more than he can describe.

Look closer to home.

The note is signed with the drawing of a robin.

Chapter 57

Maisie

Monday 1 February, 2016

She tells herself it is just her imagination. It's just her eyes playing tricks. But when she takes another look, a shiver runs down her spine and, before she can say a word, her legs give way and she lands on the floor with a thump.

It slips from her fingers and scuttles across the floor.

Maisie reaches out and folds it in her hands, holding it to her chest like a secret. She can hear him saying her name in the other room, but no matter how hard she tries, the words refuse to come.

This can't be happening.

It isn't possible.

She cups her mouth, hands shaking, eyes watering. When she looks at it again, a part of her is shocked to see the same result.

'Maisie, are you OK?' He knocks on the door, his concern seeping through the wood to greet her in her corner of shock.

'I… I… I'm fine.' The words mean nothing to her. They roll off her tongue without any meaning whatsoever. She is more than fine.

She runs her finger along it, a smile breaking across her lips, her heart beating out a rhythm she thought she'd never feel again.

'What are you doing? Are you sure you're OK? I heard a bang.' Ben's voice again.

She knows she needs to reply. She doesn't want him to worry but she also wants to hold it in her hands for a little longer, savour the moment, because the likelihood of feeling this way again, she knows in her gut, is small.

'I'm fine,' she repeats. She closes her eyes and laughs, squeezing it to her chest, marking the moments with thoughts of what awaits them in the future.

When she opens the door, she shows Ben what is in her hands, wraps him in her arms and smiles.

Because miracles do happen more than once.

Chapter 58

Miller

Wednesday 8 July, 1998

Oh, John, how it makes me cringe. The shriek fills the trees and frightens away the birds – they scatter into the sky, eyeballing the spectacle like it is a catastrophe they narrowly avoided. I follow the noise, picking out his head bopping just above the water. His arms push and swipe and flail about. His mouth opens and closes like a goldfish in a tank, eyes widening as panic and fear chase each other round his face. He splutters and coughs, hitting the water like it is a bully who must be defeated. But he never could stand up to those bullies. And he can't stand up to the water now.

I peer at him from behind a tree, basking in the panic that crackles in the air. He screams again, and I think to myself I have never heard anyone as frightened as he is now. His hands claw the air as if he is grabbing for an imaginary ladder, tears dropping into the frothing water like cubes of sugar into a cup of tea. His head submerges and his cries die on pale lips.

One.

Two.

Three.

I count the seconds on my fingers, wondering how long it will take. He can't swim; he has made sure everyone knows this.

You would be panicking right now, pulling him out, hoping against hope your friend, your dear, dear Chubs, is OK. You'd lay him flat on his back, put your soft ear to his cold mouth, listen, careful not to miss it, then you'd pinch his nose with gentle fingers and press your lips to his and breathe and breathe and breathe him back to life. The strength of you, the strength of him. And then he'd open his eyes, he'd look at you and he'd taste you, your skin on his lips, and feel the breaths you'd given him rattling in his soaked lungs. Later, you'd both joke about it, embarrassed about the kiss, but glad and grateful all the same there wasn't a death that day. Neither of you would have noticed the boy standing on the periphery, hand clutched to his chest as if his heart had just broken. That boy would have wished it was him who had been in the water, who had been given that kiss. That boy would have been me.

When his head pops through the surface, I step forward and meet his gaze, thoughts of what might have been turning my mind black with anger. He looks at me with relief, joy, and it makes me want to turn and walk away, just to hear him scream again. But I don't. I kneel down and stretch my arm towards him. He tries to grab it but I swat his hand away. It is only when I take a fistful of his hair that I think he realises. The look on his face. Oh, John! For the first time in his life, he is beautiful. Your little friend, your little pet, is mesmerising.

'Help! Hel… help me! Please!' Tears drip into the water. I watch them, all of the emotion, all of the anger draining away. Suddenly I feel calm, I feel peaceful. I feel at home.

He shouts my name then, over and over again. When he realises I'm not going to help, he starts to shout for you, John. He cries and screams for you to save him. To help him.

It is then I push his head under the water.

Shall I tell you something funny?

As he squirms and screams under the water, I turn my face to the sun and I smile.

I smile because the world, for those few moments, is perfect. And then I pull him out.

Friday 10 July, 1998

I am surprised how frightened he is of me. How he casts a wide berth not only around me but around my house, Mother, even my bike, taking care to tread carefully, casting fearful eyes around like a demon is about to jump out and carry him away. You have noticed the change in him; it worries you and for that I am truly sorry. When you ask him, beg for answers to what's bothering him, he simply shakes his head, looks at me and walks away. You sigh, shoulders slumping and wipe away a tear before anyone can see. Despite his refusals, you keep asking, keep trying to make him laugh, to right whatever wrong has taken place.

I heard you talking to your mother, you know. I was standing outside the door, peering through the keyhole, listening to your voice with bated breath.

'I think Chubs is angry with me,' you said, looking at your mother, proving, despite your age, that you still relied on her for guidance; it made my heart flutter. All those other boys, shrugging off their parents' love like a dirty shirt, and there you were, savouring yours.

'Why?' she asked, puzzled.

'I think something's happened. He's acting really weird. He's avoiding me but I haven't done anything. I… I think it's because of Jules.' You looked up at your mother, and it was then I saw how much you were hurting. I saw the pain in your eyes as easily as the scar Bessie left on my arm. It poured from your blue eyes like light from a bulb.

263

'I've noticed he's been a little strange. What makes you think it's because of Jules, though?'

The words swayed on your lips, hesitant to be spoken and become real. 'I think he loves her. He's angry with me because he feels like I've betrayed him. I didn't know, though. It only hit me the other day when we were having a picture taken. I don't know what to do, Mum. What do you think?'

'Speak to him, sweetheart.' She kissed your head. 'Speak to him. Get things out into the open. That's what I've found helps. Do you remember how you made your father and me sit down in the evenings and talk after Bess died? Well, that's what you need to do with him. Talk. Sort it out.'

You nodded and smiled at her. I was so tempted to open the door and tell you then, just to wipe that sadness from your face. I wanted to tell you it wasn't you or even Jules he was looking at when that photo was taken. It was me.

I'm sorry now. I lost control and I shouldn't have. Not with Chubby, not with anyone. But the thought of you kissing him, saving him as I stood on the sidelines, frightened me, infuriated me. It snapped the cord keeping the act in position and released a part of me which has been locked away for so long. I won't slip again, though. I'll make sure I'm more prepared, stronger, because you could so easily have been watching. And if I slip in front of you, I'll lose you for ever.

You make a vow to go round to his house tomorrow morning and speak with him. But when you open the front door, you are surprised to see men loading his family's possessions into a removal van. Once you realise what is happening, you stand there and cry. Quietly. Tears slipping down your cheeks and dribbling onto your shoes. I walk up and wrap an arm round your shoulder, comrades-in-arms, softly reminding you that I am still here. Because our friend is halfway down the road, looking back at us through the window of his parents' car, crying with you and rubbing his head as if he can still feel my hand holding him down.

Monday 18 January, 1999

I know a change is coming. I've seen you bat the idea round in your mind, worrying away at it like a stray piece of cotton sticking out of your shirt. At first, it frightened me. But now I know how to handle your idea. Now I know how to keep us close as you part from our childhood home to make your way in the world with Jules. It won't just be Jules, though. We will all do it together. Like we always have.

Before you tell me your news, I tell you mine. And you can't believe what you're hearing.

It's time to get myself a life, strive for more, go for my dreams, I tell you, palms flat, expression open, echoing what you planned to say to me. I need to do this. I'm sorry to leave you but we'll always keep in touch. Don't forget about me.

You shake your head, more in shock than as a response. Then you mutter your own news and I display the appropriate measure of surprise, then excitement. And that does it.

The recipe for our future is all set to deliver perfection.

Sunday 31 January, 1999

This is the first time since Bessie's death you and I haven't taken a trip to the sweetshop for acid drops. It became a way for you to remember her, didn't it? A way of honouring her memory and letting her know you loved her. But that tradition was never destined to last for ever. And now, as I pack my boxes into the car we both learnt to drive in, I know it ends here. Today.

Mother, you, Jules and your parents stand by the hood of the car, lined up, awaiting my farewells. All of you are smiling except for Mother. I think she is relieved to see me go; perhaps she thinks she can live out the remainder of her life freely now. I don't care, either way. You are all that matters to me.

I hug Mother and smile when I feel her shudder. Then your

parents, Jules, and finally you. I pull you into my arms and make a joke. You laugh, nod, pull away and, on the pinnacle of this life change, I see the years of our love affair shine in your eyes. It makes my heart swell with pride. I see the times by the river, the games of rock-paper-scissors, I can hear the laughter. I feel the years of knowing you brush against my skin like the night your foot brushed against mine through the duvet. I see it all. And it makes me happy.

'See you in a few days,' you say, grinning.

I nod, get in the car and start the engine. As I pull away, I send a smile in your direction.

You are waving as I drive away, into a new life, a new future. Your absence in the next few days will be torturous for me, but it is a worthy sacrifice for the rest of our lives together.

I can just see it now: you hugging your parents, getting into your loaded car and driving away, Jules's hand firmly wrapped around yours. I can see you following in my wake, joining me in a new town and a new world. You'll be worried, perhaps even a little scared. But don't be, Blue-Eyes.

I will be ready. I will be there waiting for you.

Chapter 59

John

Thursday 31 December, 2015

If someone were to see him now, they'd probably think he was a brave man, a strong, fearless man. But if they peeled back the layers they'd see the truth.

He can't say he isn't afraid. Truth be told, this is the most frightened he has ever been. He can't say he is strong because now he feels anything but. And he can't say he is brave because he knows in his bones this part of his life is drawing to a close.

The disc sits on his doormat. Scrawled across the top are the words 'The End'.

They have found them then. Perhaps they have always known where they are. Perhaps when he and Jules held each other on the sofa each night, they were spectating, peering through the window at the torment they'd created. Perhaps this 'safe house' has never really been safe.

He looks at the words scrawled across the disc. 'The End.' As if this is a story and he is one of the characters. As if this is as harmless as a game between friends. Something as inconsequential as a dream.

He picks up the disc and takes it into the lounge. The house has fallen silent around him, the air thick with a miasma that sends chills trickling down his spine. His feet shuffle a slow tune in his ears, and he makes himself walk faster, pushing through the thickness of the air.

The disc, he knows, is the weight of a piece of paper, but it feels as heavy as ten bags of sugar. He stares down at it, wondering whether, if he doesn't play it – if he simply throws it away – he'll be able to trick himself into believing Bonnie is alive. Because this disc will show his daughter's death. And John knows it won't be the end of one life; it will be the end of three.

He sits on the sofa and pushes the disc into the DVD player, wishing Jules were by his side. John closes his eyes, takes a breath and presses play.

Bonnie appears on the screen, sitting in torn, dirty clothes. Blood is spattered across her face. Her arm is hanging by her side, shoulder sticking out at an odd angle, fingers twisted like the roots of an old tree. She looks up at him, and he sees the last remnants of hope slip from those eyes like sand slipping through the neck of an hourglass. He kneels down in front of the TV and presses his hands against the screen, tears running down his cheeks.

'Bonnie…'

She looks at the floor, as if she has heard him and can't bear to look at him. John sobs, tears pattering on his hand like raindrops. 'Bonnie…'

A gloved hand appears at the edge of the screen. John jumps back, watching its progress to Bonnie's face, dread prickling the back of his neck like a cold cloth. 'Don't touch her!' He slams his hand against the screen. 'DON'T TOUCH HER! DON'T FUCKING TOUCH HER!'

Bonnie's face screws up into a thousand creases. Thick tears stream down her face. The sound of her voice carries through the room, making the hairs rise on John's arms. 'N... no. No... no. Please.' She scoots back, dragging her arm, screaming, begging, blood oozing down her nose.

'No! P... please! Please! No! Won't do it again! Won't! P... please!' She curls herself up into a ball, mouth open in a silent plea.

A hand rests on her cheek, forefinger by her right eye, little finger by the corner of her lip, and runs their nail across her eyelashes, slowly, tenderly, as if they're memorising the web of perfect lines in her skin.

And suddenly John realises.

The strength seeps from his body as if it is being sucked away. He stands up and his legs give beneath him, a noise working its way up his throat. John touches the floor as if he is trying to remind himself it hasn't fallen away. He shuffles back, away from the TV, away from his daughter, away from the man's hand, lips quivering in what looks like a silent conversation with himself.

This can't be happening? It can't be Him? He wouldn't do this? This is a mistake. John shakes his head, a refusal to believe his own eyes. 'No,' he says. 'NO!' It's Him. *It's HIM!*

Bonnie turns her head away, then the screen goes blank.

*

The darkness is blinding. The stench of blood and urine suffocating. John stumbles back as it hits him, cupping a hand over his mouth. He fumbles for a light switch, his heart thump-thump-thumping in his chest, blood cold in his veins. He doesn't care where He is. He doesn't even care if He's in the house. All he wants is Bonnie. A bang reverberates through the walls. John follows the sound down into the cellar, remembering the first time he heard it sipping tea in the lounge.

How could he have not known?

John flicks the light switch. The blood is the first thing to greet him, and he cries out, fear weaving through his muscles. Bundles of clothes are thrown haphazardly in the corner of the cellar. Opposite them sits a coffee table, knives and scissors shining under the bulb. John takes the steps one at a time, his breath catching in his throat. He glances from side to side, panic blowing through his body. Where is she?

He catches a snatch of movement from the corner and within an instant is by Bonnie's side. He pushes the mound of clothes off her and wraps his arms around her bony body. 'Bonnie! Bonnie!' Small, broken fingers fumble against his shirt as she peers up at him. 'Bonnie!'

She looks at him uncertainly, as if she can't quite decide if he is real or a dream. Her lips open a fraction and one word escapes through. 'Daddy?'

He brushes her hair back and nods, cradling her back and legs in his arms, rocking her from side to side. 'It's me, sweetheart. It's me. Daddy's here. Daddy's here now.'

She smiles. He kisses her forehead and sobs into her hair, eyes taking in every inch of her bloodied, broken mess of a body. She nestles her head into his chest and shivers. He pulls an old jacket over her chest and, as he does so, sees her feet clad in the Dorothy shoes. 'I love you, sweetheart. You're safe now. You're going to be OK.' She nods, tears snaking across her cheeks, making small trails through the blood and dirt. Her trembling body is like a small earthquake in his arms. John runs his hand over her head, smoothing down her hair and purging her mind of every pain and fear. 'I love you, sweetheart. Mummy loves you. You're going to be OK. You're going to be fine.' He wipes away the tears. 'We're going to go home and we're going to curl up on the sofa with a hot-water bottle, lots of sweets, and we're going to watch *The Wizard of Oz*. We're going to go home. OK. Mummy's waiting, sweetheart. She waiting for you.'

She nods again, then tenses and screams in his ear. John turns and feels something hit his face. His head whips round and blood trickles down his nose. Bonnie slips from his arms and he falls against the mess of clothes, chin cracking against the floor.

She screams again, nudging him in the ribs. 'Daddy! DAAADDDYYY!'

He pulls himself up and pushes Bonnie behind his leg, pain streaking through his face. His stomach lurches when he sees Him, a small part of him having been hoping he was wrong.

John wipes the blood from his nose and puts a hand out to stop Bonnie from moving out of his protection. 'Why?' he says simply.

He smiles, opening His arms like a man offering affection. His eyes peer at John from behind a masquerade mask, grotesquely distorted into a strange face, a face that would scare a child. John looks from Bonnie to Him and wonders if she even knows who this is. When He speaks, his voice is a deep, cutting sound that shreds John's memories of him like a knife. This isn't his voice.

'Because I wanted to see you cry, John.'

John grits his teeth. 'I don't understand. Why would you want that?'

'I want what's yours, John. Your life. But first I have to have all of you. I've been by your side for years. I've carried you through everything. I've seen you afraid, I've seen you in pain, I've seen you happy. I had your love, now I want your hatred too. Then I'll have all of you, every bit of you.'

John shakes his head. 'I thought… I thought you were my friend. You can't… you can't be this way. You're a good person. You would never hurt anyone.'

He smiles. 'I'm touched, John, really I am. But I'm not who you think I am. It's all been an act, Johnny Boy. The day we met was the day I knew I wanted you for the rest of my life. And I got what I wanted. I kept you close, tricked you into thinking I was a good person because, when I was a little boy, I realised that was all I had to be to get what I wanted. And I wanted you, Johnny. You're special. There have been others before but none of them were like you. I've loved you for decades but recently something happened and I realised you weren't enough anymore. I found someone even better than you, John. But you see, I couldn't give you up before I got what I wanted from you. Now I have it. Not just the love, not just the good times. I have everything.'

John stares at him in disbelief. 'Why Bonnie?'

'You already figured that out, Johnny: because it would hurt most.' He walks up to him and rests a hand on his shoulder. 'I know you're scared, I know you're hurting, mourning the boy I gave you when you were little, the neighbour. But that person didn't exist. It was only ever me with a mask, a little bit like this one, I suppose.' He gestures to his face, where only his lips and eyes are visible. 'I want you to know how proud I am of you. You grew up to be such a wonderful man. I have to kill you now. We can't both have your life, Johnny. This was always how it was meant to end. I was always going to kill you. I want you to follow you sister into heaven knowing how much you meant to me.' He rubs his cheek tenderly – a lover's touch. 'How did you know it was me?'

'The disc. The way you touched her face. I've seen it before, with Jules.'

'Ah. Clever. Very clever.'

'I don't understand. You… you were in the bathroom. You… you weren't even there.'

'I jumped out of the window, Johnny. I ran round to the front door, let myself in and knocked her out before carrying her out to my car. It was a lot easier with you both so distracted. She was in the boot while you and Jules searched the house. Then, you thought I was scouting the neighbourhood, but I was really driving her here. Do you understand now, my darling?'

John feels his legs begin to tremble as he takes it in. How had he not known? How had he missed it? 'I… I…'

'It's a lot to take in, isn't it…?' His eyes flick to John's lips, growing wider, desire flitting in and out like a bird in a cage. 'I've wanted to do this for so long. And now, I finally can…' His hand burrows through John's hair, pulling him closer, lips parting. John gasps as He opens his mouth – as if to breathe in the very essence of him – and John pulls away, sickness bubbling in his stomach. He leans forward and kisses him, lips wet with saliva, searching, savouring. John feels his throat contract as He slips his tongue along his teeth. Bonnie whimpers, horrified.

John squeezes her hand, sending a silent message to her: *don't be afraid.*

Then John bites down.

He stumbles back and screams, fingers cradling His mouth. John drops Bonnie's hand and lunges. The coffee table breaks and knives scuttle across the floor. He squirms, eyes wide with fury. 'YOU'RE NEVER TOUCHING MY DAUGHTER AGAIN!'

Bonnie screams behind him but he can't hear her. By the time John realises what she is saying and heeds the warning, he feels hands in his hair and is thrown back onto the floor. His eyes roll back as his head cracks against the concrete. Again and again and again. Pain burns through his body, tears and fear rolling through him in waves. He doesn't even realise he is crying.

He straddles John, gritting His teeth. Leaning forward, He brushes His lips against John's ear. 'I loved you so much, John. You will always be special. Just not as special as *her.*'

John gasps for breath, darkness spotting his vision. He brings his hand to his head and feels blood flood across his fingers

'Look at me, Blue-Eyes. Look at me.' But he doesn't.

He locks his eyes on Bonnie and he smiles. 'I… I love… love yo… you. Don… don't for… forget.'

She crawls to his side through the puddle of blood spreading from his head. He lifts his shaking hand and touches her fingers, then points to the door. She shakes her head. 'Daddy? Daddy?'

'Go.' He tries to push her away but she remains where she is.

John chokes back the blood in his mouth and points again, urging her to leave.

He caresses John's face, fingertips pattering across his cheeks like the wings of a butterfly flicking across the ground. 'If you're going to die, I want to feel you go. Don't worry, Blue-Eyes. I'll always be with you.'

John takes a last ragged breath and closes his eyes, realising that this is where it ends for him. He prays that Bonnie will be saved from a man he thought he knew, a man he has loved nearly all his life.

When he opens his eyes, Don has vanished and Bonnie is all he sees. She is crying, crying for him. John closes his eyes, thinking he is already in heaven, and opens them again for the last time. But she is still sitting before him, cradling his hand and smiling the smile of a girl he used to know.

As the last slivers of life fade and wither…

…as blood pools across the floor and time surrenders…

…John looks at his daughter and sends out one last prayer…

She leans forward and, with lips soft against his skin, whispers, 'Daddy, I love you…'

Chapter 60

Maisie

Tuesday 2 February, 2016

…And in room 217 Tim wakes to the sound…

…of a syringe clattering to the floor…

…A scream penetrates the walls, tearing from Watson's throat, rattling the glass and jarring the minds of those present…

…Maisie watches DCI Alice Munroe and three doctors grapple his hands away from Tim and pull him to the door, fists flying and words scraping through his lips…

'You should have died! You should have died there!'

…As they drag and heave him down the corridor, Watson's shirtsleeve rides up his skin to reveal a scar that curls into the shape of a question mark…

*

She was told they found him just in time. Any later and he would have died. Watson would have injected him before he could even open his eyes. The syringe held a lethal dose of morphine and it would have killed him instantly. She doesn't think she'll ever be able to forget the look of fury on Watson's face as they pulled him away. Or the look of confusion on Tim's.

The doctors assessed him and went through a flurry of tests. She stood by Heidi's side as they gave her his prognosis. It would take time for him to recover the use of all his faculties but, with a new team of specialists and nurses to support him, they expected him to recover. They held their breath when Heidi walked up to him, Maisie clutching Lailah's hand hard enough for the blood to drain out of it. But their concerns proved futile because, although he couldn't speak as well as he once had – his speech was something they needed to work on – a smile lit his face and it was one of recognition and love.

She later learnt Watson was a paediatrician who grew up in Saltford, Bath. When he was sentenced in court, muttering about a blue-eyed boy and the death of a girl called Bessie, his mother refused to attend. He was sentenced to life in prison. He told the judge he attacked Tim because he was in love with Heidi and wanted his life for his own. When he heard Tim was recovering, he knew he needed to take away the risk of losing all he had worked for.

Maisie had known something was bothering Heidi but she never could have guessed, with all news of it kept out of the press, that it was because, a few weeks ago, her daughter had been taken from her and abused in ways she couldn't bear to imagine. Maisie smiles as she recalls Heidi sitting her down and explaining how they had reached this point. How relieved she was when they finally found her daughter. How afraid when she thought she might lose Tim. How heartbroken to realise their oldest friend was responsible for it all. Maisie sat and listened quietly, wondering how she had coped with so much for so long.

In court, Watson proclaimed he did it all for love. But one

man's love is another man's obsession. And the judge said it wasn't a love he was familiar with.

Saturday 6 February, 2016

Maisie opens the door and takes in the scene before her.

Tim, holding his daughter and his wife in his arms, smiling, tears of happiness falling down his cheeks. The man in the Armani suit, Miller Anderson, stands by the bed, arms crossed, laughing.

'Ah, I see you've found him then. I forgot to tell you we moved him.' She is talking to Heidi but her eyes are glued to Tim.

Heidi nods, kissing his cheek. 'Yep. We found him.'

She smiles and sighs. 'Hi, Tim. Lovely to meet you. I'm Maisie. I've been taking care of you.'

He nods, a noise that sounds vaguely like a laugh rumbling in his throat. His daughter curls up against his chest, wary of the tubes in his skin, her feet tucked beneath his leg. Maisie points and smiles. 'I love your shoes.'

She grins and says, 'They're my Dorothy shoes. Daddy got them for me.'

'You like *The Wizard of Oz*?'

'Yes!'

Maisie smiles and turns to leave. 'I do too. I'll give you some space. Shout if you need me.' She takes one last glance at Tim and knows he and his family will come through the hardship of the coming months and find their way in life again. A new way.

Standing outside room 217, Maisie watches life on the ward play out around her and smiles. She lovingly touches her stomach and sends a silent message to her baby, a baby she knows will be a girl.

A girl called Polly.

Chapter 61

Sunday 14 August, 2016

Six Months Later

He and his family stand together by the water, sweet smiles sticking to their lips. Around them birds swoop and dodge through the trees as if they are bullets, the sun's spotlight drawing out the colours in the pond like freckles on a face. On this bright August day, life in Florence Park swarms across the grass and around the water, where children shrug off the worries of their young lives and embrace the sun and the water and the world.

Maisie watches the family from her bench under the brow of a willow tree, fingers tracing small lines across her bump, Ben's arm draped around her shoulders. At first she wonders if she is imagining those four figures but she can't be because Ben glances at them too. They are real. And they are here.

With a heave, Maisie rises from the bench and picks a nervous path through the dropped ice creams and red-faced parents to the family. Why she is nervous, she can't quite put her finger on. Perhaps it is because it has been so long. Perhaps it is because they began to feel as if they were more than what they were. Perhaps it's because it now feels as if they are meeting anew.

Maisie raises a hand and gently touches the man's shoulder where his blond hair curls against his collar in tiny fists. He turns and, as he does, Maisie catches the scent of soap and apple clinging to his skin. His eyes roam across her nose, her eyes, her lips, as if he is looking for someone in her face. Maisie's heart is an anchor that sinks in her chest. There is no recognition. He does not know her.

Just as she takes a step back, he takes one forward, and it is a dance that taps a sudden, frantic rhythm in her chest. She holds her breath, then lets it go in one thick exhalation as he wraps his arms around her. 'It's good to see you again, Maisie.'

Heidi turns, thick curls streaking through the air, eyes widening into bright discs. 'Oh my…' Their daughter peers round her mother's waist and beams at Maisie. Strapped to Heidi's chest is a little boy with his father's blue eyes.

Tim's voice, no longer raspy and jolting, surprises her, drawing her back in his arms. He smiles, holding her hands tight in his own as if this is the only way they can communicate. 'How are you?'

'I'm good. I'm great. I'm pregnant!' Maisie gestures to her bump as if it isn't already obvious and throws Heidi a smile she hopes she catches. Heidi's reply is a kiss blown on her fingertips.

Tim laughs. 'Congratulations.'

'Never mind me. How are all of you? How have you been? I haven't see you for months. You look fantastic, Tim.'

He smiles, and Maisie feels herself relax in the glow of his warmth. 'Thanks! We've been good. We've had our little boy, as you can see. My recovery has been a slow process – I still stumble and drop things and sometimes I struggle with my speech, but it's been good. If feels like just yesterday we were in the ICU, doesn't it?'

'Sure does. I can still remember when you came round. Just in time too.' Maisie lowers herself to the grass and stretches her legs out. They sit in a small circle, the sun slipping its warm hand along their backs, childish laughter filling their ears.

Tim scoops his daughter into his arms and kisses her head as her eyelids droop to a close. 'Me too. It was a tad too close for my liking but at least it's over now. At least he's gone…'

'I can't imagine how you both must have felt – must still feel. You knew him for years. He was your closest friend.'

Tim dips his head, a veil of anger settling like mist across his face. 'I should have known. I should have seen it. Some of the things he did when we were kids made me feel a little uneasy. Some of the things he said, how he reacted… I just should have known. But I think he was a master at hiding himself. Hiding that part of himself. Miller – you've met Miller – told us about something he did to him when he was young, the reason he left our town.' He pauses here and looks at Heidi, as if he needs her help to corral the words into a sentence. 'It's almost too much to take in… He could have died in the river that day… I'm so thankful he didn't. So thankful he found us again.'

Maisie nods, resting a hand on his and smiling at this small family who have felt the brush of something terrible yet still manage to be the good people they started out as. 'You know, I didn't think you'd recover. I thought that was it. It was over.'

'It very nearly could have been.'

She glances at Heidi. 'I knew something was wrong. I never could have guessed it was this, though. How did you cope?' She gestures to the sleeping girl curled up in Tim's arms. 'Everything she went through, everything you went through… how did you cope with it all?'

'I took one day at a time. I had my daughter back but I'd lost my husband. Some days I felt like I could barely put one foot in front of the other. Other days, I wondered how I'd ever make life good again.'

'You did it, though.'

She smiles and looks across the pond. 'I'm just glad it's all over.'

Maisie nods, following her gaze and watching a band of children skip through the water, hands clenched around their rolled-up trousers and pitched-up shirts. Their laughter permeates the air, and it feels as if it has the power to drive every shadow from every dark corner. She glances down at her bump – at Polly – and smiles, visualising the times she will bring her to this park, the times Polly will fill it with laughter of her own, the hot days when she will dance and dip through the water, and the times her parents will hold her and tell her about a little boy called Billy. The days stretching out before her send a shiver down her spine. She is excited and terrified. But she knows, just as she knows the baby inside her is a little girl, that better days are on their way.

Turning on the grass, Maisie sees Ben sinking down beside her, a spark of something bright filling her chest. He shakes their hands and waves at the sleepy baby boy curled into his mother's chest.

'Lovely to meet you, Ben. Maisie told me so much about you,' Heidi says, squeezing his hand.

'All good, I hope. It's lovely to finally meet you too.'

Tim smiles, patting Ben on the back as if they are old friends reunited by chance on a single summer's day. 'My name's John. This is my wife, Jules. And our daughter is Bonnie and that little fellow with his mum is Bertie.'

Maisie looks at him in surprise. 'I feel like I'm meeting you all over again. I'm not sure I can get used to those names.'

He laughs. 'Well, I hope you can. I think you might be stuck with us now.'

And Maisie is overwhelmed with joy because she feels in her very bones that their story together will not end here when they leave this park, just as it did not end in the ICU that day. It will stretch further and further into their lives, their children's lives. Here it will begin again.

'I hope so,' she says.

Epilogue

Watson

Seven Months Earlier

That's my story, John. That's how I found you. How I fell in love with you. If you think about it, ours *is* a love story and this is a love affair that has lasted twenty-five years.

You're probably wondering what changed. What you did wrong. The truth of the matter is, you didn't do anything. You are still perfect. But the love went out of me, Blue-Eyes. It slipped away when I wasn't looking and something else flew in.

Now, I'm standing here, thinking that perhaps you were the connection. You were the person who had to bring her to me. Do you remember when I told you my life was a series of events that led me to you, a bridge made up of moments and fleeting feelings? Well, now I see it was never you. It was her. It was always supposed to be her.

It eluded me for years. Just how special she is. How perfect. I only realised when she told me your plans. And it hit me, it hit me so very hard. She's a good one, John, and she's better than you. I love her.

I.

Love.

Her.

And I couldn't let you pack up this life we made and move to Spain. I couldn't let you take her away from me. I had to kidnap Bonnie to have the rest of you. All of you. And now you have to die for me to have them.

I don't want you to be afraid. And I don't want you to worry. I'll take care of Jules. She'll grieve, mourn you, but then she'll realise that the man who stuck by her through her husband's death is the man she really loves. And as for Bonnie? I'm sure she'll be all right in the end. After all, what could be more exciting than a new father?

I have to do this, my beautiful boy. If I don't, you'll wake up and you'll tell them it was me. I can't let you because I want what's yours, right here, right now. I want them.

Carrying you out of the cellar to my van was tricky but I managed it. Now I lie you down in the street with as much care as I can muster. It's dark, and no one is here to see us. Even if they were, they would probably think we were just two lovers locked in an embrace. How wrong they would be, John. You look so peaceful here like this. Your eyelashes bat against your cheeks, so softly, so very softly. Dried blood matts your sweet-smelling hair. Your fingers curl forward, grasping something only you can see. Are you dreaming of me, perhaps? Holding my hand, perhaps? Hoping I'm still the man you thought I was, perhaps? Sorry, sweetie. I'm not.

I pull a photograph from my pocket and lay it on your chest, right over your heart. The photograph is of the four of us together: me, you, Jules, Miller. You're wearing that red jumper you hated so much. I still have it, you know. I'll keep it as a memento of our life together. I think there is a sweet finality to this one last photo, this one last note, John. Do you want to know what it says?

It says, Goodbye. And I typed in a kiss. Our last kiss.

I push my gloved hands through your hair and take a breath.

Hold it.

Let it go.

And I crack your head against the ground. The sound echoes down the street, bouncing off the walls like beats of a drum. I am careful to remove any trace of myself from your skin and clothes; I can't have them think it was me when they find you. It has to look like you were attacked here, died here, in the dark, with the world a silent audience to your demise.

Next, I carry Bonnie down the street, carefully, carefully. In all the time we spent together, she never guessed it was me. I've always prided myself on 'putting on an act', as Mother called it. Well, I suppose I'm better at it than I thought. She will be OK, John. She'll recover and be happy in the life I'll make for her mother and I. We will be one big happy family. For ever.

I lay her down by your side like I am laying down my own heart. She nestles into your shoulder, dreams flickering behind her eyes. You both look so perfect. So sweet. Father and daughter reunited. Together. For one last time.

I'm not heartless, Johnny. I'm leaving you to die with your child, aren't I? Your precious baby. I'm still the man I've always been. I'm Donnie Watson. Best friend. Funny guy. Good sport. And this is it. My last act of devotion to you.

…Let me tell you something I haven't told you before…

Farewell, my beautiful boy…

Acknowledgements

Thank you to Dom Wakeford, Hannah Smith, Nia Beynon, Victoria Moynes and everyone at HQ for turning my dream into a reality. Working with this wonderful team has been an utter joy!

Thank you to my brilliant agent David H. Headley and to the fabulous Emily Glenister for their support and guidance. I'm so honoured to be a part of the D H H Literary Agency. *Thank you so much!*

A special thanks to Karen Sullivan and Anne Cater for their remarkable support, generosity and encouragement every step of the way. I appreciate it more than I can put into words!

A HUGE thank you to the following book bloggers for their extraordinary friendship, support, kindness, humour and encouragement. I'm so proud to be a part of the book blogging community with these wonderful people!

Shell at Chelle's Book Reviews, Kate at Portable Magic, Abby at Anne Bonny Book Reviews, Joanna at Over The Rainbow Book Blog, Meggy at Chocolate & Waffles, Anne at Being Anne, Jen at Jen Med's Book Reviews, Eva at Novel Deelights, Kaisha at The Writing Garnet, Anne at Random Things Through My Letterbox, Melissa at Broadbeans' Books, Clair Boor at Have Books Will Read, Kerry at Chat About Books, LJ at On The Shelf Reviews, Rae at Rae Reads, Nicola at Orchard Book Club, Neats at The Haphazardous Hippo, Emma at Booking Good Read, Karen at

My Reading Corner, Cleo at Cleopatra Loves Books, Jacob at Hooked From Page One, Karen at Hair Past A Freckle, Yvonne at Me and My Books, Alison at Ali – The Dragon Slayer, Claire Knight at A Knight's Reads, Sarah at Sarah's Book Reviews, Aileen at Feminizia Libros Reviews, Linda at Linda's Book Bag, Emma at Creating Perfection, Nicola at Short Book & Scribes, Jo at Brew & Book Reviews, Zoe-Lee at Zooloo's Book Blog, Emma at damp-pebbles, Hayley at Rather Too Fond of Books, Sarah at Sarah's Vignettes, Sandra at BookLoverWorm, Linda at Books of All Kinds, Becca at If Only I Could Read Faster, Joanne at Portobello Book Blog, Sharon at Chapterinmylife, Susan at Books From Dusk Till Dawn, Laura at PageTurnersNook, Mairead at Swirl & Thread, Mary at Live and Deadly, Noelle at CrimeBookJunkie, Amy at Novelgossip, Katie at Katie's Book Cave, Jill at On The Shelf Books, Sooz at the p. turner's book blog, Joanne at My Chestnut Reading Tree, Susan at BooksAreMyCwtches, Lorraine at The Book Review Café, Sandie at Sandie's Book Shelves, Drew at The Tattooed Book Geek, Abbie at Bloomin' Brilliant Books, Nicole at BookMarkThat, Faye Rogers, Lisa at Wrong Side of Forty, Julie at A Little Book Problem, Katherine at BibliomaniacUK, Kelly at Love Books Group, Kate at The Quiet Knitter, Danielle at Books, Vertigo & Tea, Zoe at What's Better Than Books?, Francesca at Cesca Lizzie Reads, John Fish at The Last Word Book Review, Janel at Keeper of Pages, Laura at Snazzy Books, Caryl at Mrs Blogg's Books, Emma at Emma's Bookish Corner, Misti at Misti Moo Book Review, Susan at The Book Trail, Nicola at Orchard Book Club, Jade at 3 Degrees of Fiction Book Blog, Kathryn at Nut Press, Chelsea at The Suspense is Thrilling Me, Amanda at mybookishblogspot, Stuart at Always Trust in Books, Nikola at Breathing Through Pages, Sam at Clues & Reviews, Abby at Crime by the Book, Nat Marshall at the owl on the bookshelf, Jo B at Jo's Book Blog, Jules at LittleMissNoSleep Daydreams of Books, Janet at From First Page To Last, Inge at The Belgian Reviewer, Tracy at Compulsive Readers, Jackie at

Never Imitate, Noemi at Book After Book, Kate at Bibliophile Book Club, Jules Swain, Rebecca at Forward Books, Rebecca Bradley at Murder Down To A Tea, Rachel at Rachel's Random Reads, Anne at Being Anne, Claire at BrizzleLass Books, Claire Huston at Art and Soul, Steph at Steph's Book Blog, Wendy at Little Bookness Lane, Caroline at Bits about Books, Paul at Half Man Half Book, Margaret at bleachhouselibrary, Adele at Kraftreader, Victoria at Off-The-Shelf Books, Renee at It's Book Talk, Sharon at Shaz's Book Blog, David at Blue Book Balloon, Ellen Devonport, Rachel Emms at Chillers, Killers and Thrillers, Vicki at Cosy Books, Liz Barnsley at Liz Loves Books, Jill at Jill's Book Café, Celeste at Celeste Loves Books, Kate at For Winter Nights, Steph at Crimethrillergirl and MANY more! Another huge thank you to all the incredible authors, publicists, editors, agents, Tweeters, Instagrammers, Facebook friends and more for your support! A thousand times thank you!

With thanks to Stuart Gibbon (Gibconsultancy.co.uk), author of The Crime Writer's Casebook, who advised me on police procedure. His help and advice was invaluable. Any errors are mine alone.

Last but certainly not least, thank you to my incredible family and friends for everything they do! I always have Team Turner cheering me on – they are the absolute BEST!

Dear Reader,

I would just like to say a huge thank you for taking the time to read my book. It still seems surreal that I'm sat here – dogs curled up next to me, cup of tea in hand – typing out a letter to you to go at the back of my book. Even more surreal that this book has been published and you have taken the time to keep turning its pages. I can't tell you how much I appreciate it. A few months ago, I could never have guessed I would be doing this right now. It's literally my dream come true. Thank you so much.

In my spare time I run my own book blog, where I review both fiction and non-fiction. Psychological thrillers, chick-lit, cookbooks and memoirs, I enjoy them all. I post my reviews on Goodreads and Amazon to share the book love. And just leaving a quick review makes a huge difference. So if you have a minute to say something about my book on Amazon or Goodreads, it would mean the world. Even if it's just a brief sentence or a single word, I'd LOVE to know what your thoughts are!

If you'd like to send me a comment, a question, a picture of the book or just say hi, I'd really like to hear from you! You can find me on Twitter, Facebook and Instagram. My timeline and pages are always brimming with #BookSnaps, reviews, dog photos, attempts at humour (one right here!) and bookish chat, so I hope these are things you might enjoy! You can also find my wonderful publisher, HQ Digital, on Twitter and Facebook too – they're always posting exciting news, fabulous giveaways and gorgeous bookish pictures.

Thank you again for reading my book. I hope you enjoyed it, and I hope to hear from you soon!

Warm wishes,
Ronnie x

🐦: @Ronnie__Turner
📘: @RonnieTurnerAuthor
📷: @ronnieturner8702
Website: www.ronnieturner.wordpress.com

Dear Reader,

Thank you so much for taking the time to read this book – we hope you enjoyed it! If you did, we'd be so appreciative if you left a review.

Here at HQ Digital we are dedicated to publishing fiction that will keep you turning the pages into the early hours. We publish a variety of genres, from heartwarming romance, to thrilling crime and sweeping historical fiction.

To find out more about our books, enter competitions and discover exclusive content, please join our community of readers by following us at:

🐦 *@HQDigitalUK*

🅕 *facebook.com/HQDigitalUK*

Are you a budding writer? We're also looking for authors to join the HQ Digital family! Please submit your manuscript to:

HQDigital@harpercollins.co.uk.

Hope to hear from you soon!

DIGITAL

If you enjoyed *Lies Between Us*, then why not try another pulse-racing thriller from HQ Digital?

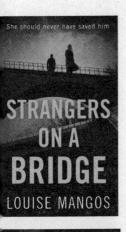

She should never have saved him

STRANGERS ON A BRIDGE

LOUISE MANGOS

DARREN O'SULLIVAN

CLOSE YOUR EYES

... and count to ten.

It's bad when the girls go MISSING
It's worse when the girls are FOUND

PRETTY LITTLE THINGS

T.M.E. WALSH

REVENGE is not always so sweet...

DECEIT

KERRY BARNES

It was the one place she should have been safe

THE CLASSROOM

A.L. BIRD

An addictive psychological suspense with a twist you won't see coming

LOVE ME, LOVE ME NOT

KATHERINE DEBONA